A
Well-Tempered
Heart

ALSO BY JAN-PHILIPP SENDKER

The Art of Hearing Heartbeats

A Well-Tempered Heart

a novel

Jan-Philipp Sendker

Translated from the German
by Kevin Wiliarty

OTHER PRESS

New York

Copyright © 2012 by Karl Blessing Verlag

Originally published in German as *Herzenstimmen* by
Karl Blessing Verlag, Munich, in 2012

Translation copyright © 2013 by Kevin Wiliarty

Production Editor: Yvonne E. Cárdenas
Text Designer: Cassandra J. Pappas
This book was set in 12.3 pt Van Dijck by
Alpha Design & Composition of Pittsfield, NH.

10 9 8 7 6 5 4 3 2 1

Library of Congress Cataloging-in-Publication Data

Sendker, Jan-Philipp.
[Herzenstimmen. English]
A well-tempered heart : a novel / Jan-Philipp Sendker ; Translated
from the German by Kevin Wiliarty.
pages cm
"Originally published in German by Karl Blessing Verlag in 2012."
ISBN 978-1-59051-640-9 (pbk.) — ISBN 978-1-59051-641-6
(ebook) 1. Americans—Burma—Fiction. 2. Child soldiers—
Burma—Fiction. 3. Burma—Fiction. 4. Burma—War—Fiction.
5. Burma—Women—Fiction. I. Wiliarty, Kevin translator.
II. Title.
PT2721.E54H413 2014
833'.92—dc23
2013015062

To Anna, Florentine, Theresa, and Jonathan

Part One

Chapter 1

THE DEEP BLUE morning sky was clear as a bell the day my life lurched off course. It was a crisp, cold Friday, the week before Thanksgiving. I have often wondered whether I ought to have seen it coming. How could I have missed it? How could I have failed so utterly to anticipate such a calamitous event? Me of all people? A woman who hated surprises. Who prepared meticulously for every meeting, every trip, even a weekend excursion or a casual dinner with friends. I was never one to leave anything to chance. I found the unexpected almost intolerable. Spontaneity held no attraction for me.

Amy insisted that there must have been early portents, that there always are. Except that we are so engrossed in our day-to-day lives, prisoners of our own routines, that we forget to look for them.

The little details that speak volumes.

According to her we are each our own greatest mystery, and our life's work is to solve ourselves. None of us ever succeeds, she says, but it is our duty to follow the trail. Regardless of how long it is or where it might lead.

I had my doubts. Amy's beliefs and my own often diverged. Which is not to say that I did not see her point in this case, at least to a certain extent. There may well have been the occasional incident over the past several months, things that ought to have raised an alarm. But how much time can we devote to eavesdropping on our inner selves just on the off chance that we might pick up some token or clue, the key to some puzzle or other?

I was not one to regard every physical aberration as symptomatic of some disturbance to my spiritual equilibrium.

Those little red pimples on my neck—the ones that developed within a few days into a painful, burning rash that no doctor could explain, the ones that vanished a few weeks later as suddenly as they had appeared—those might have been caused by anything. Likewise the occasional rushing in my ears. The insomnia. The increasing irritability and impatience, directed mostly at myself. I was well acquainted with both feelings, and I attributed them to the workload at the office. The price everyone in the firm had to pay, the price we were all willing to pay. I had no complaints.

The letter was sitting there in the middle of my desk. In a slightly crumpled light-blue airmail envelope, the kind one hardly uses anymore. I recognized his handwriting at once. No one else I knew lavished such care on penmanship.

He treated each correspondence as a miniature artwork. He gave each swooping line meticulous attention worthy of calligraphy. Each letter of each word was a gift. Two pages, tightly packed, every sentence, every line set to paper with the devotion and passion felt only by someone for whom writing is a treasure beyond all price.

On the envelope an American stamp. He must have entrusted it to some tourist; that was the fastest and safest way. I looked at the clock. Our next meeting was scheduled to begin in two minutes, but curiosity got the better of me. I opened the envelope and hastily scanned the first few lines.

A loud knock wrenched me back. There was Mulligan standing in the door, his broad, muscular frame nearly filling the space. I would have liked to ask for a moment's patience. A letter from my brother in Burma. A little masterpiece that . . . He smiled, and before I could say a word he tapped a forefinger on his chunky wristwatch. I nodded. Mulligan was one of the partners at Simon & Koons, our best attorney, but he had no appreciation for penmanship as a gift. His own scrawl was illegible.

The rest of my colleagues were already waiting. You could smell the fresh coffee; the room grew quiet as we sat down. In the coming weeks we were going to be filing a claim on behalf of our most important client. A complicated story. Copyright infringement, illegal knockoffs from America and China, damages in the hundreds of millions. Time was of the essence.

Mulligan spoke softly, and yet his deep voice resonated throughout every corner of the room. After only a few sentences I was already finding it difficult to follow him. I tried to focus on his words, but something kept distracting me, drawing me out of the room. Away from this world of charges and countercharges.

I was thinking of my brother in Burma. I saw him suddenly before me. I thought of our first meeting in the dilapidated teahouse in Kalaw. How he had stared at me and then suddenly approached me. In his white but yellowing shirt, his faded longyi, and his worn-out flip-flops. The half brother whose existence I had never suspected. I took him for an old beggar angling for a handout. I remembered the way he sat down at my table to ask me a question. "Do you believe in love, Julia?" I hear his voice in my head to this very day. As if time had stood still for this question. I had laughed—and it had not bothered him.

While Mulligan was droning on about the "value of intellectual property" I recalled my half brother's first sentences. Verbatim. "I am serious," U Ba had continued, undeterred by my laughter. "I speak of a love that brings sight to the blind. Of a love stronger than fear. I speak of a love that breathes meaning into life . . ."

No, I had eventually answered. No, I don't believe in anything of the kind.

Over the next few days U Ba had shown me the error of my ways. And now? Almost ten years later? Did I believe in a power that brought sight to the blind? Would I be able to convince a single person in this company that a person can triumph over selfishness? They would die laughing.

Mulligan was still rattling on about "the most important case of the year . . . so that we have to . . ." I was doing my best to concentrate, but my thoughts kept drifting, aimless, like scraps of wood tossed by the waves.

"Julia." Mulligan brought me abruptly back to Manhattan. "It's all you."

I nodded at him, cast a desperate glance at my notes, and was planning to lead in with a few standard openings when a faint whisper interrupted me.

I faltered.

Who are you?

A mere breath, and yet unmistakable.

Who are you?

A woman's voice. Still quiet, but clear and distinct.

I looked over my right shoulder to see who was interrupting me with a question like that at a moment like this. No one.

Where else would it come from?

Who are you?

I looked instinctively to the left. Nothing. A whisper from nowhere.

What do these men want from you?

Tense silence on all sides. I took a deep breath and exhaled slowly. I felt flushed. I sat tongue-tied, eyes down. Someone cleared his throat.

Be on your guard.

"Julia?"

Not a word. Not one. Shortness of breath. Where was this voice coming from? Who was that talking to me? What did she want? What did I have to fear from my colleagues?

"Feel free to jump right in. We're all ears." Mulligan's growing impatience. Disapproving coughs.

Take great care. Watch what you say. Be careful who you look at.

I raised my head and glanced cautiously around. Upper bodies rocking uneasily. Marc's worried expression; he felt my pain. I imagine. A smirk flitted across Frank's broad face. As if he'd always known the day would come when I would crumble pathetically under the pressure.

You mustn't trust them, no matter what they say.

That voice cinched my throat shut. I was paralyzed. Their faces ran together. Sweaty palms. My heart beat faster.

"Julia. Are you okay?"

No one will help you.

"If I may . . ." I began.

Utter silence once again. It had sounded louder than necessary. More of a cry than a polite request for attention. Their glances. The ensuing silence. I felt dizzy. On the brink of collapse.

"Would you like some water?"

It sounded sincere. Or was I fooling myself? Did I need to be on my guard?

Not a word, now. Hold your tongue.

A dark chasm opened before me, yawning wider by the second. I wanted to hide, to crawl off somewhere. What in the world was happening to me? I was hearing a voice, plain as day. A voice I had no control over. A stranger. Inside me. I felt myself getting smaller and smaller. Smaller and needier. I would not be able to say another word until it was quiet again in my head. I pressed on my ears a couple of times, quickly and sharply, the way I did when the occasional rushing got too loud. I tried another deep breath and knew right away it was pointless.

They mean you no good. Their smiles are false. They are dangerous.

Scream. Drown her out with my own real voice. LEAVE ME ALONE. STOP TALKING. STOP. STOP.

Not a word. Not one.

Mulligan and I exchanged looks. I realized it was true that no one in this room could help me. I had to get out. Immediately. I would go to the restroom, to my office, home, it didn't matter, as long as it was away from here. They were here for a presentation. They were expecting ideas and proposals, and if I wasn't up to the job, at least I owed them an explanation for my behavior. An apology. I was in no position to give them either one. I didn't have the strength. I had nothing to say. A brief hesitation, then I slowly straightened up, pushing back my chair and rising. My legs were quivering.

What are you doing?

"What the hell is going on here, Julia?"

I gathered my papers, turned away, and headed for the

door. Mulligan was shouting something, but I could no longer understand a word he was saying.

I opened the door, stepped out, and closed it quietly behind me.

Now what?

I walked down the hall past the restrooms to my office, set the documents on my desk, took my coat, tucked U Ba's letter into my handbag, and left the office calmly and without another word.

I had as yet no idea that I had unwittingly set off on my journey. On that fall day, icy cold and clear as a bell, in the week before Thanksgiving.

Chapter 2

Kalaw, November ninth
In the year two thousand six

My dear little sister,

    I hope this letter finds you in good spirits and good health. Please forgive my long silence. I no longer recall precisely when last I found the time to write you a few lines. Was it in the heat of the summer or yet before the turn of the monsoon?

    It seems that an eternity has passed since then, though little enough has transpired in my life and in Kalaw. The astrologer's wife has fallen ill and will soon die; the daughter of the owner of the teahouse where we first met now has a son. It is the same kind of comings and goings as anywhere else in the world, is it not? And yet our life here has a different rhythm from yours, as you may recall. As for me, I must confess that I am unable to imagine how quickly your world turns.

I myself am doing well. I continue to restore my old books, though the task grows increasingly strenuous and exhausting with the passage of time. It is my eyes, little sister. They deteriorate from day to day. I am gradually reaching the age of fading light. To make matters worse, my right hand has fallen further into the unwelcome habit of trembling slightly, which does not make it any easier to paste the little bits of paper over the holes bored incessantly into the pages by the ravenous vermin. Where previously three months sufficed to restore one of my books to legibility, I now require half a year or even more in the case of weightier volumes. Yet what good does it do, I sometimes ask myself, to spur myself on? If there is one thing I possess enough of, it is time. Only in old age do we fully appreciate the value of time, and I am a wealthy man. But let me not burden you with an old man's ailments! If I do not rein in my pen, you will soon begin to worry about your brother, an utterly unfounded concern. I lack nothing.

Unless I am mistaken, it must by now be autumn in New York. I read once in one of my books that autumn was New York's most beautiful season. Is that true? Alas, how little I understand of your life.

Our rainy season is gradually drawing to a close, the skies are once again dry and clear, the temperatures are dropping, and it will not be long before the first frost settles on the grasses in my garden. Oh, how I prize the sight of the delicate whiteness on the deep green blades!

Yesterday something extraordinary happened here. A woman dropped dead under the banyan tree at the crossroads. Moments beforehand, according to my neighbor who witnessed the event, she wailed in lamentation. She had been on her way to the market when she was stricken by a sudden fainting spell. Clutching her sister for support, she cried out repeatedly for forgiveness. Enormous tears ran down her cheeks, the size of peanuts supposedly, though I can hardly believe that. You know of course how people here are prone to exaggerate. She had turned suddenly away from her sister to follow an unfamiliar young man, calling out a name repeatedly that no one in the village had ever heard before. When the young man turned in surprise to see what all the racket was about, their eyes met. The woman froze and fell down dead. As if she had been struck by lightning on that clear, cloudless day. No one had any explanation for it. Her sister is inconsolable. They had shared a secluded life for years on the periphery of the village. The two of them had few friends, and even the neighbors had no information. Very odd, I must say; they generally know everything. The incident has since dominated the conversations in our little city, in the teahouses and the marketplace. Many people claim that the young man has magical powers and that he killed her with his glance. The poor fellow denies this of course and insists on his innocence. For the time being he has retreated to his aunt's house in Taunggyi.

And you, my dear sister? Have the wedding plans you cautiously referred to in your last letter, yours and Mr. Michael's, taken further shape? Or perhaps I raise the question too late and you have married already? If so, then I want only to wish you both the best from the bottom of my heart. For me, I have always regarded the few years I was fortunate enough to share with my wife as a great, even a superlative, pleasure.

And now my letter has grown longer than intended. The garrulousness of old age, I fear, and I hope that I have not taken too much of your time. I will sign off now. Dusk is here, and the electrical power in Kalaw has been unreliable for the past few weeks. The lightbulb on my ceiling flickers so badly that you might think it was trying to send me secret messages. I suspect, however that it augurs nothing more than another power outage.

Julia, my dear, may the stars, life, and fate smile upon you. I think of you. I carry you in my heart. Take care of yourself.

Yours with heartfelt affection,
U Ba

I put the letter aside. My fear that the voice would return had subsided. I was instead overtaken by a sense of intense intimacy mingled with longing and a deep melancholy. How I wished to see my brother in the flesh! I recalled his antiquated way of expressing himself, his habit of apologizing needlessly for anything and everything. His courtesy and humility, which had so moved me. His little hut of black teak, standing on stilts, danced before my eyes, the pig grunting and wallowing in the mud, the scuffed leather armchair, its cushions worn thin to reveal the outline of the springs, a couch with torn upholstery on which I had passed many a night. In the midst of it all a swarm of bees, which had moved in with him and whose honey he did not touch lest he use anything that did not belong to him.

I saw him sitting before me, flanked by oil lamps, hunched low over his desk, surrounded by books. They filled shelves that reached from floor to ceiling. They lay in piles on the planks of the wooden floor and rose in towers on a second couch. Their pages resembled punch cards. On the table was spread an array of tweezers, scissors, two little jars among them, one with a stiff white glue, the other filled with tiny bits of paper. I had watched for hours as he grasped bit after bit of paper with the tweezers, dipped them in the glue, and positioned them over the holes. Then, as soon as the glue had set, he would retrace the missing letters with a pen. In this way, over the years, he had restored dozens of books.

My brother's life. It bore so little resemblance to my own, and yet it had touched me so deeply.

My eyes lit on the shelf with the souvenirs of my trip to Burma, half obscured by books and newspapers. A carved wooden Buddha, a gift from my brother. A dusty little lacquer box adorned with elephants and monkeys. A picture of U Ba and me that we took shortly before my departure from Kalaw. I was a full head taller than him. He was wearing his new green and black longyi, freshly laundered only the night before so that it would be clean. He had wrapped a pink cloth around his head, as had previously been the custom among the older Shan. He gazed into the camera seriously and solemnly.

I could hardly recognize myself in that picture. Flush with joy from the most exhilarating days of my life, uplifted by the most beautiful love story I would ever hear, the story of my father, I beamed without a care—maybe slightly enraptured—at the camera. When I showed the picture to friends they couldn't believe it was me. When Michael saw it for the first time he wanted to know if I was standing there stoned out of my mind with my guru in India. Later he frequently made fun of my expression, claiming that I must have inhaled too deeply on a Burmese opium pipe before the shot.

Ten years had passed since then. Ten years during which I had time and again resolved to return, to visit my father's grave, to spend time with U Ba. I put the journey off from one year to the next. Twice I had booked a flight only to cancel it at the last minute when some other more pressing matter arose. Something so pressing that I could no longer even say what it had been. Eventually mundane routines took the shine off my memories; desire lost its urgency and gave way to a vague intention for some unspecified future occasion.

I could not remember when I had last written to U Ba. He begged my pardon for his long silence. It was I who owed him an answer to his last letter. And probably to the one before that. I couldn't recall. We corresponded regularly during the first few years after my return, but gradually the frequency of our exchanges decreased. He sent me one of his restored books every other year, but I have to confess that I had never yet gotten all the way through a single one. They were, in spite of his efforts, much the worse for wear: faded, dusty, soiled. I always washed my hands after handling them. He had graced them with affectionate dedications, and every one of them had lain initially by my bedside, migrating quickly to the living room and landing ultimately in some carton or other.

On a couple of occasions I had sent him money through a contact at the American embassy in Rangoon, maybe ten thousand dollars all told. He would invariably confirm receipt in a subsequent letter, casually, without putting his gratitude into so many words or even explaining what he was doing with what by Burmese standards was a tidy sum of money, which left me thinking that my financial gifts must be awkward for him. At some point I dropped the practice, and neither of us ever said another word about it. I had often invited him to come visit me in New York, explaining that I would of course attend to all the formalities and cover all the expenses. At first he demurred. Later, for reasons that were never clear to me, he declined outright, politely but very firmly, time after time.

I wondered why in all those years I had never managed to see him again, though I had promised both of us when I left that I would return within a few months. How is it that he, to whom I owed so much, had disappeared again from my life? Why do we so often put off the things that matter most to us? I had no answer. I would have to write to him at length in the next few days.

The memories of Burma had distracted and calmed me. From the taxi I had e-mailed Mulligan, blamed the problem on severe light-headedness, and promised to explain the whole thing on Monday. I considered taking the afternoon to straighten up my apartment. It was looking pretty dire. The cleaning lady had been sick for two weeks, and dust had piled up in the corners. The bedroom was still cluttered with unopened boxes; pictures waiting to be hung leaned against the walls, even though four months had passed since Michael and I had parted ways and I had moved back into my old apartment. My friend Amy claimed that the state of my apartment reflected my reluctance to accept the separation from Michael. That was nonsense. If the disarray betrayed anything, it was my disappointment with the fact that I was living in the same apartment at thirty-eight that I had lived in at twenty-eight. It felt to me like a step backward. I had moved out four years ago because I preferred living with Michael over being on my own. The apartment reminded me each day afresh that the attempt had failed.

WHY ARE YOU ALONE?

That voice again. No longer a whisper, but still muted. It reverberated throughout my entire body, made me shiver.

Why are you alone?

It sounded closer, more immediate than in the office. As if someone had stepped nearer to me.

Why don't you answer me?

I felt hot. My heart started to race again. Sweaty palms. The same symptoms as this morning. I couldn't sit still; I stood up and paced back and forth in my little living room.

Why are you alone?

—Who says I'm alone?

Would she leave me in peace if I answered her?

Where are the others?

—What others?

Your husband.

—I'm not married.

Don't you have any children?

—No.

Oh.

—What's "oh" supposed to mean?

Nothing. It's only . . . no kids . . . that's sad.

—No. Not at all.

Where's your father?

—He's dead.

And your mother?

—She lives in San Francisco.

Don't you have any brothers or sisters?

—Sure, a brother.

Why isn't he here?

—He lives in San Francisco, too.

Did you stay behind with your aunts and uncles?

— I don't have any aunts or uncles.

No aunts or uncles?

—No.

So why don't you live with your family?

—Because it's actually not a bad thing to have a continent between us.

So you are alone.

—No. I'm not alone. I just live alone.

Why?

—Why? Why? Because I like it better that way.

Why?

—You're getting on my nerves with that "why" thing.

Why do you live alone?

—Because I hate to be woken in the night by a man's snoring. Because I'd rather read my morning paper in peace. Because I don't like whiskers in the sink. Because I don't want to have to justify myself when I come home from work at midnight. Because I love not having to explain anything to anyone. Can you understand that?

Silence.

—Hello? Can you understand that?

Not a sound.

—Hello? Why aren't you talking anymore?

I stood there waiting. The sonorous hum of the refrigerator, voices in the hall, a door clicking shut.

—Where are you?

The phone rang. Amy. She could tell by my tone that I was out of joint.

"Aren't you feeling well?"

"Sure I am."

Why are you lying again?

Like a sharp blow from behind. I stumbled and nearly lost my balance.

"It . . . it's just that . . ." I muttered, bewildered.

"Julia, what's wrong?" she asked, alarmed. "Do you want to meet? Should I come to your place?"

I was dying to get out of my apartment.

"I . . . I'd rather meet at your place. When would be an okay time?"

"Whenever you want."

"I'll be there in an hour."

Chapter 3

AMY LEE LIVED in two adjacent studios on the top floor of a three-story building on the Lower East Side. She lived in one of the apartments and used the other for her art. For the past several years there had been no place where I felt better cared for. We spent entire weekends on her couch, watching *Sex and the City*, eating ice cream, drinking red wine, laughing about men or consoling each other when we suffered from heartaches.

Amy and I had met right at the beginning of law school, Columbia, emphasis on corporate law. While filling out some form or other we noticed by chance that we had been born on exactly the same day, she in Hong Kong, I in New York. She had spent the first nineteen years of her life in Hong Kong, until her parents sent her to college in America. Amy claimed that an astrologer back home had predicted she would meet someone with the same birthday who would prove to be a lifelong companion, and so it seemed that we had no choice but to become friends.

I didn't believe in astrology at the time, but I liked Amy from the start. We complemented each other in a way I had never experienced with a friend.

She was in many ways my exact opposite: a head shorter, stockier. She dyed her black hair bright colors, didn't like to make plans, loved surprises, was quick on her feet and even-tempered. She meditated, was a Buddhist, and yet regularly consulted astrologers and was so superstitious that it sometimes made me crazy. She always wore something red. Never got out of an elevator on the ninth floor. Refused to take any taxi whose license plate ended in a seven.

She was the only person I had shared my father's story with. And she believed it. Every word, without question. As if it were the most natural thing in the world for there to be people who could hear heartbeats.

In contrast to my mother and brother, who preferred to be left in the dark about my trip. They wanted to know only whether our father was still alive. When I told them he wasn't and tried to report what I had experienced in Burma and why he had returned to the land of his birth in order to die, they refused to listen to me. It was the beginning of our estrangement. My search for my father had torn the family in two. My mother and brother on one side, my father and I on the other. Amy was convinced that this split had been there all along, that I was slow to notice it or had previously been in denial about it. She was probably right. Five years ago my mother moved to San Francisco to be closer to my brother, and now we saw each other once, maybe twice a year.

Amy, on the other hand, couldn't get enough of it. When was I finally going to visit U Ba, she always wanted to know. And what of my father's inheritance: faith in the magical power of love? Had I lost it again in New York? Why had I not looked after it properly? Shouldn't I be looking for it? Questions I dodged because I had no answers, which only encouraged her to ask them at regular intervals.

Amy's heart, unlike mine, was not really in her studies. Her real ambition had been to paint, and she had gone into law only under pressure from—or out of love for—her parents, the justification changing according to her mood. Still, she was one of the best in our class. When Amy's father died in a plane crash four weeks before our last exams, Amy just jetted off to Hong Kong for two months. Back in New York she announced that her studies were over. She wouldn't spend another day at the university. Life was too short for detours. If you had a dream, you ought to live it.

Since then she'd been making ends meet as a freelance set painter on Broadway, and she refused to so much as show her work to any gallery owners. Neither exhibits nor sales held any interest for her. She was painting for herself, not for anyone else. Amy was the freest person I knew.

The door to her studio stood ajar. She loathed closed doors the same way she abhorred all locks, and she was firmly convinced that people who constantly worried about locking things up or away would eventually lock themselves out. She even refused to chain her bicycle. Curiously, she was the only one of my friends whose bicycle had never been stolen.

She sat on a rolling stool in front of a canvas that she was painting a dark orange. She had put her hair, dyed red, into a ponytail. She wore faded gray sweatpants and an over-sized white T-shirt covered with paint flecks. Her work clothes. The room smelled of fresh paint and varnish; the floor was lost beneath splotches of color, paintings rested against the walls or on easels, many of them in varying shades of red. Amy claimed that she had unfortunately got-ten mired in her Barnett Newman phase. Instead of stripes she was painting circles, and if she didn't bust out soon, I might as well start calling her Bernadette Newman. Jack Johnson was playing on her small stereo.

Hearing my footsteps on the wooden floor, she turned to face me. Her dark brown, almost black eyes widened in surprise.

"What's got you looking like that?"

I collapsed into an old armchair, my hands and feet ice cold. My eyes filled with tears. It was as if in these few sec-onds all of the stress of the past several hours was slipping away. She looked at me with a worried expression, gave her stool a vigorous push, and came rolling over to me.

"What's the problem?"

I shrugged helplessly.

"Let me guess: Mulligan gave you the boot."

I shook my head the slightest bit.

"Your mother died."

I fought back the first tears.

Amy sighed deeply. "Okay, it's something serious!"

Maybe it was her sense of humor that I liked best about her.

"Out with it then, what happened?"

"So what am I looking like?" I tried to dodge her question.

"Like a frightened hen."

I was quiet for a while. Amy waited patiently for my answer.

I found it difficult to say out loud the thought that had been haunting me incessantly for the past hour. "I'm afraid I'm losing my mind."

She studied me thoughtfully. "And what is it exactly, if I may ask, that is prompting this fear?"

"I feel as if someone is following me."

"A stalker? Is he good-looking?"

"Not a stalker. I'm hearing voices." I cringed at the sound of it. I felt embarrassed telling even Amy.

"Since when?" she asked, soberly now and without a trace of surprise in her voice.

"Since this morning," I answered, and told her what had happened at the office and back at home.

Amy sat motionless on her stool listening to me. Occasionally she nodded, as if she knew just what I was talking about. When I was through she stood up, put down her brush, and paced up and down between her artworks. It's what she did when she was thinking hard.

"Is it the first time?" she asked, pausing.

"Yes."

"Is she threatening you?"

"No, why would she do that?"

"Does she insult you?"

"Insult me?"

"Does she tell you that you're a useless slut? A lousy lawyer? That it's only a matter of time before everyone realizes what an idiot you really are?"

I shook my head, confused. "No."

"Does she order you around?"

I had no idea where she was heading with this line of inquiry.

"Does she tell you to dash a cup of coffee in Mulligan's face? Or to jump out the window?"

"No. Where are you getting such nonsense?"

Amy was thoughtful. "What does she say, then?"

"Not much. In the office she was warning me about my colleagues. Otherwise she just asks questions."

"What kind of questions?"

"Who are you? Why do you live alone? Why don't you have any children?"

A smile of relief crossed her face. "Interesting questions."

"How so?"

"I know someone else who would take an interest in your answers. Do our voices sound at all similar?"

"Quit making fun of me," I told her, disappointed. Couldn't she tell how desperately I needed her reassurance?

"I'm not making fun of you," she said, coming over to me, crouching beside me, and stroking my hair. "But these questions don't sound particularly dire. I feared something worse."

"How worse?"

"Hearing voices is often a psychotic reaction. It's a typical symptom of incipient schizophrenia. In that case the outlook is dim. Not easily cured. But in those cases the affected person feels threatened by the voices. The voices boss them around. Jump off a roof, stab your neighbor. Melancholics often hear insults. But none of that applies to you."

"How is it," I wondered, "that you know so much about people who hear voices?"

"Didn't I ever tell you that my father heard voices, too?"

I stared at her in surprise. "No."

"My mother told me about it a few years after he died. After that I read everything I could find on the subject."

"Was your father schizophrenic?"

"No. I think that for him it was a relatively harmless phenomenon."

"What did he do about it?"

"Nothing."

"Nothing?"

"I suspect that he saw the voice as someone who offered him advice from time to time." After a short pause she added: "Unfortunately, he didn't always follow it."

"What do you mean?"

"My mother says the voice told him on the day of the crash that he ought to turn back. That he shouldn't get on that plane. He even called her from the airport."

"Why didn't he listen?" I asked doubtfully.

"If only I knew. Maybe he was afraid to give it too much power over his life. Who wants to be told by a voice which planes to take and which ones not to?"

"Why didn't you ever tell me about it?"

"I thought I had. But maybe I just figured you wouldn't believe me."

I wasn't sure whether I believed her now. It made me think of my brother in Burma. "Not all truths are explicable, and not all explicable things are true," he once told me. How often had that remark come to mind during the first years after my return? In Kalaw I had at some point understood what he meant. In his world of superstitious people it had made sense to me; back in New York I had my doubts again. Why shouldn't all explicable things be true? Why shouldn't one be able to explain all truths? Maybe there were truths in Kalaw that did not hold elsewhere.

"You don't believe me," said Amy, as if sensing my doubts.

"No. Well, yes. Of course I believe your mother told you that, but I can hardly believe that a voice warned your father not to board his last flight."

"Why not?"

"You know me. I'm too rational for that."

"Your father could hear heartbeats. He could distinguish butterflies by their wing beats. How do you explain that?"

"There's no explanation for it, I know. But that doesn't mean that I have to start buying into all kinds of . . ." I searched for a way of putting it that would not offend Amy.

". . . esoteric nonsense." She finished the sentence for me.

"Exactly," I said, and couldn't help laughing at myself.

"And nor should you," she went on. "But now you are hearing a voice. Do you have an explanation?"

"No," I answered sheepishly.

We both thought for a while in silence.

"Should we go out for a drink somewhere?" she asked, straightening up.

I hesitated. "I'd rather stay here. I don't want to have to deal with strangers."

She nodded. "You want an espresso?"

"I'd prefer a glass of wine."

"Even better." She went into the open kitchen, uncorked a bottle of red wine, and brought it over on a tray with glasses, chocolate, and nuts. She poured for two and lit a couple of candles. We took two pillows and sat in silence on the floor. We were good at that. Silence lost its power to isolate in Amy's presence.

"Can you hear her now?" she asked at some point.

I listened into myself and shook my head.

"Too bad. I was hoping to have a word with her."

I cast her a slightly pained look over my wineglass. "She never explains anything. She only asks questions."

"I wonder whether this voice might also have some purpose?"

I wonder. Typical Amy-talk. She said that often when her question was really a statement. I knew her well enough to understand what she meant: *Julia! This voice has a purpose.*

"What purpose?"

"My father was uncomfortable talking about it, but according to my mother he never thought of the voice he heard as a threat. To him it was more of a lifelong companion with whom he conversed at regular intervals, I think."

I shook my head. That was not what I had been hoping to hear. Not that I could have said which words would have done me any good in this situation. Was I just looking for a bit of pity rounded out with a reassurance that I would be all better in a few days? As if I had a flu?

"I don't need a lifelong companion. At least not one that I can neither see nor touch."

Amy sipped at her wine, lost in thought. "And what if you answer her questions?"

"Why should I?"

"Maybe she'd leave you in peace. Who knows?"

"I tried that. All I got was more questions."

She rocked her head from side to side and looked at me for a long time. "Why are you afraid of this voice?"

"Why am I afraid? Because I don't have any control over it."

"Is that so bad?"

"Yes! I left a work meeting without a word of explanation. An important one!"

"A sudden fainting spell. Mulligan will turn a blind eye."

"Not if it happens again. We're supposed to be filing a pretty complicated claim in the next few weeks. We're supposed to lay out our strategy for our client, and a part of that is my job. What's going to happen if she pipes up in the middle of my presentation?"

She thought about it. "Then you just keep your cool and tell her she has to wait."

I sighed. "She doesn't listen to me."

"Then that's just the way it is."

"Amy!" Why didn't she understand me? "I can't afford to lose control like that. I have to be functional. I'm not painting pictures. I've got no other choice."

"We always have choices."

There was no topic over which we could more vehemently disagree. She was not a woman who bowed to external pressures. For Amy we were all responsible for our own fates. Period.

Everything we did had consequences for which we were responsible. The choice was ours. Yes or no.

Life is too short for detours.

If you have a dream, you ought to live it.

I emptied my glass and poured myself another. "A voice in my head is bullying me around. I want to know where it comes from. I want to know how to get rid of it. ASAP."

"Then you need to see a doctor about medication. A psychiatrist will be able to help you. At least temporarily."

I saw by her eyes, by the twist of her lip, how little she thought of that idea.

"Okay, and what would you have me do?"

"I'm convinced that this voice has a purpose."

"And what might that be?" My skeptical tone was unmistakable.

"You've been through a lot this past year. You've lost a lot . . ." She paused meaningfully.

I didn't like the turn the conversation was taking. There were things I didn't want to talk about. Not even with Amy. "I know where you're going with that. But this voice has nothing to do with what happened in the spring."

"Are you sure?"

"Positive. Why would you think otherwise?"

She shrugged. "Just a thought."

We drank our wine, ate a few nuts, and did not say anything for a long time.

"You're asking a lot of yourself."

"Don't we all."

"Nonsense. You're the most self-disciplined person I know. You haven't allowed yourself a break for years."

"We went together to Long Island just this summer," I contradicted her.

"Two days. Then you had to come back early because Mulligan needed you. When you separated from Michael and moved out you sat on the cardboard moving boxes and wrote letters to clients because there were supposedly incredibly important deadlines that simply could not be postponed."

"They were important," I countered feebly.

"You were in the middle of breaking up with a boyfriend you had lived with for four years. You're not the only lawyer at your firm."

I nodded.

"This voice might be a sign . . ."

"You think I'm hearing some kind of suppressed ego that I've chronically neglected, right? But this isn't any internal dialog with myself. The voice is real. I hear it. I can describe it to you."

"How does it sound?"

"Older than me. Sometimes a bit gravelly. Deep for a woman. Stern."

A deliberate silence was her answer.

"I'm afraid," I said quietly.

She nodded. Her eyes wandered past me to a large painting on the wall. A red cross against a dark red background on which she had glued handfuls of red-dyed chicken feathers. *Buddha in the Henhouse*, read the label below it.

"I'm going to get out of the city for a few days the week after next. Would you care to come along?"

I shook my head. Amy made regular retreats to meditate at a Buddhist center in upstate New York. She had invited me to join her many times before, but I had always put her off. It was a mystery to me how she could sit there for an hour or more thinking of nothing. The few times I had tried it in yoga classes I had had so many thoughts, images, and memories running through my mind that I could hardly stand it. My head felt as if it were about to burst. I always cut the effort short after the first few minutes. Amy thought that I just needed proper instruction, but I doubted that.

I was slowly starting to feel the wine. I was being overtaken by an almost crippling weariness.

"I guess I'll be heading home."

"You can stay here if you like."

"I know. Thank you. But I've got so much to do this weekend, and I want to get an early start tomorrow."

She smiled and took me by the arm. The physical contact felt good. I would really have preferred to stay.

I had walked hardly a block along Rivington Street when I heard her again.

Who are you?

Chapter 4

HOW THIN IS the wall between us and madness? No one knows what it is made of. No one knows how much pressure it can withstand. Until it gives.

We all live on the edge.

It's just one step. A small one. Some of us sense it; others do not.

I slept late in an effort to stick to my usual Saturday routine, not to let myself get thrown off balance. Late breakfast, leisurely newspaper, a couple of e-mails to friends, laundry. All the same, my anxiety mounted throughout the morning, hour by hour. I no longer trusted the silence within me. I had the feeling that some invisible power was watching my every move. The voice was following me; I no longer had any doubt. It was only a matter of time before she would chime in again.

Before me lay the draft of our claim. To the left and right were piles of documents and correspondence. I was looking at a work-filled weekend.

Why don't you have any children?

It appalled me anew every time. From the neighbor's apartment came the muted sounds of piano music; the elevator chimed; police sirens rang up from Second Avenue; the voice repeated its question. It sounded as if she was standing behind me and speaking directly into my ear. I wanted to defend myself. But how? Against whom?

Why did I not have children? A question I hated. Why does a woman have to justify a childless life? No one would ever think to question a mother as to why she had children. Why did she have to pick that question? I pretended not to hear.

You should not live alone. It's not good.

The voice immediately adopted a snappier tone. I had a feeling I might be able to catch her off guard. I thought of what Amy had said. Talk with her. Listen to what she has to say.

You ought to . . .

—Where are you from? I cut her short.

Silence. I repeated my question and waited. As if she owed me an answer.

I . . . I don't know, she quietly replied.

—Why not?

I don't remember.

—What do you want from me?

Nothing.

—So why do you ask all those questions?

Because I want to know who you are.

—Why?

Because I live inside you. Because I am a part of you.

—No! You are not a part of me, I objected.

Oh yes I am.

—No. I know myself.

Are you sure? Who ever really knows herself?

You're a stranger.

I wasn't budging.

I am a part of you and will always be so.

I felt sick.

—If you really are a part of me, then I want you to keep your mouth shut.

I am a part of you, but you can't simply order me around. I am my own boss.

My hands started to tremble.

What are you afraid of?

—Who says I'm afraid?

Why else would you be trembling?

—Because I'm freezing.

What are you afraid of?

I. Am. Not. Afraid.

You are. I am well acquainted with fear.

That gave me pause.

—Why are you well acquainted with fear?

Silence.

Fear was my constant companion. I've lost everything.

—What did you lose?

Everything. That's all I know.

She fell silent. I waited to see whether she would speak up again. I stood up and paced excitedly around the apartment.

—What did you lose? Where are you from? Say something.

Inside me it was quiet.

—Why don't you answer me?

What was happening to me? Who was I talking to? Was it possible that my personality had split in two from one day to the next? Was that the definition of schizophrenia?

I opened my laptop and Googled "schizophrenia." Wikipedia defined it as a "mental disorder characterized by a breakdown of thought processes and by poor emotional responsiveness." It often struck suddenly, without having presented noticeable symptoms beforehand. "It most commonly features auditory hallucinations, paranoid or bizarre delusions, or disorganized speech and thinking." I paused and briefly wondered whether it would be better just to close the computer. Hallucinations. What was that supposed to mean? I read on, ill at ease: "They include . . . the belief that thoughts are being inserted into or withdrawn from one's conscious mind . . . and hearing hallucinatory voices that comment on one's thoughts or actions . . . The primary treatment of schizophrenia is antipsychotic medications, often in combination with psychological and social supports. Hospitalization may occur for severe episodes either voluntarily or (if mental health legislation allows it) involuntarily."

I felt worse with every sentence. I was not suffering from a psychosis. Nor was I having hallucinations. The voice was real. I was not imagining it.

I searched for books on the web that dealt with hearing voices. *Curing Schizophrenia, Curing Hallucinations,* and *Hear the Voice of the Lord* were popular titles. Nothing for me there.

A search for the phrase "hearing voices" turned up more than a million results across the web. The first was for a radio program. Below that some network or other was promising "information, support, and understanding for people who hear voices." WrongDiagnosis.com provided a list of seven illnesses that could cause the problem along with appropriate treatment strategies. I opened the page.

"Causes: schizophrenia, psychosis, psychotic depression, hallucinations."

I quickly closed the page and shut my laptop. I did not want to have anything to do with that world. I did not have mental-health issues. My mother suffered from depression and took Prozac. My sister-in-law, too. Some of my colleagues. Not me.

I did not believe in higher powers or third eyes.

Working was out of the question at that point. I was seized by an internal unrest that kept me in its grip the whole day long. I cleaned up like a woman possessed. Washed the kitchen cupboards. Shined all of my shoes. Rotated out my old clothes.

I went for a jog in Central Park and I couldn't stop running. My legs would not obey me. I ran three times farther than my usual route, a distance I had not thought myself capable of. I ran without pause, in spite of aching feet and a racing heart. Something was driving me on and on. Cramps in my legs eventually compelled me to stop. I leaned against a tree on the edge of Strawberry Fields and vomited.

LATER ON THAT night I was woken by a miserable sobbing. At first I thought it was a dream. Then I thought that Michael lay crying beside me. I turned on the light and stared at the empty half of the bed. The sobbing grew to a loud whimper. I climbed out of bed and checked whether anyone lay in front of my door or whether it might be coming from a neighboring apartment. All was quiet in the hall; inside me it was getting louder and louder.

It was going to drive me mad if I couldn't put an end to it.

—Hello? Who are you?

The crying only worsened. It did not sound defiant or angry, more like a suffering that no words could express.

—Is that you crying? Why won't you answer?

Nothing but that unbearable sobbing. It was harder on the heart than on the ears. It touched something inside me. I felt an anguish, a deeply suppressed grief, and I wasn't going to be able to endure it much longer before bursting into tears myself. I turned on all the lights and blasted the radio until the music drowned out the lamentation. Pretty soon the doorbell rang. The two neighbors at the door wanted to know whether I had completely lost my mind.

That was the moment when I realized I needed help.

Chapter 5

I WAS A bundle of nerves when I walked into Dr. Erikson's office shortly before eleven on Monday morning. I had been unable to concentrate on anything all weekend. With a comment or a question, the voice quickly put an end to my every attempt at work. I had hardly slept, and earlier in the morning I had admitted to Mulligan that my condition had worsened to include severe dizzy spells and stomach pains and that I was on my way to see a specialist. I found it humiliating to lie, but the truth was not an option.

Dr. Erikson was a psychiatrist. A friend of Amy's whose younger brother suffered from a psychosis had recommended him and by chance had been able to arrange the appointment for me on short notice.

He opened the door himself. A tall, athletic man, probably five, six years older than me. His firm handshake, the quiet way he looked at me, soothed my nerves to some extent. He led me to a small room with bare white walls and two cantilever chairs, where he invited me to take a seat.

Then he took up pad and paper and asked me what brought me to him.

I told him what I had gone through the past three days. He listened attentively, taking notes and asking the occasional question.

"I can't stand it any longer," I concluded my account. "I really hope that you can help me."

He looked me straight in the eye and said quietly: "I can help you, rest assured. We have an array of new antipsychotic drugs that work true miracles."

What was intended to calm me only increased my apprehension.

"Hearing voices is not as uncommon as you might think. It can be a symptom of some physical ailment. Alzheimer's, for instance. Parkinson's. A brain tumor. Or it could be the manifestation of some psychic affliction. Or it might have other causes entirely. In most cases we can treat it with medication. Are you taking any kind of pills at the moment?"

"Now and then some ibuprofen for a backache, nothing else."

"Drugs?"

"No." I rubbed in vain at a little spot on my pants.

"Alcohol?"

"Sure, but not much."

"How much?"

"A glass of wine with dinner. Sometimes two."

"When was the last time you were really drunk?"

"Oh, God, it's been forever. In college."

He nodded quickly. "Various drugs can have a halluci-nogenic affect. They are a common cause of hearing voices."

I wondered whether he believed me.

He pondered. "Does the voice seem familiar to you?"

"What do you mean?" I asked.

"There are people who have lost a friend, a parent, or a partner who later hear that person's voice."

"I haven't lost anyone close to me since my father died fourteen years ago."

"In other words, there's no individual to whom you could assign the voice?"

"No. And it doesn't boss me around or insult me, either."

He smiled. "I see you've already done some research on the subject. Do you ever have the feeling that other people can read your thoughts?"

"No."

"Do you sometimes feel watched or followed?"

"Only by the voice."

"Do you sometimes feel that other people can influence your thoughts?"

"Don't they always?"

A delicate smile was his answer. He eyed me critically.

My tension mounted. I was entrusting my inner life to him, at least a part of it, and I did not have the feeling that it was in good hands. For a moment I considered cutting the session short. The thought of once again being plagued by the voice held me back. I needed his help.

"Where is the voice coming from?" I asked after a pause. "How do I get rid of it?"

He rocked thoughtfully in his chair. "To judge by your portrayal I would assume that it is merely a psychotic or near-psychotic reaction."

"What is that? Why would it happen?"

"It varies. That sort of thing can emerge suddenly in stressful situations, during critical phases of transition. With young adults, for instance, when they move away from home. Starting a new job. Moving. The death of a family member, as I mentioned, could be a cause. Have you experienced any extraordinary strains in recent months?"

I hesitated briefly. "No."

"Of course, I can't rule out some form of schizophrenia at this point. But the way you describe the voice, I don't really think it's likely. In order to establish a clearer diagnosis I would need to know more about you and to follow the further developments. We'll see."

He saw the fear in my eyes and added, "But don't worry. Even in that case, we have medication for it. Has anyone else in your family had a mental illness?"

"My mother suffers from depression."

"Since when?"

"As long as I can remember."

"You, too?"

"No."

"Your siblings?"

"No."

He nodded thoughtfully and took a few notes. "Is there, or has there been, to the best of your knowledge, anyone in your extended family who hears voices?"

"My father could hear heartbeats," I answered spontaneously without thinking about what I was saying.

Dr. Erikson laughed. He took it for a joke.

I was not interested in letting him string me along. He had asked, and now he was going to get an answer: "He was born in Burma. His father died young, and his mother abandoned him because she was convinced that he was the cause of her misfortunes. A neighbor raised him. He was stricken blind when he was eight years old. In compensation he discovered the gift of hearing. He could distinguish birds by the beat of their wings. He knew whenever a spider was spinning a web nearby because he could hear it." I paused to see how the doctor was reacting. He was staring at me in disbelief, quite uncertain whether I seriously meant what I was telling him. I was gratified by his confusion and continued:

"And, as I said, he was able to hear heartbeats."

"Heartbeats?" echoed Dr. Erikson, as if attempting to ascertain whether he had heard me correctly.

"Yes. My father could recognize a person by his or her heartbeat, and he discovered that every heart sounds different, and that the tone of the heartbeat, as with a voice, was a window onto a person's inner state. He fell in love with a young girl because he had never before heard any sound as beautiful as the beating of her heart."

"Very interesting," he said with a worried expression. "Do you have other fantasies, or do you sometimes see things that others cannot see?"

"The girl's name," I continued, undeterred, "was Mi Mi. She was extremely beautiful but could not walk on her own because her feet were misshapen. So my father would carry her on his back. He became her legs, and she his eyes, if you understand what I mean."

Dr. Erikson nodded. "Of course I understand what you mean, Ms. Win."

"Later, thanks to an operation, he regained his sight but lost the gift of extraordinary hearing. Not that he became deaf, but his hearing was no longer so remarkably acute."

"And you?" he asked carefully. "Can you also hear heartbeats?"

"Unfortunately not."

Dr. Erikson looked at his watch, skepticism palpable on his face.

What do you want here?

The moment I had been dreading the whole time.

—Keep quiet, I commanded her.

What do you want from this man?

—Help. I want help.

You don't need help.

—Oh, yes I do.

This man can't help you.

—Why not?

Because he didn't understand a word you said. He thinks that people see with their eyes. How is he supposed to help you?

—How do you know that?

It's plain to see.

"Is something wrong?"

"What would be wrong?"

"You've gone pale. Your lips are quivering. Are you hearing the voice now?"

I nodded.

"What is it saying?"

"That I don't need any help."

A knowing smile flitted across his face. "Anything else?"

"That you cannot help me."

"Why not? Has it revealed that to you, too?"

Tell him. He doesn't understand you.

I thought about it briefly. "No, it hasn't."

"I figured as much. The voice within you feels threatened by me. It's a typical defensive reaction."

He's crazy.

"Try to ignore it."

"If it were that easy I wouldn't be sitting here."

"I know, but try. You need to learn how. Just let the voice talk. Don't listen to it. Whatever it says is unimportant. It has nothing to do with you."

He's got no idea what he's talking about. He's nuts. Trust me. He's a typical Saya Gyi.

What was a *Saya Gyi*? I thought about U Ba. I thought about Amy. My head was spinning.

"I'm going to prescribe Zyprexa," I heard him telling me as if through a wall. "Take five milligrams later today and then the same amount every evening for the next seven days. That will help you. It can cause side effects. You're likely to feel tired and sleepy for the first few days. You should take the rest of the week off from work. Many patients also complain of weight gain. Dizziness. Constipation. In most cases it's temporary. No action without a reaction. But with this medication you'll be ready for work again just after Thanksgiving, at the latest. You should come to see me again in a week. You'll be doing much better by then. I promise."

I had what I wanted: a first diagnosis. A prescription and a confident assurance that it would work. All the same, I left the office more stressed than when I had arrived.

THE CLERK AT the pharmacy explained the side effects of the medication a second time, but I was too exhausted to pay close attention. Back at home I went straight to the kitchen without even taking off my coat. I filled a glass with lukewarm water, took the medicine out of my pocket, and pushed a pill out of the packaging.

Don't take it! Leave it alone.

Try to ignore it.

It's not going to help you.

You need to learn how. Don't listen to it.

Don't do it.

Whatever it says is unimportant.

I put the pill on my tongue and took a mouthful of water.

Shortly thereafter I was overcome by an infinite weariness. I lay down on my bed fully dressed and went right to sleep.

Chapter 6

IN THE DAYS that followed the voice continued to torment me with questions; at night she woke me with her sobbing. The lack of sleep was wearing me down. My body ached; I couldn't concentrate on anything. I would put the newspaper down after only a few minutes. Reading a book was out of the question.

No matter what I was doing, no matter where I went or what I saw, I thought of nothing but the voice in my head. Even when she was quiet.

I apologized to Mulligan in a dramatic e-mail referring to serious health problems on which I did not elaborate; further rigorous testing was going to be necessary. He replied full of concern and wished me a speedy recovery.

On one of my restless wanderings about the city I noticed a man in the Union Square subway station. He was about my age, wearing a black suit and a white shirt. A briefcase between his legs. All around him people were bustling from one platform to another. The man stood rooted to the spot.

Amid the deafening roar of the arriving trains I could just make out isolated phrases. "Hearken unto the Lord . . . we are sinners all . . . put your faith in the Lord . . . you have gone astray . . ." No one besides me paid him any mind. Even if someone had taken pity on him and stayed to listen, they would not have been able to pick up even one complete sentence. I wondered what drove him to it. Did he, too, hear a voice? Did it command him to preach to arriving trains in one of New York's biggest subway stations? What power would my voice acquire over me with time?

IN SPITE OF my fears I took the prescribed medication only twice. It was not the objections of the voice that held me back. Nor was it the possible side effects. It was the intended effect. The thought that I would be consuming a chemical substance that would overpower me. Direct me, control me. A strange heaviness had overcome me already that first time. The feeling of being a stranger in my own body.

Every fiber of my being resisted it. Under no circumstances was I willing to enslave myself to these little white pills. It had not yet come to that. There must be some other way to rid myself of the voice. I needed to try something completely different, only I didn't know what. Should I follow Amy's advice and withdraw with her to the forests of upstate New York? Meditate? I feared that the quiet there would only exacerbate my condition.

The one thing that helped was classical music. When

I lay on the sofa listening to Mozart, Bach, or Haydn, the voice fell silent. The tones of the violin, the cello, and the piano worked on her like an exorcist. As if their melodies could lay her to rest. I had to be careful, though, not to do anything else at the same time. No reading, no cleaning up, no cooking. She would chime right in. *Knock it off. Make up your mind: Listen to music or read. Listen to music or get dinner ready. It won't do to try both at once.* I was always trying to do much too much at once rather than concentrating on a single thing. That was not going to turn out well. She would not stand for it.

Thanksgiving only made things worse. For the first time in my life I would be spending the holiday alone. Amy was visiting a relative in Boston. The few other friends whose company I might have enjoyed were celebrating with their families. Half the country was going to be traveling. I had turned down my brother's halfhearted invitation to San Francisco weeks ago.

I had never seen the city so empty. Nary a car on the street, shops and cafés closed. Even the homeless man who always sat at the corner of Second and Fifty-ninth had disappeared. I called half a dozen restaurants looking to order in; not one was open.

By dinnertime the whole building smelled like roasting turkey. From the other apartments on the floor came the laughter of the revelers. The clink of glasses. The aroma of cranberries, glazed carrots, green beans, sweet potatoes, and pumpkin pie.

The miserable stench of loneliness.

I ate leftovers from the fridge and, against the vociferous objections of the voice, drank almost a whole bottle of red wine. She turned out to be right. The alcohol did me no good. I started to pity myself. I ended up huddled in tears on the couch.

On Sunday evening Amy returned from Massachusetts. We had talked on the phone several times over the past few days. She was relieved when I went off the meds, and she kept inviting me to spend a few days in the countryside with her. She was really worried about me now. Wouldn't I come with her to the Buddhist center after all? It would do me good to disengage. She promised. And if it didn't, we could be back in Manhattan within three hours. I had nothing to lose.

By that point I didn't care where we went. I was at the end of my rope. I couldn't stand to be alone anymore. I needed to get out of the city.

Chapter 7

THE TAXI TURNED around and rolled slowly back down the dirt road. The driver shot us one more look of pity, then disappeared around the bend.

Amy and I stood there surrounded by an eerie silence. No birds, no insects. Not even the wind whispering in the treetops.

I looked around. Not much color. Leafless trees, scraggy brush, boulders thrusting up out of the earth. A world in grayish brown. Vacant.

For one long moment I felt as if I had been marooned.

Amy shouldered her backpack, nodded to me, and led the way. We walked up a path and crossed through a bit of forest until a bizarre building appeared on a hill before us. The bottom part looked like a blocky, flat conference center with large windows. Above that someone had set a pagoda roof, complete with octagonal cupola, little towers, golden ornamentation, and Buddhist symbols presiding over the corners. Our path led straight to it.

A slender woman in a light-pink robe met us at the entrance. Her hair was cropped short. Her smile and her soft features masked her age. She and Amy were apparently well acquainted with each other, but she greeted me with no less warmth. We followed her around the main building to the guest quarters. Breathing heavily, she climbed up to the second floor and showed us where we would be staying.

My room was maybe eight feet by ten. There was a bed, a chair, and a little cabinet. On the nightstand stood a Buddha made of light-colored wood. Behind it, in a vase, a red plastic hibiscus blossom. On the wall hung a painting of a meditating Buddha and a plaque with some of his aphorisms: "No sorrow can befall those who never try to possess people and things as their own."

I thought of my brother in Burma. Had he internalized this idea? Is that why he could remain so serene? In spite of the poverty in which he lived?

The nun led us into the hallway and showed us where to find the bathroom and the shower. On the first floor, she told us, was a shared kitchen. The food in the refrigerator and the cabinets was available to all. There would be five other guests in the house. If we wished, we were welcome to participate an hour from now in the communal meditation that happened every afternoon at four. Dinner was at six, and, as with all the activities, participation was voluntary.

Amy wanted me to drink a cup of tea with her before the meditation, but I was not in the mood.

I put my backpack down, closed the door, and opened the window.

A world without police sirens. Without cars. Without music from the next apartment.

A silence without voice.

She had not uttered a word since our departure from New York. It had been days since she had held her tongue for such a long time. Why had she suddenly clammed up?

—Hello? Tentatively.

—Where are you? More tentatively still.

No answer.

I lay down on the bed. Waited. Impatiently. On the one hand I wished for nothing more fervently than to be rid of her for good.

On the other hand.

The vague awareness that it would not happen of its own accord. That I was going to have to get to the bottom of what was going on inside myself. Where the voice came from. What she wanted from me.

THE MEDITATION HALL was bigger than it had looked from the outside. It could accommodate several hundred people. Red carpeting on the floor. In one corner were piles of red blankets and blue meditation pillows. In three glass cases a range of Buddhist statuary; on small tables in front of them were offerings: a couple of oranges, bananas, cookies. The sweet fragrance of smoldering incense sticks filled the hall.

I arrived somewhat late. Amy and the others were already sitting in a row meditating. I took a pillow and a blanket and sat in a lotus position beside them. I closed my eyes and listened to the quiet breathing of the others. Peace like theirs eluded me. My heart beat fiercely; my breath was shallow and quick. There was a din in my head. Thoughts flitted past like clouds before a brisk wind. I thought of Mulligan with his bushy eyebrows. Of my brother's small ears, inherited from our mother. Of U Ba's threadbare green longyi. I saw an ice floe slowly melting in a lake until it vanished entirely. I thought of my shoes, which needed polishing. Of the milk spoiling in my refrigerator.

The harder I strove to concentrate, the more banal and intrusive my thoughts became. It was like the times I had tried to meditate in yoga class. My teacher's deep *Om* had not resonated with me. Relaxed emptiness, Buddhist serenity, had not descended on me. Frustration, rather. At myself. Why was I unable to sit still and do nothing? Why could I not stem the persistent flow of thoughts in my mind?

I opened my eyes. Not even ten minutes had passed. What was the point of sitting here motionless for another three quarters of an hour subjecting myself to the torment of superfluous thoughts? Could I not make some better use of my time? Going for a walk? Reading? Helping to get the dinner ready? I was just about to stand up when I heard footsteps behind me. The light, nimble gait of a child. I turned around. A monk, a short, older Asian man in a dark-red robe, head shaven, approached me and sat down next to me. Our eyes met, and he greeted me with a congenial chuckle.

As if we had known each other for years.

I could not take my eyes off him. He was wearing absurdly large glasses with thick lenses, the black frames much too dramatic for his thin face. His nose was unusually sharp, his eyes small. His full lips made me think of Botox. His smile revealed a prominent overbite. At the same time he carried himself with considerable grace. He radiated a dignity that I found impossible to reconcile with an outward appearance he was either unaware of or completely indifferent to.

He lay his hands in his lap, closed his eyes, and I could see his features relaxing further.

I also gave it another try, but now I saw the old man's face before me the whole time. From one minute to the next I became increasingly agitated. My pelvis ached, and my back was cramping up. My throat started to itch. It was torture; contemplation was out of the question.

At some point the gong sounded to indicate the end of the meditation. Relieved, I opened my eyes. The old monk beside me had vanished. I looked around the room, somewhat irritated. Amy hadn't moved yet. The others were slowly getting to their feet.

Of the old monk there was no trace.

SOON AFTERWARD WE met with the other guests for dinner. They were all from New York City. A yoga instructor, about my age. An older widower hoping through meditation finally to bid farewell to a wife who had died a year earlier. A student seeking something, she wasn't sure what. A journalist who spent most of his time talking about a book he was working on called *The Power of Silence*. I ate my vegetable curry and hoped that his writing was more engaging than his conversation. And the whole time I could not get the old monk out of my mind. Between Amy and me one look was sufficient, and a couple of minutes later we were sitting in my room.

She had brought a bag, and she had an air of mystery about her. Out of the bag emerged a candle, two small glasses, a corkscrew, and a bottle of wine.

"Is that allowed?" I asked, surprised. The lawyer in me.

Amy smiled and put a finger to her lips.

She lit the candle and turned out the light, opened the bottle quietly, poured for both of us, and sat down next to me on the bed.

"The Buddha says: 'A fool who recognizes his own ignorance is thereby in fact a wise man.'"

"I think he also frowns on drinking alcohol. Or will drinking wine turn us into sages?"

She nodded conspiratorially.

"So are you a Buddhist or not?"

"Almost."

"What does 'almost' mean?"

"The Buddha says: 'To live is to suffer.'"

"And?" I asked, now curious.

She leaned far over to me and whispered: "The master is mistaken: to live is to love."

"Love and suffering are not mutually exclusive," I quipped. "Perhaps one even implies the other?"

"Nonsense. Anyone who truly loves does not suffer," she countered, still in a whisper. An even lower whisper.

"Oh, please."

"No, really. Trust me."

She leaned back, smiled, and raised her glass slightly. "To the lovers."

"And the sufferers."

I did not wish to pursue the matter and asked whether she had noticed the old monk with the oversized glasses during the meditation.

Amy shook her head. "But the nun told me that they have a monk visiting from Burma."

"What did she say about him?" I asked, curious to know more.

"I guess he's pretty old, and in Burma he's highly esteemed and has lots of devotees. Supposedly people come from all over the country seeking his advice in difficult situations. He was forced to flee, I'm not sure why. He's been here four weeks and is leading a secluded life in a small hut somewhat deeper into the woods. They don't see him very often; she said he doesn't usually participate in the group meditation. Funny that today is the day he would show up."

We gazed silently for a while into the light of the candles.

"What does the voice have to say about our excursion?"

"Nothing at all."

"Didn't I tell you that it would do you good to get away from it all? You should listen to me more often."

"I'm not sure that it's just a matter of getting away from it all."

"What else, then?"

"Maybe . . . I don't know."

"Time will tell. Do you want to go back tomorrow, or should we stay a bit longer?"

I nodded. We clinked glasses. Quietly. We two conspirators.

THERE WAS A freeze during the night. A thin layer of frost covered the grass. The house was empty; the others had already gone to the first meditation. I saw their footprints in the lawn. Every step we take leaves a trace.

I got dressed and went outside. Cold, clear air. It smelled like winter. The bare, thin trees looked like sticks rammed by some giant into the ground.

The rising sun, a reddish sky.

I was not about to go suffer through another meditation. Better to go for a walk. A clearly marked trail led away from the house into the woods.

A brook. The first icicles on branches rising up out of the water.

The crackling of twigs under my feet.

~~~~

WHY ARE WE HERE?

Not joy, certainly not. But a curious relief.

—Because I'm looking for answers.

To which questions?

—Why I hear you. Where you are from.

Silence.

—Where have you been this whole time?

No reaction.

—What's bothering you?

I want to get out of here.

—Why?

I'm afraid, she answered in a whisper.

Of what?

I'm suffocating from fear. Help me.

There was no trace now of the intrusive, demanding tone she had bullied me with in New York. She sounded now weak and needy.

—What are you afraid of?

I don't know. She paused for a long while. *Of boots. Black boots. Polished. So shiny that I can see my fear reflected in them.*

—Whose boots?

The boots of Death.

—Who is wearing them?

The emissaries.

—Which emissaries?

The emissaries of Fear.

—Who is sending them?

Silence.

—What can you remember?

White pagodas. Red flecks. Everywhere. On the ground. On the wood. Red fluid running out of mouths. Coloring everything. My thoughts. My dreams. My life.

—Blood? You remember blood?

It's dripping onto my face. Into my eyes. It burns. Oh, how it burns.

She cried out briefly. I winced.

—What's happening?

It hurts. So much.

—What hurts?

The memory.

—Which memory? Where are you from?

From a land you know well.

—Where exactly?

From the island.

—Which island?

Thay hsone thu mya, a hti kyan thu mya a thet shin nay thu mya san sar yar kywn go thwa mai.

—What did you say?

She repeated the unfamiliar sounds.

—What language is that?

I can't go on. Please help me.

—How can I help you?

Leave this place. I don't want to go back.

—Back? Back where?

To the island.

—We're not going to any island.

Oh, yes we are. We're headed there right now.

—I don't understand what you're talking about. You have to explain it to me.

She fell silent again.

—Don't leave, stay here. Try to remember.

No answer.

How was I supposed to piece together those fragments of her memories? A land I know? Boots of Death? Emissaries of Fear? What did it all mean? I hadn't the foggiest.

Suddenly a small hut appeared among the trees. A cabin built of dark-brown timbers, an A-frame. On both sides the roof reached clear to the ground. On the porch a monk's robe was hung over a line. From the chimney, snow white billows. I walked right to it without any hesitation.

As if someone had called me.

Through the large front window I could see the monk from yesterday. He was sitting in the middle of the room on a tatami mat reading a book. In a wood stove behind him a fire was blazing.

I knocked and opened the door without waiting for an answer.

He looked up and set his book aside.

"How nice to see you," he said in a distinctly British accent. "Come in."

I took off my shoes and went in, closed the door. I stood before him, uncertain. What was I doing here?

"Come closer. Please, sit down." He gestured to a spot on the floor in front of him.

I hesitated, embarrassed.

Neither of us spoke. He was a master of the art of waiting.

Eventually I took a few steps forward and sat down.

"Do you know who I am?" I asked tentatively.

"I am a monk, not a clairvoyant." He smirked.

More silence. The crackle of the burning wood. He looked at me. A gaze that harbored no demands. Gradually I felt as if I was arriving in the room.

"You are from Burma?"

The old monk nodded.

"So was my father."

He nodded again.

"I've heard that people in Burma come to you when they need advice."

"Sometimes, yes."

"How do you help them?"

"I listen to their stories and remind them."

"Of what?"

"Of a few truths that we all know but sometimes forget."

"Which truths?"

"Aren't you in a hurry!"

"Is that bad?"

"Grass does not grow more quickly for pulling on it. Have you ever meditated?"

"Yes, yesterday. Next to you," I replied testily.

"You sat there and did nothing. That's not the same."

"How do you know that?"

He smiled. "If you like, I will help you."

"With what?"

"Coming to rest."

I had no reason to refuse.

He slid over to me until he was sitting right in front of me. Knee to knee. He did nothing but wait patiently again. Behind him the fire blazed in the stove. He gave me the feeling that I had all the time in the world. My breath, much too quick, gradually slowed. He took my cold hands, which I willingly let him do. As if I had been waiting for it to happen all along. He examined them slowly from both sides. I closed my eyes and let it happen. Heard his even breath. Felt his warm fingers. His soft, wrinkled skin. The sensation of falling. Like a leaf drifting to the ground from a great height. Unhurried. Inexorable. Calmly fulfilling its destiny.

He was supporting my hands. And me.

I lost all sense of time.

When I returned to the guest house Amy was already cleaning up from breakfast.

"Where were you?"

"In the woods," I answered spontaneously.

"Meditating?"

I nodded.

"With the old monk?"

I nodded again, astounded afresh at how well Amy knew me.

"Pity he's not a bit younger," she said with a wink.

~~~~~~

THE NEXT MORNING I woke before sunrise. I would have liked more than anything to go straight to the old monk, but I waited until all the others had left for the meditation hall. Then I got up, dressed, and set off.

"Come in, sit down," he said, not in the least surprised to see me again. "Or lie down, if you prefer."

I took off my shoes and stretched out on the floor. Only now did I notice how cold I was and that I was shivering all over. He spread a blanket over me and squatted right behind me. He put his hands briefly on my temples and then tucked them like a thin pillow under my head. They were wonderfully warm. I closed my eyes. My breathing slowed, the shivers dissipated, and a feeling of calm stole over me that I had only ever experienced with my brother U Ba. As if I could entrust everything to the hands of this old man. The weight of my entire world.

"What is troubling you?"

Sometimes one question is enough.

And so I began to tell. Of an oversized love and my longing for it. Of unlived lives. Of butterflies one could recognize by their wing beats. Of the *Book of Solitude* and its many chapters. Of the mighty wings of Deceit, which darkened the heavens until they were black. Of the many colors of grief. And of dread. Of the voice and her questions. And mine. Of my fear of her. And of myself.

I felt the tears streaming down my cheeks. Flushing out things I had thought buried forever.

He said nothing.

I knew that he understood every word. When I was through, he brushed the hair out of my face and gently stroked my brow. His fingers had the softness of a child's.

"Something extraordinary has happened to you. In my entire life I have only ever encountered this phenomenon one other time." He spoke slowly and quietly, but his voice suddenly betrayed an urgency. "You know that we Buddhists believe in rebirth. The body dies while the soul, if you will, lives on. It departs the body and slips into a newly born being. We call the process reincarnation. The karma from one's previous life determines the future life. If you have done good, then something good will eventually come your way. If you have mistreated your fellows, you will have to bear the consequences. Nothing vanishes. Many Buddhists think that people with bad karma can be reborn as monkeys or lice. That is not my belief."

The monk paused. He was talking in riddles. I had no idea what he was getting at or what it might have to do with me.

"In your particular case, there's something." He faltered. "I can think of no way to say it that will not seem like quackery to you."

He sat for a while in silence. "In your case, something went wrong, to put it bluntly, during one of these processes of transformation. I'll try to explain it to you."

He stood up, put another log on the fire, and sat down beside me again.

"You are hearing a woman's voice?"

"Yes."

"She remembers white pagodas and red stains on the ground? She is afraid of black boots?"

"Yes."

"Yesterday she uttered phrases in a strange language, something like *Thay hsone thu mya, a hti kyan thu mya a thet shin nay thu mya san sar yar kywn go thwa mai*. Did I understand that correctly?"

"It sounded something like that, yes."

"It's Burmese. It means 'The Isle of the Dead. The Isle of the Loving. Of the Lonely.' Given all you have told me of this voice, given the things she knows and doesn't know, I suspect that she lived in Burma. She must have been a troubled spirit. A restless individual whose soul could not find peace after death, but took refuge in you instead. Which means that two souls now live in your body."

I sat up abruptly. Astonishment in his eyes. Doubt in mine.

"Two souls?" I asked.

"Yes."

"I don't believe it."

Not all explicable things are true.

Not all truths are explicable.

"I can't say that I blame you. It is a most unusual story. Yet I am convinced that it has happened just that way."

"How long will this soul stay inside me before she moves along?"

"Until you die."

"Forever? I'll never be rid of her?"

Swaying back and forth a bit with his upper body, he took my hands. "There is one possibility to lead her back . . ."

The monk paused and looked at me for a long while. "You would have to find out who this woman was. Find out why she died. In that way and only that way will she have a chance to find peace. Then she would be able to leave your body again. But you would be setting off on a long journey. A journey whose destination is unknown to you. Are you ready to do that?"

Chapter 8

A WARM WIND played in my hair; the blinding sun stood almost directly overhead. I stood in the shadow of an airplane's tail, one hand over my eyes, surveying my surroundings. Heho Airport consisted of a single tiny terminal, one runway, and a tower that did not rise above the treetops. Ours was the only plane. It stood on the airfield like an intruder from a very strange, very distant world.

The pilot had powered down the engines, and I heard nothing beyond the rushing of the wind. The other passengers, a tour group from Italy, a few Burmese, and two monks, had gone ahead and were gradually disappearing into the little arrivals area. Three men were pulling a baggage car behind them loaded with suitcases, bags, and backpacks. A gust of wind stirred up a thin light-brown dust devil and chased it across the airfield. I picked up my bag and hesitantly followed the men. Again and again I stopped and looked around. As if reassuring myself where I had landed.

I had spent the days since my conversation with the monk in a kind of trance. My decision to follow his advice. Amy's encouragement, as if she feared I might reconsider. My hasty travel preparations. The long flight to Bangkok, the delayed arrival, the missed connection to Rangoon. Waiting for hours in a lounge. I had drowsed my way through a large part of the trip.

Now I was shedding stress with every step. My exhaustion and weariness were falling away. The anticipation was too intense. I could hardly wait another minute to see my brother again. With his help I would be able to sort out the fate of the voice inside me.

There was nothing at all going on in front of the airport. One old, dented Toyota waited with rolled-down windows on a patch of sand in front of a shack. The driver sat sleeping behind the wheel. Someone had painted the word "Taxi" in black paint on the door. I knocked hesitantly on the hood. The driver didn't move. A second knock, more assertive. He lifted his head and looked at me through groggy eyes.

"Can you take me to Kalaw?"

The man smiled cheerfully, yawned and stretched. He stepped out, retied his longyi, opened the trunk with a screwdriver, stowed my backpack, and tried, in spite of the broken lock, to close the trunk. When that didn't work, he enlisted the help of a bit of wire that he wrapped around the fender and passed through a hole eaten into the metal by rust. He reached through the window to open the door for me from the inside. The springs had worn deep circles in the shabby upholstery. Up front there were no controls and no dashboard, just a wild chaos of black, yellow, and red cables and wires. I hesitated.

He nodded encouragingly, and I got it. Soon we were stopping at a stand by the side of the road. The driver bought a bag of betel nuts and a freshly woven garland of white jasmine, which he hung from the rearview mirror. For a moment, the fragrance filled the car.

The wind on the road was cool and dry. I tried to roll up a window, but the handles were missing on both sides.

I felt how the driver was watching me in the mirror.

"Are you cold, Miss?"

"A little," I replied.

He nodded. For a few seconds he reduced his speed, only to pick it up again around the next bend.

"Where may I take you in Kalaw, Miss?"

"Is the Kalaw Hotel still there?"

"Of course."

"That will do, then."

Our eyes met in the mirror. He wagged his head slightly and smiled. His teeth were stained bloodred from chewing betel nuts. "If Miss would like, I can recommend other hotels."

"What's wrong with the Kalaw Hotel?"

He was quiet for a moment. "Nothing, Miss. It's just that we natives would not like to stay there."

"Why not?"

"Word is there are ghosts there."

I might have known. "What kind of ghosts?" I asked, sighing slightly.

"Oh, it is a very sad story. The hotel served as a hospital during the war. Unfortunately several English died there. Their ghosts still roam about the house, it is said."

"I don't believe in ghosts. Have you ever seen one?"

"No, of course not."

"You see?"

"But I do not stay in the Kalaw Hotel." He wagged his head again and smiled.

"Have you ever spoken with anyone who has seen one?"

"No, Miss. My passengers do not sleep there."

"I have already stayed once at that hotel, for two weeks, and I did not meet a single ghost."

I suspected he was getting a higher kickback from other hotels and left it at that.

We drove through a hilly landscape where farming could not have been easy. Not far from the road a man with a water buffalo was plowing a field. It must have rained not long before. The ground was slippery; man and beast were covered with mud. The emaciated buffalo plodded through the mire; the farmer, clad only in a drenched longyi, drove the plow with all his strength. Both looked as if they might collapse at any moment.

A couple of hundred yards away a golden stupa sparkled in the sun. Hidden among the hills and fields, between the trees or in bamboo groves, I glimpsed pagodas, monasteries, and temples.

On one occasion we stopped abruptly for two stubborn oxen whose cart was blocking the way.

A good hour later we pulled into the driveway of the Kalaw Hotel. The driver stopped before the entrance, fetched my backpack from the trunk, gave me a card with his name and address, in case I reconsidered and wanted other accommodations, wished me a pleasant stay in Kalaw, and went on his way. Hotel employees were so far nowhere to be seen.

The door stood wide open, so I climbed the few steps and entered the building with a pounding heart. One glance at the reception area was all it took for the memories to come flooding back. The clocks on the wall showing the local times in Bangkok, Paris, Tokyo, New York, and Myanmar, all of them incorrect. The plaster flaking off the walls like skin after a sunburn. The key cabinets, in which I had never seen a single key. Not during my previous stay, and not now, either. The cold neon light. Highly polished floors. Yellow drapes billowing sedately in the breeze.

A sense of returning home. As if I had spent years of my life in this hotel.

"Hello," I called, but got no answer.

In an adjacent room a television was playing, a young man sleeping on the bench in front of it.

"Hello," I called again loudly, knocking on the door frame. The young man woke and looked at me in surprise. A guest was apparently the last thing he had been expecting.

My room, 101, had not changed.

Large with a high ceiling, whitewashed walls, two beds, a little nightstand between them, a table and two armchairs in front of the window, even the Korean mini-fridge still occupied its former location. Still out of order.

The young woman at the reception desk was very friendly. She knew a few English phrases. She did not know U Ba.

I set out to find the teahouse where I had met my brother for the first time. Someone there would certainly know where he lived. I walked down the street that led from the hotel to the middle of the town. It was bordered by poinsettia, oleander, and elder bushes, and it was in better condition than what I remembered. Leisurely pedestrians ambled along, most hand in hand or arm in arm. Almost everyone greeted me with a smile. A young boy on a bike that was much too big for him rode toward me and called out: "How are you?"

Before I could answer he had disappeared around the next corner.

I came to a fork in the road. I stopped and tried to get my bearings. On the right was a park populated by the overgrown remains of a mini-golf course. At the entrance two horse-drawn carriages waited in the shadow of a pine. On the left the main artery led to the city center. I followed it and walked past a school with children's voices spilling out the open windows.

And then I discovered U Ba. I recognized him from a distance. I knew him by his gait, by the slight spring in his step. By the way he held up his longyi a little with his right hand in order to be able to walk more quickly. He was walking in the street and coming right toward me. I felt my heart race. Every ounce of me remembered.

My eyes welled up with tears. I swallowed, pressed my lips firmly together. Where had I been so long? Why had I never given in to my longing for U Ba, for Kalaw? How hard it is to follow one's heart. Whose life had I been leading these past ten years?

He looked up and spotted me. We both slowed our steps. Paused briefly, then continued on until we stood face-to-face.

One of us tall, the other short. One of us not so young anymore, the other not yet so old. Brother and sister.

I wanted to hug him, to press him to me, but my body would not obey. It was U Ba who broke the tension. He took one small last step toward me, stretched out his arms, took my face gingerly in his hands. Looked at me out of tired, exhausted eyes. I saw how they turned wet. How they filled, drop by drop, until they overflowed.

His lips were quivering.

"I took my time," I whispered.

"You did. Forgive me for not meeting you at the airport."

"U Ba! You didn't even know I was coming."

"No?" A smile, just a brief one.

I put my arms around him. He stood on tiptoes and put his head on my shoulder for a moment.

Some dreams are big. Some small.

"Where are your things?"

"At the hotel."

"Then we must fetch them later. You'll stay with me, won't you?"

I thought of his hut. I thought of the swarm of bees, of the sagging couch, of the pig under the house. "I don't know. I would hate to be a burden."

"A burden? Julia, it would be an honor." He faltered briefly and then continued quietly and with a wink: "Aside from the fact that the people of Kalaw would never speak to me again if they heard that I made my sister stay in a hotel after she had traveled around the world to visit me. Out of the question."

U Ba took my arm in his and led me back in the direction he had come from. "For a start, let's go drink some tea and have a bite to eat. You must be hungry from your long trip, no? Do they give you anything at all to eat in those airplanes?"

We crossed the street and made for a restaurant. It had a large patio with umbrellas, low tables, and tiny stools, and it was very full. We sat under an umbrella at the last free table. My knees stuck up above the table.

Beside us sat two women in animated conversation, on the other side two soldiers in green uniforms. U Ba greeted them with a quick nod.

"This establishment belongs to the same people who owned the teahouse where we first met," he said, coughing.

I thought of the shabby old shack with its dusty floor

and greasy display cases full of fly-ridden pastries and rice cakes. "It's a big improvement."

"You brought them luck," replied U Ba, beaming at me.

My brother observed me for a long time without saying a word. The tea came in two espresso cups. There was a dead insect floating in mine. "Oh, so sorry," said the waitress when I pointed it out to her. She took a little spoon, fished the creature out of the tea, and tossed it over the railing. I was too surprised to say anything, and she shuffled off.

"Would you like a new one?" asked U Ba.

I nodded.

He deftly swapped our cups.

"That's not what I meant," I said, embarrassed.

The tea had a very distinctive flavor that I had only ever encountered in Burma. Very strong, a hint of bitterness, overlain by sweetened condensed milk.

U Ba sipped at his tea without taking his eyes off me. It was not a gaze intended to provoke. Not an evaluation, an analysis or examination. It simply rested on me. I found it unsettling all the same. Ten years had passed. Why were the words not bubbling out of us? *How are you? What are you doing?* Didn't we have anything to say to each other after all that time?

I was ready to break the silence between us, but he intimated with his eyes that I should wait a moment yet. The waitress brought two steaming bowls of noodle soup.

" 'Defy ephemerality. Wander not always ahead of yourself in thought, but neither dawdle in the past. It is the art of arrival. Of being in one, only one, place at one time. Of absorbing it with all of your senses. Its beauty, its ugliness, its singularity. Of allowing oneself to be overwhelmed, fearlessly. The art of being where you are.' I read that once in a book I was restoring. I think it was called *On Travel*. Do you like it?"

I nodded, even if I wasn't quite sure what he meant.

He tipped his head to one side and smiled at me. "You are lovely. Even lovelier than my memory of you."

I laughed, embarrassed.

"Today is the fifteenth. Quite a coincidence," I said, hoping he would understand the allusion.

"I know. How could I forget?" A shadow passed across his face.

"Do they still hold the procession to honor Mi Mi and our father?"

U Ba shook his head gravely and glanced uncomfortably around the establishment. He leaned over to me and whispered: "The military has forbidden it."

"What!?" I said. Loudly. Much too loudly. "Why?"

He suppressed a wince. The soldiers at the next table got up and looked at us with curiosity on their way out. In front of the teahouse they climbed into an army Jeep and drove off. They left behind a cloud of dust that drifted our way and then settled drearily among the stools and tables. I gave a short cough.

My brother, by contrast, was breathing easier. "The army does not like demonstrations."

"Not even when they commemorate two lovers?" I wondered.

"Then least of all." He sipped at his tea. "What are people with guns most afraid of? Other people with guns? No! What do violent individuals fear most? Violence? I should say not! By what do the cruel and selfish feel most threatened? All of them fear nothing as much as they fear love."

"But people were just bringing flowers to Mi Mi's house. What was so dangerous about that?"

"People who love are dangerous. They know no fear. They obey other laws."

U Ba wanted to pay. The waitress said something I didn't understand in Burmese; my brother said a few sentences back, and they both laughed.

"They don't want our money. It's on the house."

"Thank you."

"She is thanking *you*."

"What for?"

"For allowing her to show you a kindness."

I was too exhausted to follow that logic. I nodded amiably and stood up.

"Shall we hire a carriage to take us to the hotel? I'm sure you are tired after your exertions."

"No, that's all right. It's not far. I can make it."

U Ba coughed again. A dry, piercing cough.

"Do you have a cold?"

He shook his head and took me by the arm. We strolled along the main street toward the hotel. I thought I could feel my brother gently holding me back every time I started to walk faster.

The sun was casting long shadows and would soon dip behind the mountains. The air was noticeably cooler.

In the hotel U Ba waited at the desk while I went to the second floor and got my things together. As a courtesy I paid for two nights.

U Ba, deaf to all objections, shouldered my backpack and sped on ahead.

Chapter 9

I WAS DYING to see whether my brother had renovated or modified his house. With the money I sent him he ought to have been able to rebuild it completely.

We followed a narrow path down to the river, which was lined by papaya and banana trees. U Ba stopped frequently to catch his breath, but still he would not let me carry my own pack. A wooden bridge crossed the water. We climbed a steep bank, passing huts that looked as if the next cloudburst would carry them off. Their crooked walls and roofs were woven out of dried palm leaves, bamboo, and grasses. In many yards there was a fire; white columns of smoke rose unswerving into the evening sky. There were children playing everywhere who fell silent and watched us curiously as soon as they spotted us.

My brother's house lay hidden behind a gigantic bougainvillea hedge covered completely with red blossoms that had laid claim even to the gate. We forged our way with difficulty through his garden. His house stood on stilts five feet off the ground. Black teak with a corrugated tin roof and a small porch. A pig wallowed below. True to my memory.

We climbed the steps to the porch. At first glance, the interior had not changed much, either. The brown leather chair was still there, the two couches with their tattered upholstery, a little coffee table, the dark cabinet, even the oil painting of the Tower of London. The red altar on the wall was new, with a picture of Mi Mi and another of Tin Win in New York that I had sent to U Ba. In front of the photos lay red hibiscus blossoms and some rice. Unless I was mistaken, a Buddha had occupied this location on my last visit. I wondered in which unopened moving carton my own framed picture of our father might lie hidden.

I noticed several plastic buckets distributed without a discernible pattern around the house. I looked in vain for the beehive.

"Where are the bees?"

"Alas, they have flown on and taken up residence elsewhere," my brother explained as he set my pack down.

I sighed with relief.

"In their stead two snakes moved in."

I froze. "Two what?"

"Two cobras."

"You're not serious."

He looked at me, surprised. "We divvied up the house."

"U Ba! Cobras are extremely poisonous snakes. One bite and you're dead."

"They have done me no harm," he replied calmly, apparently surprised that I was so upset.

"Where are they now?" I wanted to jump onto the table in front of the couch.

"I don't know."

"You don't know?" I was on the verge of hysteria.

"One day they just disappeared."

"Disappeared? What does that mean? When did you see them last? Last week? A month ago?"

U Ba thought hard. "I'm not sure. As you know, time does not play much of a role in my life. It must have been a year ago. Maybe two."

"So you mean they're not here anymore?" I wanted to confirm.

He was visibly baffled by my questions. "Yes, that's what I mean. What else?"

I breathed a little easier. "Weren't you afraid?"

"Of what?"

My brother was not teasing me. He truly did not understand my fear. I saw it in his eyes. Small, brown, I-wish-I-knew-what-she-was-talking-about eyes.

"Of what? Of being bitten. Of dying."

He gave his answer long and careful consideration. "No," he said at last. "No, I was not afraid of that."

I believe I envied him.

"Of course you will sleep in my bed." He drew a faded green curtain aside to reveal a small room with a wooden shelf, a nightstand, a chair. From the ceiling hung a flickering bare lightbulb. "I even have a mattress," he declared proudly. "My greatest luxury."

He let the curtain fall back into place. "Now I shall make us some tea."

He went into the kitchen; I followed. In an open cupboard stood a pair of white enameled tin bowls and plates. On the bottom shelf were eggs, a few moldy tomatoes, garlic, ginger, and potatoes. In one corner some smoldering logs. Above them hung a sooty kettle. U Ba knelt down, piled a bit of kindling on the embers, and blew forcefully a couple of times until the dry wood ignited. The smoke exited through a hole in the roof.

What had I gotten myself into? Was I really going to manage living in this hut? Using a latrine, bathing at the well in the yard. I was wondering what excuse I could offer my brother for the move back to the Kalaw Hotel.

On a tray he set a thermos of tea, two mugs, and a plate of roasted sunflower seeds, and then we went together into the living room.

It had cooled off. I dug a fleece out of my pack and put it on. In the process I accidentally kicked one of the pails. "Why do you have so many plastic buckets scattered about?"

He looked around as if noticing them for the first time. "Oh yes, the buckets. My house is old; the roof leaks in several places. But don't worry, the bedroom stays dry."

"Why don't you have a new roof put on?"

"It's very expensive; the price of wood has exploded . . ."

"But with the money I sent you," I interrupted, "you ought to have been able to build a brand-new house."

He tilted his head to one side and looked at me thoughtfully. "That is true."

"So why didn't you? What did you do with the money?"

The question just slipped out. In a tone that immediately made me squirm. As if he had to justify himself. I wasn't looking for him to give me an account of himself. The money had been a gift.

All the same.

"Of course it's your own business, but I expected . . ."

U Ba furrowed his brow in thought. "You are completely correct, little sister. It is a good question: Whatever did I do with all that money? Let me think. Some of it I gave to the owner of the teahouse so that he could afford the new establishment. My neighbor's wife was very ill. She had to go to a hospital in the capital and needed money. The son of a friend was studying in Taunggyi; some of it went to him."

I hoped that was the end of the list. My shame deepened with every example.

"A few years ago we had a decidedly dry year, and the harvests were bad. A few families needed a bit of help. What else?"

He was quiet for a moment. "Yes!" he suddenly cried out loudly. "I also bought something for myself. Something truly marvelous."

U Ba went to the bookcase and pointed proudly to a cassette recorder. "I bought this for myself with your money, and every time someone goes to Rangoon they come back with a new cassette for me. Half a moment."

He loaded a cassette into the player, pressed "play," and shot me a proud, expectant look.

Horns and strings started to play, something classical.

"Sometimes my neighbors come, and they bring their neighbors," he said in a solemn tone, "until there are so many of us that we sit in tight rows on the floor listening to music together. All evening long."

I concentrated on the piece and attempted to decipher what the orchestra was playing. It sounded simultaneously familiar and utterly bizarre. As if drunken musicians were attempting Beethoven or Brahms. It sounded like a Chinese-made tape recorder—tinny, shrill, and very uneven.

"I think the speed is fluctuating."

U Ba was taken aback. "Really?"

I felt unsure and nodded cautiously. It hurt my ears.

"Do you really think so?"

I nodded again.

He was quiet for a long while. "It doesn't matter. I find this music beautiful all the same." My brother closed his eyes and followed the melody of a violin. "Besides, I have no point of comparison," he declared, his eyes still closed. "That is the secret of a happy life."

I saw how intensely the music moved him. He opened his eyes for a moment and cast me a grateful look, closed them again, and with every note the flutter and wow mattered less until I hardly noticed them myself. In the middle of a delicate solo the violin dropped out suddenly. It was so dark that I could no longer even make out my brother's silhouette. For one moment I heard nothing but the humming of the insects. Then the neighbors' voices.

"The power," sighed U Ba in the darkness. "It has failed frequently these past few weeks." He stood up, and a moment later I saw his face illuminated by a flickering match. He lit several candles and distributed them throughout the house. Their glow bathed the room in a warm, soft light.

"Sometimes we have electricity again after a few minutes, sometimes not until the next day," said U Ba, refilling my mug.

I sipped at my tea. The strains of the road were beginning to tell on me.

"Has life," he asked, having again sat down, "have the stars smiled upon you in recent times?"

I'm fine, thanks. Dandy. Wonderful. No complaints. Could be worse. In my mind I ran through all the pat responses I would have called on to answer a similar question in New York. With my brother any one of them would have been an insult.

"A good question," I replied evasively.

"A stupid question," he contradicted. "Forgive me for posing it so thoughtlessly. We often discover only many years later whether life and the stars were smiling upon us or not. Life can take the most surprising turns. What seemed initially to be a misfortune can turn out later to be a blessing, and vice versa, no? I really wanted only to know how you are faring? Whether you are happy? Whether you are loved. The rest is immaterial."

I looked at him in the candlelight and fought back the tears. I didn't know whether it was out of sadness that I couldn't answer his question with a loud, resounding yes, or because my brother touched me so deeply.

Was I loved? By my mother, of course. In her way. By my other brother, I wasn't sure.

By Amy.

Two people. Two very different forms of love. No one else came to mind.

Was that enough? For what? By how many people must we be loved in order to be happy? Two? Five? Ten? Or maybe only one? The one who gives us sight. Who takes away fear. Who breathes meaning into our existence.

There was no one like that for me.

When does love begin? When does it end?

U Ba's gaze rested on me. He stole a look at my hands. My ring finger. I knew what he meant.

"Sir Michael is a long story," I said. Sighing.

No lifelong love. But still a wish for it.

My brother sensed my discomfort. "Forgive me for asking. How presumptuous of me. How could I have asked so directly and carelessly when you have barely arrived at my house. As if there were no tomorrow. As if we did not have all the time in the world to tell each other whatever we have to tell. I am terribly sorry. It must be the excitement. And the delight finally to see you again. Of course, that does not excuse my behavior, either. I can only hope for your indulgence." He put a finger to his lips. "And not another word this evening about these intrusive questions."

His way of expressing himself made me laugh. "Promise. But I think that I need to go to bed anyway."

He jumped up. "Of course. Another oversight on my part. I will prepare your bed at once."

I insisted that I sleep on the couch. After a bit of back and forth he accepted my decision, dug a warm blanket and pillow out of a chest and blew out one candle after another. He put a flashlight on the coffee table for me in case I needed to find my way to the latrine in the night. He asked repeatedly whether I was comfortable, whether I had everything I needed for a good night's sleep, wished me a good night and stroked my face once gently in the light of the last candle.

I could still hear him doing something with water in front of the house, then coughing his way up the porch steps and climbing into his creaking bed. Moments later he blew out the candle.

The couch was more comfortable than I expected. I remembered now how well I had slept on it the first time around. Tonight, though, despite my exhaustion, I was finding it difficult to fall asleep.

I was thinking about my father, and for the first time in a long time I wished he were sitting next to me, holding my hand, talking to me in his soothing voice. I had left someone out of my tally. The love of a dead person counted, too. No one can take that away from us.

A reassuring thought, but still I could not sleep. I sensed that I would soon have company. It took a few minutes of lying quietly on the couch and listening to insects before I heard her.

Please, leave this place.

It was the first time she'd had anything to say since my departure. I knew what she wanted. She had warned me repeatedly in New York against this trip.

—Not a chance. I'm staying.

Don't do it. Leave. Quickly. Before it's too late.

—Why?

I know this place, where we are now. It will bring you grave misfortune.

—What kind of misfortune?

They will come to get you.

—No one is coming to get me.

That's what you think. You don't know them.

—Who?

The black boots. They come by day. They come by night. They come whenever they please. They take whomever they wish.

—Not me.

You, too.

—My brother will protect me.

No one can protect you from them.

—I am a foreigner.

They don't care. They take the elderly, women and children, if they wish.

—What do they do with them?

You hear all kinds of stories. Few there are to tell them. Those who return are changed.

—Did they get you?

Not me.

—Who then?

My son. That's much worse. Those left behind are changed, too.

—Where will I find the black boots?

They find you. When they come, don't look them in the eye. Don't look them in the boots.

—Why not?

Because they have magical powers. In them is reflected all of the cruelty, all of the evil we are capable of.

—Who are "we"? I interrupted her.

We humans. In the world you see reflected in that shiny, polished leather there is neither love nor forgiveness. In that world is only fear and hatred. There are sights we cannot endure. They turn us into a different person. Don't look there.

She had never before revealed so much about herself. I waited a long while to see if she had more to tell.

—Who are you? Where do you come from?

Silence.

It was always the same. As soon as I wanted to know something about her history or origins, she would clam up. What's your name? Where were you born? Where did you live? She had not once offered even a shred of an answer to any of these questions. Now I knew, at any rate, that she was acquainted with Kalaw, that she had had a son, and that the black boots—whoever they were—had come to get him.

Don't tell him about me. Not a word.

—Who?

Your brother.

—Do you know him?

Silence.

—I'm going to tell him everything. That's why I'm here. He's going to help me find you.

There is no me anymore. I am dead.

—Find out who you were. Why you died.

I forbid it.

—Why?

It will only make things worse.

—What? Tell me!

I can't tell you. It must remain secret. Forever.

—You're trying to frighten me. It's not working.

I'm not trying to frighten you; I want to warn you. You must not search for me. You must fly back to New York tomorrow.

—Then tell me how you died.

No. Never.

—Did someone murder you?

Silence.

—The black boots? Did they kill you?

Nothing.

—Was it an accident? Were you old and sick? Did you kill yourself?

Unrelenting silence.

—If you don't tell me I'll just find out on my own.

I did not expect an answer.

Eventually my eyes fell shut.

I was wakened in the middle of the night by the droning sound of a violin. Beethoven's violin concerto. Now, half asleep, I recognized it instantly.

The power was back on.

I heard my brother cough, rolled over, and went back to sleep.

Chapter 10

I WOKE TO unaccustomed sounds. Birdsong, the pig snuffling, roosters crowing. Children's voices. It took a few seconds for me to place them and to remember where I was. I must have slept a long time. The sun was high in the sky. It was warm. My stomach growled with hunger.

Someone was sweeping in front of the house. I stood up and went to the unglazed window. U Ba was cleaning the yard. When he saw me he put his broom aside and hurried up the steps.

"Good morning. Did you rest well?"

I nodded sleepily.

"You must be near starvation."

I nodded again.

"Then I shall prepare breakfast at once. I do not have a shower, but you can wash at the well in the yard."

He gave me a longyi and an old towel, then disappeared into the kitchen. I undressed and slipped the cloth around me, pulling it so high that it reached from my knees to my armpits. The well was a thin water pipe that reached over the hedge from the neighbor's property and ended over a large concrete sink. Beside it were two red plastic buckets and a large white enamel bowl. I filled the bowl and poured it with both hands over my head. The water was bitter cold despite the mild air temperature. After the third round I had gotten used to it, and after the fifth I was enjoying the refreshing chill. After washing from head to toe I was wide awake.

When I got back to the house, breakfast was waiting on the coffee table in front of the couch. Two mugs with hot water, beside them a bag of instant coffee, two sugar cubes, and canned milk. U Ba had made scrambled eggs with tomatoes and peppers. Thick pieces of butter melted on slices of toasted white bread were arranged on another plate.

"It looks wonderful. Thank you. How kind of you. Where did you get the butter?"

My brother smiled with delight. "I got it this morning from a friend in a hotel."

We sat down. The egg was delicious. Even the coffee tasted good. Only after the second slice of toast did it occur to me that my brother was eating nothing. "Aren't you hungry?"

"I will wait until you are finished."

"Why would you do that?"

"One does not dine together with guests. One waits until they are satisfied. That is our custom. Not so in the States?"

I had to laugh. "No, that would be very impolite. We all eat together at home. Besides, I'm not a guest; I'm family, aren't I?"

He smiled in agreement and self-consciously helped himself to some egg and a piece of bread.

We ate together. Silently. It did not seem to bother him. I was again unnerved by the quiet.

"How did things turn out for you?" I asked in order to break the silence.

My brother considered the matter so long that I grew anxious for his reply.

"Well," he said at last.

"Well?"

"Yes, well. The Buddha says: 'Health is the greatest gift, contentment the greatest wealth, faithfulness the best relationship.' I am healthy and content. My faith is unshakable. And, as you can see"—he spread out his arms and let his gaze sweep once across the room—"I lack for nothing. What cause would I have, then, to complain?"

I looked around the room myself. "I can think of a few things you might find a use for," I said, half in jest.

"Really?" he replied, surprised.

"A shower, for instance. Hot water. A hot plate, maybe?"

"You are right. Those things would make my life more comfortable. But do I need them?"

U Ba contemplatively scratched the right side of his head with his left hand. I had seen my father do the same thing when he was thinking hard about something. "I think not."

He covered his mouth and coughed.

"How long have you had that cough?"

"I don't know. Probably a couple of weeks. Perhaps a bit longer."

"Do you have a fever?"

"No."

"Runny nose or sore throat?"

"No."

"Any pain?"

"None to speak of."

I couldn't help but think of Karen. A colleague at the firm, a couple of years older than me, the only female partner at Simon & Koons. She had put up for weeks with a nagging dry cough that sounded similar to my brother's. Karen had no fever, no other cold symptoms, and, assuming it was an allergy, she had not gone to a doctor. When she finally went, the radiologist discovered a pulmonary mass, an indication of lung cancer. Follow-up examinations confirmed the diagnosis. Six months later she was dead.

"Have you been to a doctor?"

He shook his head, smiling. "It appeared on its own, and when the time has come, it will disappear the same way."

"All the same, you ought to see a doctor, just to be on the safe side."

"I fear that would be an utter waste of time, and though I may possess enough of it, I am loath to squander it. We have no doctors here who specialize in dry coughs. We have only the two hospitals: one for emergencies, the other for the army. The former cannot heal the sick, and the latter helps only its own. Don't worry; it's nothing serious. It will be gone in a few days. Tell me instead whether I can help you."

"What gives you the idea that I need help?"

"I see it in your eyes. I see it in the way you smile at me. I hear it in your voice, and our father would presumably insist that he could hear it in the beating of your heart."

I nodded mutely.

I thought of everything the voice had told me the previous night. What if she was right? If my search for her would prove dangerous? If there was some secret behind her life and death that ought not to be revealed? Who could protect me if things got rough? Certainly not U Ba. The American Embassy in Rangoon was far away. I did not even have a telephone so that I could notify them of an emergency. But I hadn't traveled halfway around the world to be daunted. I had to know the hidden fate of the voice within me.

"You are right; I am not doing so well."

Breathless, I told him.

Breathless, he listened.

Now he furrowed his brow in concern, scratched his head, and closed his eyes.

His lanky body sank into the leather armchair. His cheeks were slightly sunken, his eyes deep in their sockets. His thin dark-brown arms, capable of carrying more than they let on, hung limp at his sides. He looked vulnerable.

"I think I can help you," he said abruptly, looking at me soberly.

"Do you know the voice?" I asked in surprise.

"No."

"Do you know who the black boots are?"

U Ba hesitated. Then he shook his head very slowly without taking his eyes off me.

I wasn't sure whether he was telling me the truth.

"But I know where our search must begin."

Part Two

Chapter 1

U BA WAS deep in thought. All bounce had faded from his step. He strode swiftly through Kalaw, almost as if hunted, paying little attention to anyone who greeted us and answering my questions so brusquely that I stopped asking.

We walked past the teahouse, past the mosque and the monastery where our father had lived as a novice. We turned left at the big banyan tree and followed the road until we struck a well-beaten path that led us up a hill to the other end of the city.

We came to a halt before the overgrown, dilapidated remains of a garden gate. With one arm my brother pushed the branches aside, and we stepped into the yard where, beside a hut, banana, papaya, and several palms were growing. The little house with walls of dried grass stood on bamboo poles just about three feet off the ground. A few steps led up to a tiny porch where a red longyi and a white blouse hung over the railing to dry in the sun.

U Ba called out a name and waited. He called it a second time.

Khin Khin was a woman whose age I could not guess. She might have been fifty, or maybe eighty. Her dark eyes were small and narrow. Deep wrinkles creased her cheeks and forehead. A wide scar divided her chin into two asymmetrical halves.

An entire life in a face.

Around her head she had wrapped a pink cloth. In her hand she held a billowing cigar.

Why had my brother brought me here? What bound my fate and hers?

She greeted U Ba with a surprised smile and gestured encouragingly for us to come in. Her hut consisted of a single room. In one corner lay rolled-up blankets and a few clothes, above them a little altar with a recumbent Buddha, in front of that some rice and a vase with a wilted flower. A kettle of boiling water hung over a little heap of wooden coals. We sat down on a straw mat. Without letting me out of her sight, she set out three cups and served tea from a thermos. I suppose she was asking herself the same question: Why did U Ba bring this strange woman into my house?

My brother began to tell a story in a rhythmic singsong. We both listened attentively. She understood the lyrics, I only the melody and his voice. It sounded like a passionate, well-constructed plea. Sometimes urgent, almost demanding, then beseeching again, and in between cheerful and light.

She wagged her head in disbelief from time to time, puffed on her cigar, made brief comments, smiled or gazed at me in astonishment. When his song was finished, she shook her head deliberately and laughed.

My brother was not to be distracted. He continued to speak, as if it were the second movement, the adagio, of some grand composition. He spoke softly, leaning over, letting his words ring out, whispering. Their gazes met often, and neither avoided the other.

She had become thoughtful, furrowing her brow, letting her cigar burn out, and looking at me for a long time. When U Ba fell silent, she sipped at her tea. A look at him. A look at me. A quick nod.

My brother leaned over to me. "She is prepared to tell us of her departed sister's life," he said quietly. "I will translate for you."

"What makes you think that her sister, of all people, has anything to do with the voice inside my head?" I whispered back, amazed.

"You will understand once you have heard her story."

Chapter 2

A SMALL FARMER'S wife. A big heart with surprisingly little room to spare. But it was the only one she had.

Two young boys and their mother. A vast love that nevertheless brought happiness to no one. But it was the only one they had.

Or perhaps the story began much earlier. Perhaps it began in that first week, when Nu Nu encountered death for the first time in her life. Her father had woken with a piercing headache and a high fever. Just the day before, he had suffered from minor diarrhea. The herbs recommended by the local medicine man, brewed by Nu Nu's mother into a foul-smelling concoction, had no observable effect. Similarly ineffective were the stones warmed in the fire that she laid on her husband's stomach, and the tincture that she massaged for hours at a time into his feet and calves.

The fever rose. Regardless of what he ate or drank, he could keep nothing in his steadily weakening body. Life flowed out of him. In a watery brown stream that eventually ran dry.

Nu Nu encountered death for the second time just two weeks later when her mother died under identical circumstances.

The neighbors say that she sat motionless beside her dying mother for three days and nights, holding her hand. Without a word. Afterward she looked as if she were carved in stone. A small, gaunt body, frozen, eyes open wide, gazing mutely straight ahead. Even when the men carried the body out of the hut she did not move. She stood beside the grave without shedding a single tear.

Nu Nu knew about these things only from hearsay. She had only vague memories of the weeks during which she first encountered death. A silence, quieter and quieter, was all she could recall. A fire that went out. So that a dying fire was ever after a sight she could not bear.

And a warm hand. Colder and colder.

Nu Nu had just turned two at the time.

Her father's brothers and sisters did not want her. A child orphaned so young must have bad karma. A harbinger of misfortune who could bring only calamity. Not to mention the fact that they already had hungry mouths to feed at home.

In the end one of her mother's brothers took her in. He was young, lived in the same village, and, having married only recently, he had as yet no children of his own. He was a hardworking, capable farmer whose luck with vegetables was often good. At the same time he was an extraordinarily un-excitable sort, who possessed one virtue in excess: patience.

Nu Nu marveled early at her uncle's equanimity. How could he keep an even temper when rats had again plundered the family's supply of rice? When the rains came too late, when the dry earth was cracking open and the entire harvest was at stake?

How could he look on calmly while his wife put their money again and again on the elephant in a game of chance at a pagoda festival? While mouse, tiger, and monkey kept coming up until she had gambled away their last kyat, at which point the elephant appeared three times in a row?

Such spiritual serenity was unthinkable to her. Hers was the soul of a child who knew too much. Of life. Of death. Of warm hands, and how quickly they can grow cold.

Her moods were as variable as the weather during the rainy season. One moment she was stubborn and contrary, and the next moment she was anxious and insecure.

She was temperamental, her sorrow flaring up as easily as her joy. A spilled plate of rice might lead to bitter tears. A false assertion, or a thoughtless, casual insult uttered by the child next door might occupy her for days. Even her skin re-acted impulsively. At the slightest excitement red splotches would develop on her arms and legs, often on her stomach and chest, too, red splotches that itched as if all the mosqui-toes in the Shan States were attacking her at once. Nu Nu would scratch herself raw and wake up in the night covered in blood. No medicine man knew what to do; salves and incantations were useless. After a while the rash would just disappear on its own.

When Nu Nu was playing with other children in the woods and was stricken from one breath to the next by disproportional grief, she would not be able to identify any rhyme or reason. Deep black clouds would gather over her during the next few hours; the world would go dark for her more swiftly than in the minutes before a severe storm. A dead butterfly by the side of the road was enough to bring her to tears. At which point she would desire above all to be alone. Any activity required too much energy: playing, lighting a fire, chopping vegetables, even looking the other children or her aunt in the eye. On days like this she wanted only to lie on her thin straw mat and speak to no one.

The next morning the clouds would have cleared as quickly as they came.

On other days, by contrast, she was filled with an almost unbearable lightness, and she would dispatch without ado even wearisome chores, such as weeding the vegetable beds, or hauling the heavy water bucket.

Nu Nu had no explanation for this.

She was troublesome, her exhausted uncle would say from time to time. What did that mean, she wanted to know one time. He thought for a while and answered gravely: that her spirit had some troubles.

Later she sometimes imagined that was the reason she had always felt out of place in the family. Not undesired. Not at all. But different. Kin, but not kindred.

She would often lie awake late into the night listening to the soothing crackle of the fire, her aunt's and uncle's dampened voices and later the measured breathing of their sleep. She did not doubt that her relatives loved her. They were very caring. Never demanded more of her than she was capable of. Were never cross. Aunt and uncle had long since become mother and father.

And yet.

As if there were some invisible wall dividing them.

Nu Nu had a recurring dream in which, as a young girl, she was walking beside a lazy river. Her parents were waiting on the opposite bank. She was afraid, felt lonely, and longed above all to cross the waters. Yet she feared the current and the crocodiles that lay in wait for her. As her distress mounted she ran up and down the bank looking for a shallow spot. She called and waved, but her parents barely acknowledged her. When they turned away and made to leave, Nu Nu forgot her fear and leapt into the river. She immediately felt an uncanny power pulling her into the depths. Nu Nu resisted, swimming with short, powerful strokes, just as her father had taught her. When she reached the middle of the stream she saw the predators approaching from behind. She swam faster and faster, but still they closed in on her. Five strokes away from the shore and salvation. And nearer. Four more. And nearer. Three more. Just as the crocodile, maw agape, was about to swallow her up, she would wake up. Sweating. Breathless with fear.

Her aunt and uncle laughed when she told them about it. Silly girl. There are no more crocodiles in the Shan States. For a long time Nu Nu dreaded sleep for fear of the dream.

Nor did her sense of estrangement diminish as over the years two brothers and sisters came into the picture. They had inherited their parents' even temperament.

Five serene spirits and one troubled one. With red splotches.

Maybe that was the reason why Nu Nu yearned early on to start a family of her own. Her dream was not a house of stone. Not a well-sealed roof. Not a journey to the provincial capital. Her only wish was to find a husband and have a child with him. Her child. She would carry it inside her for nine months. She would give birth. She would nurture and protect it. A part of her even after the birth.

A kindred spirit.

Chapter 3

NU NU WAS seventeen when the first young suitor sought her hand in marriage. She had grown into a beautiful young woman, turning the heads of the men from other villages at the market. Catching the shy but desirous eyes of the young men in the fields. She was slender and tall, and despite her size, she always stood up straight, even when balancing a heavy burden on her head. Her features were pleasing: an unusually high forehead, full red lips, and large, very lively, very brown eyes.

The young man did not make it an easy decision for her. Besides being polite and modest, he also had the most beautiful and, at the same time, the saddest eyes she had ever seen. They had grown up together in the village and had liked each other even as children. He was half a head shorter than she was, and because his left leg was somewhat shorter than his right, he limped. He, too, was frequently alone. When the young men came back at twilight from working in the fields, he inevitably lagged a good ways behind.

When they played soccer, he would wait patiently until the teams had been selected. And if no one picked him, he would sit on the sidelines hoping that someone would lose interest and that he might be allowed to jump in for them.

He was the only one with whom she had spoken of unseen walls. Of darknesses that sprang up suddenly. Of dead butterflies by the roadside. Of her fear of dying fires.

She could tell by the way he looked at her, listened to her, asked a question now and then, that he was not unacquainted with troubled spirits.

With warm hands. Slowly growing cold.

That he knew what affinity meant.

And how important it was.

Exchanging only a glance, they could often tell what the other was feeling.

She broke out in tears when he asked her to be his wife.

She sensed that if she refused him, he would never have the courage to ask another woman. She hesitated. Asked for some time to consider. Until the next morning. Spent a sleepless night sitting by the fire trying to bring order to her heart.

Beside her slept five serene spirits. There was not one among them she could ask for advice.

By the time the birds announced the new day she had decided.

Love knew many foes. Among them pity.

He was a friend. She would never find a better one. A lover he was not.

Nor did the second suitor stand any chance. He was the son of the richest rice farmer in the province. He came because he had heard of Nu Nu's beauty. He was handsome, and his manners impressed her parents, but she knew within minutes that he understood neither groundless sorrow nor groundless joy. How could her love grow where it had no place to take root?

She might almost have overlooked Maung Sein.

Not because he was small of stature. On the contrary, he must have had some English ancestry; how else could one explain his light skin, or, more than anything, his athletic frame? Maung Sein had a broad chest, extraordinarily muscular biceps, and hands so big that her head nearly vanished in them.

Nu Nu was partial to tall men, but on that market day she had been thoroughly preoccupied with her little sister. Khin Khin had a high fever and lay wearily beside her under the umbrella. Before them, stacked in orderly piles, were the fruits of her father's labor: tomatoes, eggplants, ginger, cauliflower, and potatoes. It was hot. Nu Nu dipped a cloth in a bowl of tepid water every couple of minutes, wrung it out, and laid it on her sister's brow. While her sister was dozing, she thought she would seize the chance to bring an order of tomatoes, several pounds, to a nearby restaurant. In her haste she stumbled, lost her balance for a moment, felt the basket of vegetables slip from her head, and watched as they spilled in every direction. Across the road, into the tall grass, and deep under the bushes. She crawled after them on all fours. When she got back to the basket it was full again. Beside it stood a young man, smiling bashfully. He looked first at her and then shyly at the ground.

It was a smile she would never forget. Warm and sincere, but tempered by the realization that not every sadness needed a justification.

Caught up as she was in concern for her sister, she might even then have thanked him perfunctorily and thought no more of him. As it was, she had observed several unusual things in the preceding days.

Nu Nu wondered how people could live under the delusion that there was nothing real other than what we could perceive directly with our senses. She was convinced there were powers beyond our knowledge that nevertheless had an effect on us and that occasionally left signs for us. One needed only know how to notice and interpret them. Nu Nu studied extensively the silhouettes of the banana and papaya trees at dusk, the outlines of the smoke rising from the fire, and the configuration of the clouds. She spent many hours gazing at the sky, observing and reading their formations. She was fascinated by their fleeting existence. They were constantly shifting form, shaped by an unseen hand, only to disappear one or two moments later into the infinite expanse out of which they had arisen.

She pitied anyone who saw in all of that only clouds, portents of nothing more than fair weather or foul. In them Nu Nu could make out monkeys and tigers, ravenous maws, broken hearts, tearful faces.

Over the past weeks she had spotted several elephants in the sky, tokens of energy and strength. A few days earlier a white cloud had transformed itself suddenly and directly above her into a bird. She had taken it for an owl, a symbol of luck, stretching its wings. To Nu Nu it was a clear sign that someone or something was approaching her from a great distance.

Yesterday in the field she had uncovered a fist-sized stone with a highly unusual shape. She had turned it this way and that, and depending on how she held it, it had reminded her of one thing or another. It could be a funnel. A stupa. Or, with some imagination, a heart. She was not sure what it really represented.

Today, there was Maung Sein standing before her.

He had come from a far-off province to spend a few months helping an uncle clear a field.

She asked if he might be able to bring the tomatoes to the restaurant, since she needed to be looking after her feverish sister, described to him the location of the vegetable stand, and asked him to deliver the money there.

He shouldered the basket without a word.

A short time later, when he stood in front of her for the second time, she noticed his large hands.

He held out a kyat note and a few coins for her and asked whether he could assist her in any other way.

Yes, she said, without missing a beat. Her little sister was sick. If he could help bring her home in a couple of hours she would be much obliged. Perhaps he would not mind returning near the end of the day?

It would be no trouble at all for him just to wait there, replied Maung Sein. Provided, of course, that she would permit it. He did not wish to be in the way.

Nu Nu nodded, surprised.

He hunched beneath the sunshade at her sleeping sister's feet while she held Khin Khin's head in her lap.

Maung Sein offered to fetch fresh, cold water. She gratefully declined; it would only warm up quickly. She did not want him to leave.

People walked past them, many of them exchanging knowing looks at the sight of the athletic young man sitting by her side. Again and again customers would stop, buy tomatoes, ginger, or eggplants, eyeing the stranger critically all the while.

Maung Sein was only peripherally aware of all the interest he was arousing. He sat up straight, as if meditating, eyes lowered most of the time, hardly believing what he had done. He, who was otherwise so shy that he clammed up the moment a girl was in the room or even in the vicinity, he had suddenly had the audacity to ask this young woman, the most beautiful he had ever seen, if he might sit with her. He did not know where the source of his newfound courage lay. It had simply been there. As if bravery needed only a suitable occasion to make an appearance. Who knew, thought Maung Sein, what he was really capable of.

From time to time Nu Nu would ask him a question, which he would answer courteously, though he found he had to repeat every second sentence, so quietly did the words pass from his lips.

Maung Sein was an unusually quiet individual who on many days uttered little more than a couple of sentences. Not because he was rude, morose, or disaffected, but because he felt the world was better explained through actions than through words.

And because he treasured silence.

He had spent his youth as a novice in a monastery. There the monks had taught him not to attribute too much meaning to this, his life. It was, after all, but one in an infinite chain. The justice and happiness that eluded an individual in one life would be granted him in the next, if he deserved it. Or in the one after that. The exact details were beside the point.

What's more, they had taught him to be friendly and helpful to others. Not because he owed it to them. Because he owed it to himself.

These were two of the maxims by which he sought to lead his life. The rest would follow.

Or else it was not important.

Maung Sein cast about for something he would like to tell the young woman beside him.

About his work as a lumberjack? He could not imagine it would interest her. About his uncle who had just fathered a child with the neighbor's daughter, thirty years younger than himself? No, he would be hard-pressed to find a topic more ill-suited to the occasion.

About himself? His family at home, where Death was a frequent guest. A silent visitor to whom one addressed no questions, who took whomever he wished. To his youngest brother he had appeared in the guise of a snake. The boy had reached innocently to pull that stick out of the underbrush. What does a four-year-old understand of the art of natural camouflage, of the secrets of mimicry?

Death had jostled his eldest brother out of the crown of a eucalyptus tree. An eight-year-old boy who wanted to know what the world looked like from above.

Only wings could have saved him.

No, he would rather talk of Happiness. She was no stranger to him, even if she was a less frequent visitor than Death, more fleeting. He would see her at regular intervals as long as he kept a sharp eye out for her.

Today she had come to him in the form of a tomato rolling across his path, along a trajectory that led him back to an overturned basket.

He might also have chosen to pass by. One must not be deceived by the many disguises of Happiness.

The more he thought about it, the more clearly he recognized that he did not wish to say anything at all. It was enough simply to sit there. To be near her. To be able to glance at her from time to time, and to get a response.

Nu Nu enjoyed his silence, even though it cost her considerable effort to keep her curiosity in check. She was convinced that she would learn all that mattered when the time was ripe.

She could see during the brief moments when their eyes met that he would not be startled by tears for a dead butterfly; he would make sure there was always a log on the fire.

As the market drew to a close Nu Nu packed the remaining vegetables in a basket. It was heavy, and she asked Maung Sein to set it on her head. He raised it with an effort and declared that she would never be able to carry such a burden by herself. The way he said it made clear to her that he would sooner make the trip two or three times than let her carry the basket. He would be able to provide for her. In every respect.

They took the basket between them, one on each side. He set her sister gingerly on his shoulder, which Khin Khin accepted without complaint. And thus they set out.

When they parted he asked permission to see her again the next day.

That evening Nu Nu lay awake for a long time. She remembered the stone from earlier in the day. She knew now what shape it had been.

Chapter 4

NU NU LAY beside her sleeping husband, listening to the rain. She could tell by the sound what it was pattering on. The thick leaves of a banana tree rang out deep and powerful. The small, thin bamboo leaves were bright and gentle. The puddles in the yard gurgled. Her old roof swallowed the drops with a dull sound only to spit them out again as a burbling rivulet into the gutters. The mats of dried grasses and palm leaves that covered her house leaked in several places. Nu Nu heard the appalling splashing on the floorboards. There was no money to repair them. They would have to serve for another year. At least.

From a neighbor's house the tones of a tin roof, loud and furious. She would never be able to sleep under that, she thought, no matter how practical it might be.

It had started to rain the previous afternoon and had not stopped since. That was unusual. At this time of year the rains generally pelted from the heavens in bursts that lasted one, maybe two hours, making the air heavy and humid.

The ground soaked up the moisture, and the sun devoured whatever was left with its merciless rays. In a short time the ground would again be dry, waiting impatiently for the next downpour.

Outside, dawn was gradually approaching. The first beams of light were falling through the cracks in the wall. Nu Nu snuggled again against her husband, throwing her arm across his chest. For a few minutes she savored the warmth of his body, the even rhythm of his heart beating beneath her hand, his breath on her skin. Then she got up, fanned the smoldering fire, hung a kettle over the flames, sat down in the open doorway, and watched the water turning their yard into a growing pool of mud.

She loved the rainy season. She loved these months clad in silver-gray when the earth awoke, when life throve in the unlikeliest places and nature, uninhibited, covered everything in a veil of green. It was also a time when she need not rise before the sun just to get to the fields on time. When she and Maung Sein had a few hours to themselves because there was nothing to do but listen to the sound of the rain. Or to weave a basket.

Or to follow one's passion.

She felt desire kindling within her and briefly considered lying down with her husband again and seducing him the moment he woke, but she decided against it. The way things looked, they would have the whole day for that, and the novices would be standing in front of their hut expecting their daily offerings in one hour at the latest. She stood up, went to the hearth, put rice on, and picked out a handful of especially large tomatoes and eggplants for a vegetable curry. Only the best for the monks, even though food was in short supply in their house at times and Maung Sein occasionally grumbled about her generosity.

Nu Nu felt a deep sense of gratitude and humility when she thought about the past two years and she wanted to show her appreciation however she could within the modest means at her disposal. She wondered what she had done to deserve such joy. What good deed might she have performed in a previous life to warrant such a rich reward in this one?

Thanks to a loan from Maung Sein's uncle when they got married, they had been able to buy this old hut, the attached property, and a field. It lay in a village two days on foot from her birthplace. The hut offered sufficient space, and there was a room with a cooking pit in one corner. On a wooden shelf behind the fire stood bowls, tin plates, cups, and a few sooty, dented pots. The cutlery and two cooking spoons were stuck into the wall of woven palm fronds. Beside the shelf sat their few supplies: half a sack of rice, tomatoes, ginger, eggplants, and one jar of fish sauce.

Above the door Nu Nu had hung an old clock whose hands had frozen at six o'clock long ago. On the opposite wall hung the altar with the wooden Buddha. Between the wooden beams her husband had installed two bamboo poles where they could hang their few things. A towel for each, a longyi, a shirt, some T-shirts and underwear. That was all they owned.

In the yard grew two lanky papaya trees, bananas, bamboo, and palms. Behind the hut there was room for tomatoes and other vegetables.

Out of Maung Sein, the lumberjack, her father had made a farmer whose enthusiasm compensated somewhat for his lack of native ability. He was often among the first in the field, and he had made a point of helping his father-in-law in order to learn from him. With modest results. His vegetables never really flourished. The cabbage was skimpy, and the tomatoes didn't taste right. The yields from his rice field, too, fell far short of what the neighbors harvested.

Some days they were so hungry that Maung Sein doubted whether he would ever be able to provide for a family. He thought about working as a lumberjack, but there were not many of the mighty teak trees left in their region. He would have had to travel to more distant provinces and would have been away for several months of the year. Neither he nor Nu Nu wanted that. Every hour they spent apart was an hour wasted.

A life of privation did not matter to them; it was the only one they knew.

Together they had discovered something entirely different: their bodies.

The first shy touches had given way to an almost unquenchable longing.

Nu Nu's desire had driven out her unfathomable sorrow. During the first months there had still been a few days when it crept up on her, and Nu Nu had done her best to stave it off and hide it from her husband. But Maung Sein had an impeccable sense for his wife's moods. One look into her eyes was enough. When he saw how much energy it took for her simply to get out of bed in the morning, how much trouble she had preparing a meal, chatting with a neighbor, or going to the market, he would redouble his care for her without peppering her with questions or chastising her. As if it was the most natural thing in the world that a person should suffer from time to time a sadness so great that it exhausted and discouraged her.

Now she could not even remember the last time she felt heavyhearted.

A serene spirit and a troubled one gradually finding peace.

Since meeting her husband Nu Nu had been firmly convinced that certain people belonged to one another.

Kindred spirits. Soul mates.

Later, much later, she sometimes wondered if she had used up most of her happiness during the first two years of living together with Maung Sein. Was that possible? Was there such a thing as a limited supply of lucky breaks? Did people come into the world with an allotment of good fortune that they could enjoy during their lives, some earlier, others later? Ought they to have been more sparing with their intimacy? But how can a person guard her happiness? Or was everything that happened mere caprice and chance? Were we balls to be kicked around by forces that followed no rules, that did with us as they pleased, like a raging river with a little branch that eventually is crushed in the flood?

In that case nothing in life would make any sense or have any meaning. But one look at her sleeping husband—and later into her son Ko Gyi's eyes—was enough to reassure her that it could not be so. A token of love, a gesture of compassion, a helpful deed—regardless how big or small—was all it took to let Nu Nu know that her doubts were unjustified, that there was a power that lent each and every one of us our particular value.

Nothing was futile. Nothing was in vain.

Maung Sein and his love had convinced her of that to the very core of her soul. Until those things happened that caused her again to have doubts. Forever. About everything.

Sapped her life of meaning the way salt draws liquid from a body until it destroys it.

But that was later. Much later.

Now the curry and the steaming rice stood before her. She filled a mug with tea and squatted again in the doorframe, waiting for the procession of monks or for her husband to wake up, to stretch and turn to her, to look at her through drowsy eyes until a smile swept across her face.

The rain was gradually slackening, and Nu Nu noticed a few dry leaves falling from a tree into a puddle at the bottom of the stairs. Tiny messengers, rocking in a storm, hounded by bean-sized raindrops that sank one leaf after another.

Only one refused to go under, no matter how often it was hit. Nu Nu closed her eyes and counted to ten. Should it—against all likelihood—still be afloat when she opened her eyes, she would know it was not mere chance, but a sign.

She intentionally counted slowly. At five she started to feel nervous. At eight she contemplated what it might mean. When Nu Nu opened her eyes there was the grayish-brown leaf still floating in the middle of the puddle. She walked down the steps, plucked it from the water, and thoroughly examined its form and patterning. At first glance she did not make out anything remarkable. She flipped it over. On the back were two black spots staring at her like little eyes. The stem continued into the middle of the leaf. It resembled a spinal column. She held it up to the gray sky, and against the light she could clearly see the branching stems running like veins through the leaf.

Eyes. Spinal column. Veins.

Did this dry leaf presage a child? Why not? It was meant to be discovered and deciphered by her; why else did it refuse to go to the bottom like the others?

Nu Nu wanted some confirmation of her suspicion. She examined the leaf one more time and then leaned over and let it slip from her hand. Should it fall in the puddle and there weather a second bout of rain, that would end all doubt. The normal trajectory of the leaf ought to have carried it somewhere under the steps, but the wind changed direction. It sailed right back to the puddle, in which a further handful of new leaves now floated. Nu Nu closed her eyes and counted to twenty-eight, just to be sure. Eight was her lucky number. The two in front of it doubled her luck.

When she reopened her eyes all the leaves but one had vanished. She recognized it at once.

The world was full of signs. One needed only to know how to see and interpret them.

For two years Nu Nu had been waiting for a child, a son, to be precise. She had imagined that after the wedding, pregnancy would be a matter of weeks or at most a few months. After six months, when she still could detect no changes in her body, she asked her mother, who urged her to be patient.

At the end of a year she called upon the advice of the local medicine man, who attempted to treat her with various herbs and teas, to no avail.

She consulted the astrologer, who made very careful calculations regarding the best days for her to conceive, days that she took full advantage of, with the sole result that Maung Sein had sore genitals.

She thought nothing of walking for a day to get to the nearest city to visit an astrologer renowned for his extraordinary abilities. He, too, consulted books and tables, reassuring her that she would bear a healthy son who would soon be followed by an equally healthy brother. He could not say when, exactly. The indications pointed in contradictory directions. It might be a while yet. Maybe even a few years.

Nu Nu returned to her village deeply disappointed. She wanted nothing as much as a son. The neighbors' daughters and her friends were mostly mothers already. A few years, the astrologer had said. An almost unimaginably long time. Or perhaps he was mistaken, and she was one of those unfortunate women who could never have children, no matter what they tried?

There were days when she thought of little else: a person who would belong only to her. Who would need her like no other, who could not live without her. How would he look? Tall and lean like his mother? Or with his father's muscular build, his light skin and curly hair?

Would she bring a serene or a troubled spirit into the world?

Maung Sein was nonplussed by his wife's impatience. Whenever they had a child, be it a boy or a girl, they were not going to have much influence over whether it came into the world healthy or ill, whether it would live past its first birthday or, like so many other newborns, die before the age of one. The essential things in life were predestined. In his view, trying with all one's might to influence them was dangerously presumptuous and could bring nothing but misfortune. He refused to drink the sundry concoctions his wife prepared according to the medicine man's instructions, apparently in order to make both of them more fertile. He did not accompany her to the astrologer's, because he did not wish to know anything about the future. He could not alter it anyway. Maung Sein implored his wife repeatedly to exercise greater patience, to find the equanimity without which life was unbearable. And even if for some reason they never did have a child, it would not be a tragedy. It was just one existence. One among many.

She would agree with him, only to besiege him with questions again two days later. Why she wasn't pregnant. Whether he would try a potion after all that some midwife had brewed for her. Or what he thought of a particular name.

For a long time it was the sole point of contention between them.

Nu Nu heard the wood creak and looked up. Her husband sat on the sleeping mat in the half light, rubbing his eyes and yawning. She admired his muscular torso, the powerful arms that could lift her into the air as if she were a child, the hands that caressed her so tenderly or held her so firmly that that contact alone was enough to arouse her. It took all of her self-control not to go to him.

"Have the monks been by yet?" inquired Maung Sein. As if he had guessed her thoughts.

"No."

"Let me guess . . . still raining?"

"Yes, but it's slowing down. Are you hungry?"

Her husband nodded. He stood up, retied his longyi, pulled on a fraying T-shirt, got two tin bowls, spoons, a mug, gave her a kiss on the forehead, stroked her face tenderly, and squatted down beside her.

Nu Nu's heart was racing with excitement.

He poured himself a tea, gazed at the lead-gray sky, the low-hanging clouds, and the muddy yard full of puddles. "We've got a lot of time today."

"A whole lot," she replied as coyly as she could.

Maung Sein did not react. He filled the bowls with rice and vegetable curry, handed one to her, and began to eat in silence.

It was not long before they heard the monks asking for alms at the neighbor's house.

Nu Nu took the large plate of rice and the curry, laid a cloth over them, descended the steps, and waded through the muck to the gate.

The rain was warm. The water ran down her face, neck, back, and breasts. In a matter of moments shirt and longyi clung to her skin. A long procession of young men filed past with their shaven heads and their soaking-wet dark-red robes. She devoutly deposited a small spoonful of rice and some vegetables in each wooden bowl. She accepted their grateful expressions and mumbled blessings, her thoughts all the while on Maung Sein's body and the passion it aroused in her.

When she turned around her husband was gone and the curtain was across the door.

Her legs quivering with excitement, she stayed at the gate until the last monk was out of sight. She went back to the hut, climbed the stairs, and pushed the curtain aside.

Maung Sein was lying on the mat waiting for her.

Chapter 5

SHE KNEW.

She knew immediately and beyond any shadow of a doubt.

As if she could sense something that for her body was imperceptible.

As if she could see what to her eyes was invisible.

A part of him would remain inside her. Implant itself. Grow.

Even if her husband would later smile indulgently and object that it was impossible. That no one was that sensitive.

What did he know of a woman's body and feelings?

Something about this morning had been different. It was not the way he moved, although he had been especially ardent and passionate. Nor was it the way he had inflamed and then quenched her lust.

Her body had been saturated with a feeling she had no name for and could not describe.

When it was over they lay beside each other breathing heavily. Nu Nu was quivering, and tears were running down her face, though she did not notice it right away.

Maung Sein was worried and asked whether he might have hurt her in his abandon.

No, she said, not at all.

Why she was crying, then?

For joy, she explained. For joy.

He took her in his arms, and she only cried harder.

Later she would often reflect on this moment and ask herself whether those were truly tears of joy that morning. Or did she already have an inkling in her heart of hearts of how it would all end? That every great happiness entailed a correspondingly great sorrow. That every beginning already contained its own end, that there was no love without the pain of parting, that every hand eventually turned cold.

Had she, in spite of the many travails of her early years, only now fully understood what the Buddha taught? To live means to suffer. Nothing is permanent.

"Say something," whispered Nu Nu.

Maung Sein propped himself on his elbow and stroked her hair solicitously.

"What should I say?"

"Anything," she implored. "I want to hear your voice."

"I love you."

She clutched her husband. Maung Sein did not utter these words often. The way he said it now, it sounded like a gift.

"Once more. Please."

"I love you."

She clung to him with all her might, as if she were afraid of sinking. Never in her life had she felt so vulnerable and defenseless. Why now, at the moment when her most fervent wish was starting to come true? Why could she not simply welcome the new life?

"I love you, too."

NU NU CONTINUED to be extraordinarily sensitive for several days. She had difficulty falling asleep and woke up earlier than usual. At the market and in the field she avoided looking anyone in the eye, and she was happiest when no one other than her husband spoke to her. Her skin revolted. Red spots everywhere. She scratched until the blood ran down her arms and legs.

Worse still than the gloom and the itching were the anxieties that plagued her, seemingly for no identifiable reason. It was a ubiquitous fear that constantly sought new justification. Sometimes she dreaded that Maung Sein, having stepped on a cobra, would come home dead from a short visit to the neighbors. Sometimes she woke in the middle of the night and flew into a panic, convinced that Maung Sein had stopped breathing as he lay there beside her. The sight of a well would alarm her because it led so deeply into the darkness, the heavy rains because they could wash away the entire village. The world had always been full of danger and threats. Now it was just a question of when she would fall prey to one of them.

Maung Sein took greater than usual pains about his wife during these weeks. He would get up before her in the morning to cook for the monks. He fetched the water from the village well, accompanied her to the market, talkative like never before, in order to distract her from the sorrow whose cause he could not fathom. In the field he would never let her out of his sight. As soon as it seemed to him that the work was overtaxing her, he would bring her home and stay by her side.

In the end, though, it was not Maung Sein who helped her. It was the certitude that something was developing inside her. It was the sensation of giving life even when on the outside there was no indication of it at all. A gentle twinge in her belly early in the morning, a slight pressure in her breasts—these were at first the only signs that something had changed.

But her confidence in what was happening to her increased daily, so that two months later both anxiety and sadness had fled. She was going to have a child. A son. He would be healthy, and she would survive the birth. It was more than the astrologer's prophecy; she felt it herself. Her fears gave way to an optimism that she had never experienced before, not even during the most blissful hours with Maung Sein.

It did not take long for him to notice what was happening with his wife. It was not only the belly that caught his attention as it started to swell, but also the calm that she suddenly radiated. As if all her troubles had evaporated overnight. Her eyes beamed, her prominent lips were just a bit fuller, her slender body acquired curves, and he got to see a side of her he had never experienced before: her laughter.

In the field and at home he had to work against her desire always to be active, because he worried she might run herself down to nothing. She wanted to borrow money to re-thatch the roof. To plant additional tomatoes in a fallow corner of the garden. To build a little chicken coop.

One night Nu Nu felt a first movement in her belly. She wanted to wake her husband but then reconsidered. This moment should be hers alone.

Hers and her son's.

She held still and listened into her body, breathless. Had it just been her imagination? A few seconds passed, and then she had the sensation again that she had felt something. A gentle tremor, the beat of a butterfly's wing.

Whenever she thought no one was watching she would lay both hands on her torso, stroking it and talking to her son. Telling him of a hut in which there was little more than love for him. Of a father who worked from dawn till dusk to keep the hunger away. Of a mother who was so looking forward to him that she took little interest in anything else. Of a life that would not be easy, he should be clear about that, but that nevertheless—in all its beauty and tribulation—was a life worth living. Mostly, at least.

The larger her belly swelled, the more time she needed for herself and her child. Bending over to work in the field became wearisome. Every step taxed her. She found the housework increasingly challenging. Her legs swelled. At night there was no position in which she could lie comfortably. Regardless of how she moved, something always hurt. She liked best of all to sit on the top step with a thermos of tea, leaning against the porch, a blanket at her back, rubbing her belly and feeling her child.

For once Maung Sein could not help her. On the contrary, there were moments when his presence annoyed her. When he tried to take her into his arms before falling asleep in the evening she would turn away from him because the physical proximity was too much for her. When he came home from the field drenched in sweat she hoped he would go straight to the river; the same smell of him that she had loved not long ago now repulsed her.

One evening—they had already extinguished the candles and were lying beside each other in the dark—she heard him grinding his teeth. Maung Sein did that only when restless and nervous.

"Nu Nu?"

She felt inclined to feign sleep.

"Nu Nu?"

She couldn't resist that pleading tone. "Yes?"

"Is something wrong?"

She knew how difficult that sentence must have been for him. Her husband was not one who liked to ask questions. But there was no way she could tell him what she was going through. She did not wish to offend or hurt him. "No. Why do you ask?"

"You are so . . ." He searched a long time for the right word. "Different from before."

"I have our child inside me," she answered, hoping it would be the end of the conversation.

"I know, but that's not what I mean."

"What then? How am I different?" She would have liked to turn to him and kiss him reassuringly or stroke his head, but she could not do it.

"I don't know. Different. You hardly look me in the eye anymore. You don't like it when I stroke you."

"No, really, I do." She was not a good liar.

"You don't like the way I smell anymore."

"That's not true. What makes you say that?" she replied weakly.

"And now you are telling lies."

She heard how hurt he was. How much he needed her. Nu Nu briefly considered telling him how she was feeling. He wouldn't understand.

She herself did not understand.

"Nu Nu?"

She did not want to talk. She wanted to rest and be alone. Just mother and child.

It was a strange, irritating feeling that she preferred not to think about. She had often heard of women who experienced bizarre mood swings during pregnancy. She did not want to create trouble. It would go away on its own.

"It's okay. Don't give it another thought. Let's just go to sleep."

"Is it something about me?"

"No," she answered so brusquely that he held his tongue.

Maung Sein lay awake for a long time that night. He did not understand what his wife was going through and could explain her behavior only as having to do with the pregnancy. He was sure their old intimacy would return after the birth.

Chapter 6

DEATH STOOD WAITING at the door. Tall and lean. She could make out his dark silhouette clearly against the light of the rising sun. He had pushed the curtain aside and was about to step in.

Nu Nu clamped down on the cloth the midwife had thrust between her teeth to stop her biting her lips bloody from the pain. She knew that her body could not take much more. She had been suffering already for a day and a night. It had started at dawn with a powerful contraction while she was distributing alms to the monks. Maung Sein had been with her and had been able to calm and distract her during the first few hours. When a gush of water had coursed out of her he had run full of concern to get the midwife. Two older women later came to her aid. They had reached inside her repeatedly with their long, bony fingers to determine the baby's position and to feel the head. They were still full of optimism; it wouldn't be long now, they said.

Later they made an effort to shift it and turn it, to dilate her with their hands. Nu Nu had let it all happen, followed their instructions, stood, lain down, knelt, crouched on all fours. They had tried herbs, tinctures, and compresses. They had massaged her, and she had inhaled mysterious vapors, all to no avail.

Her child did not wish to enter the world.

Nu Nu could see in the women's faces that it was getting serious. She was losing blood. She felt colder and colder. There was no doctor who could have cut her open, no anesthetic that could have eased her pain.

The baby was not moving.

For months she had felt it every day. The kicks, the thumps and rumbling in her belly had become a part of her.

Now she could not feel it anymore. She had the feeling that she was carrying a weighty stone inside her that grew heavier by the minute and would pull her irresistibly into an abyss.

The pains did not relent. The child had to come out, or they would die. Both of them.

The women whispering. Their helplessness. They sensed what would unfold in the next few minutes. This year alone five women in the village had died in childbirth. It was the risk every pregnant woman took.

The price one paid to give life.

Nu Nu clamped down on the cloth again. Someone pushed the drenched hair out of her face and held her head.

One of the women hurried out to fetch Maung Sein. He had left the hut in the middle of the night when he could no longer bear to watch his wife's misery. For hours they had heard him chopping and sawing wood in the yard, in the dark.

The next contraction came. She felt dizzy.

Death still stood at the door, exuding his vile stench. Why did he not step in? What was he waiting for? Why did he torture her like this?

She called to her husband. Called his name with all her might. Again and again. Why wasn't he coming? She wanted him to be with her when she died. She wanted to be held by him, and only by him.

The midwife stuffed the cloth into her mouth again. She heard Maung Sein's footsteps.

He sat behind Nu Nu and wrapped his arms around her so that her upper body was in his lap. When the next contraction came and threatened to carry her off for good, she clutched his knee, spat out the cloth and bit with all her strength into his forearm. Maung Sein cried out in pain and squeezed her with such force that it took her breath away.

She had no memory of the next few minutes.

When she came to again she heard the excited voice of the midwife.

And the whimpering of a child.

IN THE FIELDS or at the well few of the women she had spoken to could say much about the hours following a delivery. They were happy to have survived. They had older children to care for or had simply wanted to forget the torture. Not so Nu Nu. She remembered every detail even years later, in spite of her exhaustion. The blood- and slime-covered bundle that lay on her breast. Maung Sein's distorted face, his arm and the big, gaping wound in it. He was missing a thumb-sized piece of flesh just by his elbow.

Her quivering body, the almost unbearable pain.

The smoldering fire with the big kettle where the women were boiling towels for her.

Her son's racing, thumping heart, his quick breath. His wrinkly little fingers and the way he looked at her out of his puffy dark-brown eyes. She would never forget that sight. Or the happiness that she felt.

She hugged him tightly and was never going to let him go. He was a part of her and would remain so forever.

Like it or not.

Then she lost consciousness.

Chapter 7

NU NU SPENT the weeks following her son's birth in a no-man's-land between life and death. She was aware only in a blur of the hut, the fire, the smoke, and the faces bending over her. There was no more boundary between night and day. She slept long, to be woken only by a dreadful thirst or the whimpering of her hungry child. She nursed, ate and drank whatever Maung Sein offered her, then went to sleep again. The ministrations of the midwife, the juices she pressed for her, the salves Maung Sein massaged her with, she let them wash over her without stirring.

She spent her few waking hours in a fog, too exhausted to stand up or even to exchange a few words. In her nostrils the sickly-sweet smell of decay.

Maung Sein prepared the food. He boiled towels and clothes, changed her, washed her sweaty body, squatted beside her and talked at her in the hope that his voice might help her. Now and again, while his son was sleeping, he would lift her carefully and carry her in his arms into the yard for a few minutes. He was taken aback to find how light she had become. Hardly heavier than a sack of rice. Although she opened her eyes only briefly and hardly responded, he would take her slowly around the house. She ought to see how the bougainvillea was blooming. The poppies. The yellow hibiscus, whose color she so loved. How the tomatoes he had planted for her were growing, the fruit on the banana plants.

She ought to see how life was waiting for her. How sorely he needed her. Death was a silent visitor to whom one addressed no questions.

Who took whomever he wished. But not Nu Nu. She mustn't go. Not without him.

In the evening—the midwife had long since gone home—he would sit alone at the head of her bed, trying to meditate. Without success. Instead he would gaze in the candlelight at the faces of his sleeping wife and son. He recalled the words of the monks he had lived with for so many years. He had learned from them everything he knew about life: that every individual is the author of his own fate. Without exception.

But Maung Sein did not feel at all the master of his fate in these weeks. He was driven, not the driver. A slave to his fears.

What crime must he have committed that he deserved to lose his wife and child? He did not wish to blame anyone other than himself for his sorrows, but was it really his fault if he wound up a young widower? What mistake had he made?

Maung Sein knew the answer to his questions: He ought not to have married. He ought not to have lost his heart to Nu Nu. Had he not, then he would not now be suffering, he had to admit. Was that what the Buddha preached in his infinite wisdom? If he and Nu Nu had never conceived, he would not now need to fear for his child's life. But what kind of existence would that be? A life without attachments. A life without people one feared to lose. The life of a monk. Not his. He feared nothing more than Nu Nu's death.

The price of love.

He was no Buddha. Was not even on the right path, no matter how much he meditated. He was a human being. A simple, vulnerable human being, full of hopes and fears, full of desire and longing, whose happiness was fragile. He was sure he would eventually acquire a heart that he could not lose.

But not in this life. Not as long as there was Nu Nu.

Nu Nu was aware of almost nothing during all this time. She had the impression that Death still stood at the door, exuding his stench, on the verge of stepping in. Uncertain yet whom he would take. The mother or the child? Or both?

She was not afraid. She lacked the energy even for fear.

She perceived little more of her son than his lips sucking at her from time to time. His gentle breath on her skin. The short, pitiful cries that grew quieter and weaker rather than louder and stronger. His skin was wrinkled and limp. She could feel it as she dully stroked his tiny body.

The midwife did not give Maung Sein much cause for hope. She had seen too many mothers and newborns die.

Danger lurked everywhere after such a difficult birth. Nu Nu had lost far too much blood. She was too weakened, just like the baby, and the world was full of germs, bacteria, viruses, and parasites just waiting for an opportunity to infect them. Their fate would be decided in the coming days, perhaps weeks, and beyond the care she was already giving them there was not much she could do. To be safe she was bringing a small offering twice a week to the spirit who lived in the fig tree near the house. Rice. Bananas. Oranges. She did not know whether it was in his power to heal Nu Nu, but it could hardly be a mistake to incline him favorably.

Later, when Nu Nu and her son had gotten through it, she would call it a miracle. At one point during the birth and then one other time thereafter she had taken the child for dead and had given up on Nu Nu. There was no saving a woman with a lifeless child in her womb. And no saving a woman with so little blood, either. They were on their way to a new existence; she had never before seen a mother and child recover once so far gone.

One morning Nu Nu awoke and knew that Death had changed his mind. For the first time since the birth there was no stench of decay in her nostrils, only the sweet aroma of ripe mangoes. For the first time since the birth she could feel her body without freezing. She breathed deeply in and out and sniffed her son's hair as he slumbered at her breast.

He smelled different. A hint of almonds and honey. The scent of life.

She looked around the hut. The doorframe was empty; she had a clear view of the papaya tree and the palms in the yard. Two butterflies danced in the sunbeams that fell through the windows. Maung Sein squatted by the smoldering fire, stirring a pot. Beside her were towels, a yellow hibiscus blossom in a vase, strewn in a circle beside it the petals of a red rose.

She tried to sit up but felt too weak. She called to him. He did not react. For a moment she thought it was all a dream. Perhaps this was not a return to life but the moment of final farewell. A terrible fear gripped Nu Nu. She did not want to die. Not yet. Not with her son in her arms. She mustered all her strength and called his name again. Loudly and clearly. He turned to her. Puzzled. As if not believing his ears.

"Nu Nu?"

"Yes," she whispered.

He stood up, walked over to her with careful steps, and bent over her.

"Nu Nu?"

She smiled faintly.

Chapter 8

THE FIRST TIME she left the house with her sleeping son in her arms, still unsteady on her legs, gripping the railing tightly, she surveyed the yard, astonished. It was at once familiar and strange. Something was different, though she could not immediately put her finger on it. The morning sun beamed through the bushes. The leaves of the banana plants seemed greener, their fruit larger and yellower. The hibiscus and the bougainvillea had never looked so beautiful. A warm breeze caressed her skin. Maung Sein was perched on a log below her, chopping kindling. Stroke by stroke he would split branches as thick as a fist. The uniformity of his movements radiated something infinitely reassuring.

Nu Nu looked at Ko Gyi in her arms. He had her nose. Her mouth. Her cinnamon skin. She cautiously took one of his little hands. It was warm. And would always remain so. Suddenly he opened one blinking eye, and then quickly the other. He had her eyes, too, without a doubt. Ko Gyi regarded his mother earnestly, intently. She smiled. His deep brown eyes did not move. They looked for a long time at each other. Then a quiet smile drifted across his face. No one had ever smiled at her that way. No look had ever moved her so.

She was back.

In the weeks that followed she recovered more and more of her strength, and it was not long before she could assist her husband with simple chores. She would buy food at the market, balancing the big basket of rice and vegetables on her head all the way up to their hut with Ko Gyi wrapped firmly on her chest. In contrast to all the other young mothers in the village, she did not like to carry him on her back. She wanted to see him. She wanted to smell his hair. She wanted their hearts to hear each other.

She managed all of the work in the house with a single hand. She fanned the fire one-handed, cooked, swept the yard, pulled weeds out of the tomato beds, washed longyis and towels, and even developed a technique to wring them out one-handed—all because she did not want to put her son down. Not for one second. They had together been ordained to die, and together they had returned. It would be a long time before she was ready to let him out of her sight even for a few minutes.

The most beautiful part of Nu Nu's day began when Maung Sein set off for the fields in the morning. If Ko Gyi was awake she would unwrap him and gaze at his small, perfect body. The most beautiful she had ever seen. A full head of hair, a round face with strikingly large eyes and comely lips. She marveled at his soft skin, smelled him. Took his tiny hands and feet in her mouth, rubbing his belly again and again, seeing in his eyes how much he enjoyed every touch. His tiny fingers gripped hers tightly, as if they would never let go. She noticed changes every day, however small they might be. His grip was getting stronger. His eyes were bigger, his gaze more alert, his kicking more boisterous. The first rings of fat appeared on the thighs and little arms that had previously been so thin. His gaze began to stray from her, to wander. Fixating on shadows on the wall. Marveling at his own little hands that appeared suddenly like shooting stars sweeping across his field of vision only to disappear again mysteriously. Until he learned to control them and put them in his mouth. With each passing day his soul came a bit farther into the world, thought Nu Nu. A bud unfolding slowly.

Whenever he started to cry she would carry him all around the house and yard; the motion was soothing to him. All the while she would be telling him in detail about everything they saw. The gleaming yellow hibiscus and the ripe tomatoes. The plump insects. The singing birds.

In a matter of seconds Ko Gyi would settle down and listen attentively to his mother's voice.

After she had seen and described everything for the second time she would think up stories of her own. It was a steady stream of talk that she hoped would envelop and transport her son, a melody to accompany him through life and to protect him in need.

While nursing she would often sit on the porch with a cup of tea, letting Ko Gyi drink until he fell asleep, holding him in her arms or on her lap and watching him while he drowsed. Taking delight in every smile that dreams might charm from his lips. Every sigh. Every breath.

As soon as Maung Sein got home he would join her, but he would grow impatient after only a few minutes. He did not understand how his wife could stare at someone just lying there motionless with his eyes closed.

"Don't you ever get bored?"

"No."

"Why not?"

She shrugged.

"What do you see when you look at him?"

Nu Nu thought about it. "Everything."

"What everything?"

"The Riddle of Life. And its solution."

A disturbed expression was his only reaction.

She wondered what her son had done to her. Even her skin had settled down since his birth.

She examined her forearms again and again in disbelief. Her legs. Her neck. Her midriff. Nowhere did she find even the slightest hint of a red splotch.

Nu Nu felt so strong and confident that she no longer paid bad omens much heed. She attributed no special significance to the dead cat she found lying in the road with foam on its snout on her way to the market. When Maung

Sein injured himself carving a wooden fish for his son, she wrote it off as a mishap.

Nor was she distressed when the neighbor's sow bore six piglets on her birthday, one of them with two heads. For a short time she felt herself immune to the threats and vagaries of life.

Until that evening.

Sometimes it is a matter of seconds.

Chapter 9

SHE KNEW FROM the very first moment.

Just as she had known the first time around. Beyond any shadow of a doubt. A part of him would remain inside her. Implant itself. Grow. Something about this night had been different. Her initial passion had given way to uneasiness. She was loathe to surrender herself to him. She did not wish to be touched. In any way.

Maung Sein did not seem to notice, or perhaps he believed that his own desire would ultimately excite her. He kissed her neck tenderly. He caressed her and touched her with his fingers, but everything that usually aroused her felt to her now increasingly unpleasant.

As if she sensed already that anything they did that night would come to a bad end.

She thought of asking him to stop but did not want to disappoint him. What did it matter if for once they did not share equally in the pleasure? If she went along with it just to please him?

Later, when he entered her, she felt a stabbing pain in her abdomen, a pain that grew more intense with the ardor of his movement. Again she thought of asking him to stop, hesitated, and then let it happen.

To her.

When it was over, he lay panting beside her, and Nu Nu barely managed to suppress her tears. A part of him. But this time she did not want it. The thought of something growing inside her repulsed her from the very start.

She wanted more than anything to go outside and shove a finger down her throat, to vomit until she had expelled all foreign elements from her body.

She did not want a second child. Not now. Later. Perhaps.

Ko Gyi was enough for her. Ko Gyi and her husband. The distance they had felt during the last months of the pregnancy had gradually given way to their former intimacy. She was happy when he came home from the field, sweaty as he was. She needed his proximity. His calm. Nu Nu could not imagine loving a new child as much as those two. There was not room in her life for another person. Later. Perhaps. For now it would bring only sorrow.

During the early days she hoped she had been mistaken. Ko Gyi was still nursing, and she felt no great change in her body for some time.

Then came the morning sickness, the twinges in her abdomen.

Nu Nu pleaded with her body to cast away that little nothing. Seal up. Just stop nourishing it and then at some point wash it away in a gush of blood.

When that did not work she tried willpower. She would squat down several times a day, close her eyes, breathe deeply, and concentrate only on that foreign matter inside her. Go away. Away. Away. Out. Out. Out.

She sought support every morning from the spirit who lived in the fig tree, bringing him papayas and bananas as offerings. Perhaps he had the power to end the life growing within her.

Nu Nu recalled the words of the women in the field. During her first pregnancy they had advised against carrying anything too heavy lest she endanger her child. Now she threw caution to the wind. With her son on her back she would take on the heaviest work in the field and at home, so that Maung Sein exhorted his wife to be mindful of her condition. Ko Gyi needed a healthy mother.

She gave him no answer, but hoped that the physical exertions would eventually have the desired effect. Possessed by rage and doubt, she would drum her abdomen with both fists until her arms wearied. To no avail. Her belly swelled, and she took to ignoring her condition as best she could. As if through her indifference the child might cease to grow and vanish from her life.

One evening they were sitting in silence by the fire, Ko Gyi was asleep, and Maung Sein gazed for a long time at his wife. The arch of her belly was now impossible to miss.

"Aren't you happy?" he asked, almost casually, scraping rice from a bowl with a tin spoon.

Nu Nu stared into the flames. She felt paralyzed. She was short of breath. She drew shallow drafts of air and exhaled them rapidly. Her heart raced. Fear had returned. The effortlessness of past months was nothing but a faint memory now. Why was her body ignoring her? Why had it not eliminated that something inside her weeks ago?

She summoned all her courage. "No, I am not happy."

He nodded, as if he had expected this answer.

"Why not?"

She briefly considered asking him whether he did not feel the same way. Whether in his heart, too, there was no room to spare. Whether they might together find some solution. There were a number of young women in the village who could not conceive and who would be delighted to have a child.

"I don't want a second child."

"Why not?" he repeated without looking at her.

"It's too soon." Later. Maybe.

"Are you afraid of the delivery?"

She shook her head. "No."

"Of what then?"

If only she had an answer.

"How can I help you?"

"To be happy?"

He nodded, and she saw the sincerity in his eyes. If only it were that simple.

"And you?" she inquired hesitantly.

His laughter in the firelight.

"I am happy. Very, in fact. Nothing could be more wonderful." After a short pause he added: "Not for me."

"Aren't you frightened?"

"No. Of what?" He looked at her intently. "Should I be?"

She pursed her lips and shook her head again, quickly. "I wonder if we should think about . . ." Nu Nu did not finish the sentence.

"Think about what?"

"There are women in the village . . ." She saw the happiness in his eyes. He would have no understanding for that train of thought.

"What's troubling you?" he asked anxiously.

She shrugged. Helplessly. How could she explain something she did not herself understand?

Maung Sein edged over to his wife and put an arm around her shoulders.

"I love you," he whispered tenderly in her ear.

Three words that otherwise never missed their mark.

"I love you," she echoed softly.

A chill ran down her spine.

"Don't worry. The second child is always easier. I asked the midwife."

Nu Nu nodded. A moment later she felt a sharp kick that made her flinch.

This was no tentative wriggling as she had known it with Ko Gyi; this was a ferocious punching and lashing out.

Maung Sein lit a candle, set it with a bit of wax on a tin can, and lay down beside his nursing wife. He listened to the gurgling sounds of his son's eager suckling. When Ko Gyi had fallen asleep exhausted, Nu Nu swaddled him in two cloths and laid him on the far side of her husband. For a while they rested wordlessly side by side.

"Do you think that a person can shed?" she asked suddenly.

He looked at Nu Nu in the flickering candlelight. Perplexed. She could tell by his eyes and lightly furrowed brow that he had not understood. "What do you mean, 'shed'?"

"Shed. Like snakes. Or amphibians."

Thinking his wife was joking, Maung Sein smiled. He pinched her arm and tugged softly at her skin. "Not you, anyway. Yours is on there pretty tight."

Nu Nu eyed him gravely. "I don't mean our bodies. I mean our souls."

"Our souls?" he replied in surprise.

"I want to know if we can strip away a part of ourselves once something else has grown in to replace it. Like an old snakeskin. Can a troubled spirit transform into a serene one? A sorrowful spirit into a joyful one? A solitary spirit into a sociable one? Not just for an evening or a week. For eternity."

Maung Sein crossed his arms under his head and looked at the ceiling. It was not a question he had ever considered. He pondered how the monks would have answered it. They might have said that the true essence of every individual resides in the soul; that this essence is not static but dynamic. That each person is free and that no one but ourselves can harm, rescue, or change us. Of that much he was convinced. And if we possessed the power to change ourselves, if the essence in our souls was not set in stone, then a troubled spirit could also transform itself into a serene spirit.

"Or," he heard her asking, "are we stuck with who we are?"

"No," he answered confidently, "we are not."

She laid her head on his chest and gazed pensively at her son as he lay sleeping beside his father. She hoped fervently that he was right.

Chapter 10

THAR THAR WANTED to live. He defied his mother's every attempt to be rid of him. Obstinately he had implanted himself within her and started to grow. In spite of her exertions and punches.

After toughing it out for thirty-nine weeks and five days he could wait no longer: Thar Thar was anxious to come into the world.

The delivery lasted less than an hour and proceeded without complication. The amniotic sac broke near dawn; the sun had not yet risen over the mountains when the water flushed him out onto a few wet cloths in a little shack. Nu Nu never even really had to push.

She discovered quickly that Thar Thar was not one to depend on the help of others. He was heavier and taller than his brother. His first cries were so penetrating that even the farmers living on the other side of the valley would swear years later they had heard them clearly.

A strong and healthy boy, she heard the midwife say. And a handsome one, like his mother. Someone laid him on her belly. Nu Nu lifted her head. The resemblance escaped her. She saw nothing but a blood-smeared, pointy-headed creature howling in fury. With all his might. Shrill and piercing. Ko Gyi had never wailed like that. Not once.

The soothing voices of the women around her. Maung Sein wiped the sweat from her face with a moist cloth. They took her son, washed him, tried to calm him with rocking and patting. In vain.

He must be hungry, she ought to nurse him, said the midwife.

Nu Nu did not want to. She was too tired. Later.

Not be resisted, the midwife laid him at her breast.

It hurt from the very first. He did not drink. He guzzled. He sucked at her furiously, voraciously, as if hoping to drain his mother utterly, looking up at her with clenched fists all the while.

"An unusual child," the birth attendants declared unanimously, congratulating her. She could be proud. She was now the mother of two healthy sons. Such good fortune! Every woman in the village should be so lucky!

Nu Nu did not want to hear it. She did not wish to feel thankful. She wanted only to be left alone.

His bawling woke her in the night. Maung Sein was already up, having lit a candle, kneeling beside his son and watching him, full of concern. Thar Thar's body was stiff like a dead animal's, his mouth and eyes wide open, his lips quivering. He was belting out cries that shook his whole body, each one eerier than the last. What suffering could cause him to make such dreadful noises?

"Maybe a nightmare," said her husband, looking at her helplessly.

Nu Nu wondered what a newborn might dream about.

"Or he's hungry?"

She slid over to her son and tried to put him on the breast, but he turned away, screaming all the louder.

Her husband rubbed his head and belly but got no reaction. "Do you think he's in pain?"

Nu Nu shrugged, confounded. To her ears his bellowing sounded less like suffering and more like an irate, desperate denunciation.

"Maybe he doesn't want to be with us?" she muttered as if to herself.

"Where else would he want to be?" snapped her husband.

"I don't know. Ko Gyi never cried like that."

Maung Sein shook his head, daubed tiny droplets of sweat from Thar Thar's brow, took him in his arms, and carried him around the shack. He sang. Whistled. Swayed, turned in circles.

No matter what they tried, their son remained beyond their reach. In the end he would fall silent from exhaustion. His little body would twitch a few more times, then his eyes would close. Even in his sleep he would sob deeply a few more times.

The midwife examined him the next day but could find no reason for his complaints and recommended patience. Every child is different. Some babies cry more, some less. She mustn't forget his long journey here. Her firstborn seemed so calm to her only because the two of them had hovered for weeks between life and death.

Within three days her breasts were so inflamed that she could feed neither Thar Thar nor his brother. Ko Gyi was old enough to eat rice porridge and vegetables, but Thar Thar was nursed by a young woman from the village who had recently delivered a child of her own. Nu Nu was happy every time Maung Sein took him away and for a while quiet prevailed in the hut once again.

Thar Thar would make his impending return known even from afar.

Nu Nu felt the tension in her body.

She marveled at her husband's patience. Between carrying, rocking, and singing he was now almost always able to soothe his son. A calm that never lasted long.

When his wailing continued undiminished, the midwife examined him a second time. Pressing his stomach, she could feel a bit of gas. With a few deft movements she was able to entice it out of him in the form of a long, loud fart. Checked his mouth, ears, and nose; no sign of an infection. He could focus on her finger and follow its movements. His reflexes were in order; arms and legs, hands and feet were as they should be. Thar Thar lay naked before her, looking with interest at the strange woman and tolerating her examination without protest.

"He is physically healthy," she said, wrapping him back up.

"So why does he cry so much?"

The midwife shrugged. "I don't know."

Nu Nu thought back to the hours she had spent awake at night wishing that the life within her would cease to grow. Was it possible that he understood something of that?

Of the rice, the papayas, and the bananas she had offered, hoping for his death? Of her black tears? The desperate punches to her abdomen? Did he know of her wish to give him to some other family? Impossible. He was just a few weeks old. What an absurd idea.

All the same Nu Nu asked the midwife as casually as she could whether she thought that infants could remember things.

The woman gazed at her as if astonished by the question. "Of course," she replied.

"Do you really think so? My parents died when I was two," Nu Nu countered doubtfully. "I couldn't even tell you now what they looked like."

The midwife nodded. "That's a different matter. Images can fade. Sounds and smells disappear from our memory. But our heart forgets nothing. A child's soul knows everything."

Nu Nu felt a shiver run down her spine.

"Why do you ask?"

"Just curious." She left it at that.

But the midwife's words stayed with her. What if she was right? If in some part of his heart the knowledge lay hidden that he had not been wanted? What might it do to him? Would it be forgotten over the years, the way she forgot mundane things? Or would it follow him his whole life long?

She asked her husband if he believed that thoughts alone could cause harm.

"Everything has consequences," he replied.

"Even thoughts?"

"Everything."

"Even thoughts from long ago?"

He could not understand what she was talking about.

"I can't believe it," she said after thinking it over awhile. "I believe thoughts simply disappear unless we act on them. Like clouds. Or water that seeps into the ground."

Maung Sein smiled. "Just because you don't see it anymore doesn't mean the water is gone. Plants live off it. The bananas we eat. The rowanberries that poison us. Nothing is lost. Even thoughts have consequences."

In the weeks and months following this conversation no one could have claimed that she did not do everything in her power to help her son. She wanted to be a good mother to him the way Maung Sein was a good father.

Nu Nu sang for him. Talked to him. If Maung Sein was working in the field, she would carry Thar Thar around with the same patience his father exercised. He would lie in her arms, but he found no peace there.

Why did he cry when she held him? Why was he so sparing with his smiles? Why did he so often kick and punch?

Even his gaze made her uncomfortable. He looked at her penetratingly. With a wrinkled brow. Much too serious for a child. Or was it mistrust she read in his dark, nearly black eyes?

A child's soul knows everything. A heart forgets nothing.

She had bonded with Ko Gyi at first sight, but Thar Thar was still a stranger to her.

Maung Sein implored her to stop comparing the children. "Comparison is the mother of discontent."

Nu Nu wondered whether troubled spirits were born or made. A question to which she found no satisfactory answer, regardless of how long she pondered it.

In Thar Thar's case the birthmark under his chin might offer a clue. She had first noticed it one day after his birth, when she had not given it a second thought. Now she realized who it reminded her of: her father's brother, a drunkard who had squandered every kyat he ever earned on rice wine. His wife and children had abandoned him, and he had disappeared from the village one night shortly thereafter, never to be seen again. Perhaps he had died recently, and maybe his spirit had been reincarnated in her son? A birthmark of that size on the same part of the body. Could that be a coincidence?

Maung Sein was incensed when she cautiously shared her thoughts with him. Said uncle, if the stories could be trusted, would have amassed so much bad karma during his lifetime that he could never have been reborn as their son. Crippled, perhaps. Or blind. Or the son of some other drunkard. Not as the son of two parents who loved their children and cared for them as they did. Did she really think it a punishment to be born into their family?

He had a point.

But still.

How does a mother share out her love?

If it came in the form of beads or leaves or grains of sand she could count them and allocate them evenly.

If she wanted to.

If it came in a big, warm, soft lump like a rice cake she could divide it into pieces of equal size.

Or in a viscous, fragrant extract that she could measure drop for drop into glasses and offer to her two children.

But love does not know justice. Love follows its own laws. Even a mother's love.

Chapter 11

THAR THAR DID not make it easy for anyone. Not for his father. Not for his mother. Least of all for himself.

He remained a glum and fretful baby who regarded his surroundings with suspicion. Maung Sein alone could coax the odd chuckle out of him with his antics.

He was becoming an impatient child, for whom nothing happened quickly enough. He wanted to sit upright before his body had the strength for it, and he would burst into a rage the moment he fell over. He wanted to crawl before his muscles would carry him, and he bawled when his energy flagged after only a few feet.

He had trouble settling down, twitching while he slept as if plagued by pains and starting frequently out of his sleep during the night.

A tiny spirit. A gigantic fear. Nu Nu lay beside him. With a heavy heart. And a conscience heavier still.

As soon as he finally learned to get around on all fours he scorned being carried. It seemed to his mother that his crawling always had a singular purpose: to get away. Away from her. If she laid him down beside her it was only a matter of seconds before he was off to some other corner of the hut, most often toward the door, without ever looking back. He was deaf to Nu Nu's cries. She would have to hurry after him, scoop him up, and haul him back, a furious, struggling child. No sooner had she set him down than he would resume his battle with her.

In contrast to his brother. Ko Gyi was happiest in close proximity to his parents. He would rather be carried than walk himself, and when he explored his environment, he did so cautiously and deliberately, never straying more than a few yards away and turning back at the first word of warning. When Nu Nu crouched beside him and rolled an orange across the floor he would waddle after it, swaying, squeaking with delight. The moment he had caught up with the fruit he would take it in both hands and carry it proudly back to show his mother. Mother and son would frequently race around the hut. Or she would hide behind a wooden beam. His joy when he found her!

Thar Thar was not interested in their games.

On one occasion—Nu Nu was preoccupied with Ko Gyi—he crawled clear across the hut to the fire. He squatted in front of it and gazed in fascination at the flickering flames and the glowing coals. Listened to the crackling. Curious, he leaned forward and reached for an ember the size of an egg. Nu Nu reeled in terror. Thar Thar closed his hand around it.

The smell of burnt skin.

He cried out briefly, dropped the ember, looked in astonishment at his fingers, at that glimmering something in front of him, then back at his hand, now bright red. Rather than wailing in pain, he turned around and looked at his mother. Outraged.

As if she were to blame.

Nu Nu rushed over to him, took him in her arms, and plunged the burned hand into water, blew on it with all her might, tried to comfort him. It hurt her even to look at the wound.

Thar Thar, on the other hand, exhibited no further reaction. No crying. No moaning. A serious injury. A silent child. A bewildered mother.

He was and remained a mystery to her. In the years that followed she was frequently disquieted by his ability not to feel pain, or not to let on that he felt it, she wasn't quite sure which it was.

But she was also comforted.

Who was this person she had given birth to? A troubled spirit, to be sure. Not the only one in the family. But what might have brought mother and son together served instead to divide them.

Nu Nu did not have the same patience with him that her father had shown with her. Without patience a troubled spirit can never come to rest.

It is our own flaws that we are least ready to forgive in others.

As soon as Thar Thar was confident on his feet he set about investigating the world. All warnings and prohibitions notwithstanding. He crawled again and again through the thick hedge that bordered the yard and roamed about the village. After he had fallen into the well a second time—whence he was rescued only by chance—and after Maung Sein and the neighbors had vehemently berated her for her negligence, Nu Nu took a rope and tied one end around his waist and the other to one of the pilings that held up the house. As soon as Thar Thar understood that his world had been reduced to a five-yard radius, he took up a raging outcry of protest the likes of which the village had never heard before. She ignored him in the hope that he would eventually stop of his own accord.

She threatened to tie him directly to the post if he did not settle down. When he did not, she made good on her threat. She would not untie him until he calmed down.

Thar Thar was not a child to be impressed by punishments.

That evening Maung Sein heard his son's bawling as soon as he came near the village. It was the familiar mixture of rage and desperation. At home he found a distraught Ko Gyi and two captives. One tied to a post, the other not.

He had never seen his wife so riled up.

He wanted to know what had happened. Nu Nu had no answers to his questions.

That evening she was heavyhearted as never before. She felt that her world and whatever good fortune remained in it were crumbling bit by bit. Ko Gyi retreated ever further into silence. She and Maung Sein, exhausted by the sleepless nights, fell to quarreling. The relatives who might have helped her lived two days away on foot. The neighbors had their hands full with their own fields and their own children.

A short time later Maung Sein had an epiphany and took Thar Thar with him to the fields. From that day on father and son left the hut together every morning just after sunrise and often came back only after darkness had fallen. Thar Thar would walk the first mile or so on his own. After that he wanted to be carried. Hands full with heavy tools, Maung Sein would set his son on his shoulders. The lad would cling to his father's hair and sway in rhythm with his step. Sometimes he would hold his father's eyes shut, and Maung Sein would pretend that he could no longer see. He would start to stagger or walk straight toward a ditch or tree, only to turn on his heel at the last moment while his son on his shoulders would squeak with delight. Now it took him an hour longer than previously to get to the field. Time that he might have spent working.

In the field he built a shelter for Thar Thar out of bamboo and palm leaves, a protection against sun and rain, and he showed him a bit of land that was his own to "farm."

During the first few months he made animals out of clods of dirt and played with them day in and day out. Later he loved to dig holes and little caves with his bare hands, selecting the bigger stones out of the ground, dragging them to the edge, building dams and levees and creating a minia-ture irrigation system. He was utterly disinterested in his surroundings. Maung Sein could have worked in some other field for hours; Thar Thar would not have noticed. Maung Sein found it touching to see how engrossed his son was in his work. With what devotion he would rebuild trenches and dikes, without a word of complaint any time a rain shower had washed them away.

At lunchtime they would crouch together in the shade of the shelter, eating their rice, drinking water, and gazing without a word across the fields to the green mountains in the distance. They heard nothing but their own breath and—during the rainy season—a babbling brook. Some-times a big black bird with a long, sharp beak would land not far from their refuge. He would strut back and forth looking greedily at the grains of rice that fell next to their bowls. Thar Thar would edge his way closer to Maung Sein, who would put his arm protectively around the boy. After their meal they would rest together. With his head on his father's chest Thar Thar would fall asleep within minutes.

At moments like these Maung Sein had to wonder why mother and son had never bonded. Were there people who simply did not belong together? Who loved each other, but who were nevertheless happier when they were apart? Cer-tainly not a mother and her child. It would just be a matter of patience and self-composure on Nu Nu's part.

Every evening on the way home both of them would be so tired that Maung Sein would have to carry Thar Thar all the way, pausing several times to rest. Twice it happened that they fell asleep arm in arm by the side of the road and made it home only because passing farmers woke them.

Chapter 12

PERHAPS THINGS WOULD have turned out differently if Maung Sein had stayed at home. Perhaps the intimacy and bond with his father would in the long run have given Thar Thar the peace and security he could not get from his mother.

Perhaps it might have helped his heart to forget.

But two much-too-dry rainy seasons and Maung Sein's ineptitude as a farmer were enough to turn an already low-yielding field into so much worthless acreage. No matter how he drove himself, Nu Nu and the children were going to bed hungry with increasing regularity.

"I've got to find some other work," he said one evening while the children slept and they sat by the fire.

How often Nu Nu had feared that sentence in the last few months. While secretly knowing it was true.

"What kind of work?" she asked tentatively. There was no one in the village but farmers.

"As a lumberjack."

It was the only answer that made sense. Still, it was not the one she wanted to hear.

"Maybe one of the neighbors could use some help?" she offered without much conviction.

"They certainly could. But what would they pay me with?"

"Maybe you could . . ." She never finished the sentence because it had no predicate. She knew there was no work for him in the village.

For a long time they said nothing.

Nu Nu did not want him to go away. Every fiber of her being bridled at the thought. She already missed him when he was away in the fields a whole day while she stayed in the village with Ko Gyi. Since their wedding they had not spent a single night apart. She needed him to go to sleep. She needed him in the morning to find the strength to face the day. She needed his laughter. His even temper. His faith that we are not powerless against the vagaries of fate, but determine fate ourselves. Now more than ever with Ko Gyi and Thar Thar. And they needed their father. Especially Thar Thar.

As a lumberjack he would travel about the provinces. He would be on the road for weeks, probably months at a time. How often would they see each other? Twice a year? Three times? The very thought was unbearable. She felt the pressure mounting in her eyes. She felt her heart constricting.

"No, I won't have it," whispered Nu Nu, hoping he would fail to notice that she had started to cry.

"Do we have a choice?"

"We could go with you." For a brief moment a glimmer of joy in her voice.

"Hauling the children from village to village?"

"Why not?" Don't say No. Please don't. Say Maybe.

"I'll never be in one place for very long, my love. I'll be working in forests throughout the country. How could we ever manage that?"

When she had no answer he added: "Besides, someone needs to stay here to look after the tomatoes and the fields. Even as a lumberjack I won't earn much."

"So why do it, then?" she challenged.

As if he were to blame.

Nu Nu searched long for a solution. Any solution. Anything would be better than living here alone with her sons.

"We could send Ko Gyi and Thar Thar to a monastery," she blurted out.

"They're five and six years old, much too young to—"

"We could give it a try for a few months," she interrupted him in her desperation. "And if it didn't . . ."

"No."

Yes. Yes. Yes. "Maybe just one of . . ."

"Nu Nu!"

"Why not?"

"Because, because . . ." He looked at her, his voice faltering.

By the light of the fire she looked into his face.

Maung Sein's eyes were bloodshot, and his face contorted.

Chapter 13

HE HAD NOT taken proper leave of them. A white truck had arrived before sunrise to collect him and one other man from the village. Maung Sein had not wanted to wake his sons. The evening before, he had not been able to bring himself to say good-bye.

Nu Nu accompanied him with quivering knees to the well in the middle of the village where the truck was waiting.

They did not say much by way of farewell. Neither was in the mood for talk. Take care of yourself. You, too. I love you. I love you, too. Come back soon. I will. Promise.

Maung Sein climbed onto the bed of the dented vehicle, tucked the small bundle of his few possessions between his feet, and stared at the ground.

Nu Nu took a step toward him. It was all she could do not to climb into the pickup herself. And she felt her resistance waning. She was already standing next to him, clenching the tailgate.

The truck set off slowly. Nu Nu walked beside it, not letting go. Her husband sat less than three feet away. She could still jump in.

Maung Sein lifted his head. One desperate, imploring look.

It was the moment when Nu Nu realized with certainty what she had suspected since the day Thar Thar was born: that her good fortune was not limitless.

She let go of the metal, took a couple more steps, and stopped. The darkness quickly swallowed up the truck.

When she told the children later in the morning that their father would be away for many weeks and that she did not yet know when he would be back, Thar Thar refused to believe her.

Would he be back that evening, he wanted to know.

No, in a few weeks, repeated Nu Nu. At the earliest.

Had he gone to the next village to take care of something?

No.

Was he working in the fields?

No, she replied with a sigh. A truck had picked him up. He was gone. Far away.

Thar Thar ate his rice in peace and looked at his mother as if she were talking about a neighbor.

Half an hour later he had disappeared. He was not to be found in the yard, nor in the little chicken coop where he usually liked to hide. She waited awhile in the hope that he had gone to play somewhere. When near midday he still had not appeared she went to look for him in the village. None of the neighbors had seen him. She went several times to the new well and to the old, exhausted one. She walked to both of the ponds outside the village and made inquiries of the monks at the monastery. By evening half the neighborhood was involved in the search, but there was not a trace of Thar Thar. What could have befallen him? Maybe he had fallen out of a tree while playing and was lying somewhere with broken legs. Had he climbed up to one of the nearby caves, despite her having forbidden it explicitly, and not been able to find his way back out? Or perhaps a stray dog had molested him? Only last month a child in the next village had fallen prey to a rabid dog.

She spent a long, sleepless night.

The next morning some farmers found him on the edge of the field that the family cultivated. He was sleeping in the shelter that his father had built for him.

Nu Nu explained to her sons again that Maung Sein was not working as a farmer anymore, but cutting down trees, and was very far away and would come back sometime. Thar Thar still did not believe her. There were trees here, too. You didn't need to go away just to cut down trees. For one whole week he scoured the village for him, going from house to house and asking everyone he met if they had seen his father, or if they knew where he might be. When he had finally convinced himself that Maung Sein had actually disappeared, for some mysterious reason, he withdrew. Nu Nu had worried that he would in his anger and spite become even more rebellious and impulsive. Quite the opposite. Thar Thar fell silent.

He stopped quarreling with his brother.

He stopped contradicting her.

He slept long and had no appetite.

While Nu Nu and Ko Gyi were eating he preferred to retreat to the hen house, being satisfied later with the leftovers.

He felt no urge to get away. On the contrary, he often sat silently in the yard whittling at an old tree stump. For hours.

Nu Nu watched his behavior with concern while secretly also feeling relieved. She savored the peace in which he left her, and the time she spent with Ko Gyi. His attachment to her helped to dampen her longing for her husband. When she woke in the night with him lying beside her she even had the sensation that he smelled like his father.

Now and then she would catch Thar Thar observing them out of the corner of his eye. With a guilty conscience she would ask whether he wanted to come eat with them or sit by the fire or play in the yard with them. It would be so much nicer all three together. He only shook his head and looked at her in a way that made her so uncomfortable that she had to avert her eyes.

A child's soul knows everything.

Only when he strayed about the village with other children did he get into more trouble than before.

He climbed the tallest trees, jumping from branch to branch or rocking so violently in the crown that the children below screamed in alarm. He alone would brave the darkness of the cold, damp caves; he alone dared to somersault from the bridge into the river. The older boys feared him because he let no one push him around and never shied away from a scuffle.

There was no test of courage that he did not pass.

At home he was gradually starting to lend a hand. Though a year younger than his brother, Thar Thar was bigger and stronger. He had inherited not only his father's wavy hair and light skin, but also his powerful build. One day, Nu Nu thought, he would be a fine and handsome man. When she asked him for anything he would help without complaint. He hauled firewood from the yard into the house, gathered kindling in the woods. As soon as he understood which wood was best for lighting a fire, how to break it and tie it in little bundles, he preferred to go without her into the woods, staying away for a long time and returning with armfuls of dry branches. On market days he would carry small but much-too-heavy baskets full of tomatoes and ginger to the market while Ko Gyi was still holding his mother's hand. Thar Thar spoke little throughout it all. If his mother asked him a question, he would answer simply and succinctly.

WHEN, AFTER SIX months, Maung Sein returned home for the first time for two weeks, it was Thar Thar who spotted him first. He was stacking wood beneath the porch when he heard the creak of the front gate. For a few seconds

Thar Thar did not move. Maung Sein spread his powerful arms wide; his son set the log carefully on the ground without letting him out of his sight. As if not believing his eyes. As if fearing that a single blink would be enough to wash his father away as suddenly as he had appeared. He took one step toward him, hesitated briefly, then turned and ran behind the hut and hid. Despite many calls and pleas he did not come out of hiding until the evening. The next day he ignored his father completely. On the second day he would look at him, but would not say a word. On the third day he asked him a question: How long are you staying?

When he heard the answer he fell back into silence.

On the following days, too, Thar Thar avoided his father's every attempt to approach him. He would go with him to the fields and deftly carry out whatever tasks Maung Sein assigned him. Pulling weeds, turning the soil over, sowing seeds. And saying not a word.

All told they did not exchange more than a few sentences.

On the last evening Maung Sein had to search long before he found his son in the chicken coop. When he refused to come out even after lengthy entreaties, Maung Sein managed to squeeze himself inside through the tiny opening, in which he nearly got stuck. Thar Thar lay in one corner on a bed of straw. All around him the hens were cackling, disturbed by the unfamiliar visitor. Little brown feathers fluttered in the air. It was hot and stifling and stank of dung. Maung Sein wondered how his son could stand to be in there. He lay down beside him and waited.

"Why are you hiding?" he asked after a spell.

"I'm not hiding."

"What are you doing here, then?"

"Visiting my friends."

"The chickens?" Maung Sein asked, surprised.

"Yes. They like me." He stretched out an arm. One of the birds landed on it at once and picked at his hand with her beak. It was not a greedy hunt for food but more a gentle nibble. Thar Thar's face lit up with an unaccustomed smile. "You see?"

Maung Sein nodded. "Mama says you spend a lot of time here."

"Yes. Sometimes I even sleep here."

"Why?"

"Because it's beautiful. Because they're my friends. Because they need me and sometimes they ask me to stay with them."

"You talk with them?"

"Of course. I know all their names."

"They have names?" Maung Sein wondered.

"I gave them names. That's Koko." He pointed to a lanky brown bird. "Her eggs taste the best. That's Mo, she's the cheekiest, and above her is Mimi. She especially pays attention to me."

"What do you tell them, then?"

"Everything."

"Do they listen to you?"

"Of course." His son made an odd sound and all the hens immediately fell silent. From the remotest corner Mimi strutted forward. Thar Thar stretched his hand to her and she, too, nibbled at it delicately.

Maung Sein imitated his son, but hardly had he moved his arm when the birds startled off to hide. A few words from his son sufficed to calm them again.

"They don't like Mama, either." A second smile. Stranger still.

Maung Sein was delighted that the birds loosened his son's tongue, and he hoped it would last, although he was not quite sure what he should talk to him about. He wanted just to talk. To hear Thar Thar's voice before he left again. He waited a long time for a clarification, but it was quiet again in the coop.

"I'm leaving again tomorrow," Maung Sein said finally.

His son stared mutely at the ceiling.

"Tomorrow, before sunrise. You'll still be asleep."

"I want to go with you," said Thar Thar suddenly.

A second hen came up and nibbled at his bare feet. Now it was Maung Sein's turn to be silent. He wondered whether there was any possibility of bringing him along, but a lumber camp was no place for children. "You can't."

"Why not?"

"Because I'm on the road so much, and I have to work the whole time."

"I can help you."

Maung Sein smiled. "That would be nice. But felling trees is not easy and also a bit dangerous."

"I'm not afraid."

"I know. You can come with me when you're a little bigger. Promise."

Thar Thar did not reply. Maung Sein watched him in silence, and the longer he looked at him the sadder he felt. In the light of the candle his son's face lost all its youthful aspect. His lips were thin like the tail of a field mouse. He pressed them together the way he often used to do. His eyes looked tired. Was it just his imagination, or were those early wrinkles at the corners? It was not the weariness of a child after a long day that Maung Sein beheld; it was the exhaustion of a sad, lonely adult.

"Besides, Mama needs your help when I'm not there."

"She doesn't need me."

"Sure she does," contradicted Maung Sein. "You're wrong about that. She told me how industrious you are and how much you help her. That's very kind of you."

"Mama has Ko Gyi. She. Doesn't. Need. Me."

Maung Sein had to swallow twice. He wanted to give some answer, but nothing occurred to him. It was the way he said it that most alarmed Maung Sein. Grave and cool.

If only it had been a complaint.

Chapter 14

SHE WANTED TO surprise him. A little treat for him and the children. That was all. For his sons who always found it hard to see him go. Especially Thar Thar, whose most sincere wish was to go along when his father took to the road. Now he would have a chance to see what a difficult and dangerous trade Maung Sein practiced.

One of the last tall trees in the village needed to be cut down. It stood at the main intersection. Beetles had eaten away at its trunk. It was old and unsound, and it threatened to fall on the nearby houses in the next storm. Before it could be cut down, someone had to prune the crown. Otherwise it would fall on huts at the end of the street.

Maung Sein was the most experienced lumberjack in the village. He gladly volunteered.

The men were amazed at how deftly he scaled the tree with a saw over his shoulder. He shinnied right up to the top. They closed the street, he started to saw, and no one could say afterward exactly what happened then. A first branch came whooshing down. Then a second. All at once they heard a creaking and rustling, quietly at first, then louder and louder. Everyone looked up, many held their breath, out of a few mouths came short, high cries. The dull thud of the impact. No one who was there would ever forget it.

Most of the villagers were convinced that the spirit who lived in the tree had cast him from the crown out of vengeance. Others thought he must have stepped on a rotten branch. Several claimed to have seen him leaning too far forward to give a final kick to a branch that did not want to fall. A small number insisted that he had carelessly neglected to hold fast and then lost his balance. Or maybe for a moment he had let his guard down.

Everyone agreed there was nothing anyone could do about it. A tragic mishap. A twist of fate. Everyone has the karma he deserves.

Nu Nu knew better.

It was her fault. She had distracted him. She had seen him from a distance sitting in the crown of the mighty tree. Thirty, maybe forty yards off the ground. He had already lopped off two big branches. A black spot amid the green leaves.

She pointed him out to her sons, marking his position with her finger until they could discover him. They looked up at him full of pride and wanted nothing so much as to run right to him.

When they came to the barriers all three of them looked up and recognized him clearly among the branches and called his name in unison. He had not noticed them approaching and looked down in surprise.

They waved to him.

He waved back.

The children hopped and waved and clapped for joy.

He leaned forward to see them better. Waved. With both hands.

There was a creaking and a rustling in the crown of the tree.

Chapter 15

IT LASTED TWO years. Two years after which Nu
Nu could not say how she had survived. Two years
during which hardly a day passed when she did not fear
that she would fall into madness. Not a single day on which
she did not ask herself why this tragedy had stricken her of
all people. What had she done to deserve the fate of a young
widow? Why not the village leader's stingy wife? Or the
greedy, cantankerous wife of the rice merchant? Why her
with her two little children? Why was life so unjust?

There were many weeks during which she never left the
hut and hardly ever got out of bed. Neglecting the laundry.
Cooking nothing for her sons. Not even preparing alms for
the monks. She was wakeful all night and slept the whole
day. At times, believing it was all just a dream, she would
go to look for her husband. Ko Gyi in hand, she would wander the village with empty gaze, grimy longyi, and dishev-
eled hair. Her ramble ended every time at the stump of the

beetle-ridden tree at the crossroads. There she would squat in the dust and remember.

See him waving.

With both hands.

Eventually Thar Thar would arrive, take her by the hand, and lead them both back home in silence.

The brothers responded completely differently to their father's death. Ko Gyi clung to his mother. He slept next to her. By day he would not let her out of his sight. He begged her to get up when she simply lay there. He entreated her to say something when she was silent for days. He followed her every step the moment she left the house. As if, having lost his father, he feared now also to lose his mother. Most of the time, though, he simply crouched beside her and waited.

And waited.

Thar Thar, by contrast, driven by an inner unrest, was out and about from dawn till dusk.

He fetched water from the well, making sure that his mother and brother had enough to drink and that they ate at least once a day. He looked after the chickens. At regular intervals he would take a tub of laundry so heavy that he could barely carry it down to the river, where he would find a spot beside the women in the water. Then he would lug the wet things, now even heavier, back home, where he hung them on the porch to dry. He walked to the market and bought rice, and when their last kyat had been spent, he slipped through the hedge to the neighbors to ask for help. He tended and harvested the tomatoes and planted additional vegetables behind the house. He cooked every day. His curries tasted good. Better than hers.

Nu Nu could not figure out where her eight-year-old son found the energy. Sometimes she wondered if, with Maung Sein's death, some of the father's vigor, care, and love had passed into Thar Thar.

One afternoon more than two years after Maung Sein's death she lay exhausted on her blanket and watched how he cleaned the vegetables carefully, keeping the fire ablaze, tending to wood and kindling. With a clumsy movement he accidentally knocked over a kettle that fell with a clatter into the flames. Thar Thar disappeared behind a cloud of white steam. The fire went out, hissing loudly. He regarded the mess, sighed once briefly, and started to separate the dry wood from the wet. He went to the yard to fetch wood chips and little twigs and calmly lit another fire to boil water for the rice. The big barrel in front of the house was empty and he had to walk to the well in the village.

Nu Nu marveled at his equanimity. She would doubtless have been upset at her clumsiness. Would have gotten annoyed. Would have retreated discouraged to her sleeping mat. What had happened to Thar Thar? Where was the impulsive, hot-tempered boy who spent all his time in the chicken coop?

What had the father's accident done to the child's spirit? What had the elder taught the younger?

She thought about Maung Sein. Her husband was dead. There was nothing she could do about that. But whether the loss led to despair, whether it broke her, that was up to her alone.

Nu Nu straightened up and tried to stand. She found it easier than expected. She put on a clean longyi and added a fresh log to the fire. She watched as it started to smolder and eventually caught fire. Nu Nu squatted beside it and hesitantly picked up the little knife, testing the blade. Someone must have sharpened it. She took a cutting board and somewhat clumsily cut up spring onions and tomatoes, sliced zucchini and carrots, peeled and diced the ginger. With every movement the work came more easily and she felt improved. The sharp smell of the fresh ginger rose into her nose. How long had it been since she smelled it?

Ko Gyi sat beside her. Watching her. Speechless.

Suddenly Thar Thar stood in the doorway behind her with a pail of water.

"What are you doing?" he asked in surprise.

"I'm helping you," she replied.

He thanked her with a smile.

They put rice and vegetables on and then went, all three of them, into the yard to wash the tin plates and to fetch water for tea.

She noticed now for the first time that the roof in one corner of the hut had fallen in. The boards below, moist from the rain, had rotted. This part of the hut would not survive the next rainy season. Nu Nu looked around the yard. It was swept clean. Big tomatoes were thriving in the beds. Beside them Thar Thar had also planted carrots and eggplants, and he had skillfully weeded. The banana plants hung full of fruit, likewise the papaya and avocado trees. The bougainvillea, though, had utterly overgrown the gate, and she could see by a gap in the hedge what alternative exit her son was now using instead.

And she asked herself why she neither saw nor heard any sign of the chickens.

"Where are the chickens?"

Thar Thar swallowed and lowered his eyes. "In the coop."

"Are you sure? They're so quiet."

He nodded without looking at her.

Nu Nu walked over to the coop and listened. Not hearing anything, she squatted down and peered in through the little door. In one corner she spotted three birds.

"Where are the others?" she asked, puzzled, as she stood back up.

"Gone," whispered Thar Thar, turning aside.

"What do you mean, gone? Did they run away? Did dogs get a hold of them?" Nu Nu knew how much the chickens meant to her and she couldn't believe that he had not looked after them better.

Thar Thar shook his head mutely.

Nu Nu looked in doubt from one son to the other.

"He sold them," said Ko Gyi in a muted voice. "One after another."

"Sold them?"

Thar Thar, still silent, stared at the ground. She put a hand under his chin and cautiously lifted his head. Two tears ran down his cheeks. His lower lip quivered. He closed his eyes and the tears increased.

"Why?"

Silence.

"Why?"

A profound, almost unbearable silence was her answer.

"Because the neighbors were no longer willing to lend us money or rice," murmured Ko Gyi.

"Because otherwise we would have starved," said Thar Thar, turning away and running as fast as he could back into the house.

Nu Nu was still trying to understand what had happened. A thought crept up on her, so sad that she wanted to forget it again immediately. "But the neighbors have their own chickens," she said, looking to Ko Gyi for an answer. "It doesn't make sense. Can you explain it to me?"

He nodded. "It's true. They didn't want them, and they offered him a terrible price." He paused awhile. Softly, very softly, he continued: "He slaughtered, plucked, and dressed them and sold them at the market."

Chapter 16

WHEN NU NU awoke near dawn she could hear someone already busy with the pots. It was barely light yet, but the birds were already atwitter. She rolled over. Beside her Ko Gyi was asleep. Soon afterward she heard the monks at the gate, and she wondered why they had not long since ceased to ask for alms where there was nothing to be had. Nu Nu saw Thar Thar hurry down the steps with the big rice bowl in his hands. Had he been making offerings? All those months? How could he have conjured up the rice when they had hardly enough for themselves? She was too exhausted to ponder the question for long, and she fell back asleep.

It was light when she awoke again, and the birds had fallen silent. She rose. Ko Gyi was still asleep. Beside the fire she found rice and a lukewarm curry.

There was no sign of Thar Thar. Alarmed, she ran into the yard and looked into the chicken coop. Three chickens ogled her as she stuck her head through the door.

All at once her son's voice rang out from the neighbor's yard. Nu Nu shoved her way through the hedge and saw him sitting in the shadow of a massive fig tree. Beside him, as tall as a man, stood a pile of dried bamboo leaves and grasses. In front of him a woven mat on which he was working.

"What are you doing there?" she asked in surprise.

"I'm helping U Zhaw," he said softly. As if it made him uncomfortable.

"Your son is the most gifted weaver I've ever seen," called the neighbor's wife as she came out of the house. "And the most productive," she added with a look at the mother that said as much as: hard to believe, given his mother. "He can make half a roof in less than three days."

Nu Nu watched her son. Only now did she notice how nimbly his fingers moved, how deftly they intertwined the leaves and the tufts of grass. She saw the neighbor's new roof and another already finished half of a roof leaning against a tree.

"Your house looks nice," she said suspiciously, and gestured to Thar Thar's work. "Who is that for?"

"We'll sell that one."

"Sell? To whom?"

"Whoever needs it."

"For how much?"

"Two hundred kyat."

"How much does my son get?"

"Twenty. He's working off the money we've lent you."

"Twenty kyat?" Nu Nu found it difficult to conceal her outrage. She tried to catch Thar Thar's eye, but he kept his gaze lowered.

"How much longer?" she wanted to know.

The woman did some reckoning. "If he keeps up this pace, it won't be more than four weeks."

THAT EVENING SHE noticed her son's callused hands. The nails were lacerated, the fingertips reddened and bloody in places. They crouched with Ko Gyi by the fire. Nu Nu had a lot of questions, but Thar Thar was loath to answer. How long had he been working for the neighbors? When exactly had the money that Maung Sein had saved as a lumberjack run out? Did they have other debts? Instead of answering he just poked around in the embers with a stick.

Nu Nu wondered how they would get by in the future. Even if all three started to weave roofs and walls, the paltry pay would not amount to much. Their few savings were spent. They had nothing to sell besides the last three chickens and Maung Sein's rusty tools. Their field lay fallow. None of them had sufficient experience as a farmer. Any relatives that might have helped them lived too far away. They could not count on the support of the village. The family's fate was her bad karma, earned through her numerous misdeeds, and now there was nothing to do for it. Helping them out of pity or sympathy was, in the eyes of others, entirely inappropriate. Nu Nu knew that. She would have behaved no differently.

"We have to cultivate our field," said Thar Thar suddenly, as if he had been reading her mind.

Nu Nu nodded. "But how?"

"The same way everyone else does," he replied. "How else?"

"It's not so easy. Trust me."

"I know. But I always watched how Papa did it."

"That was a long time ago."

"I still remember a bit."

"That won't be enough."

"We've got to try," interjected Ko Gyi.

Thar Thar agreed with his brother. "The field is big enough. If we do it right, it can feed us."

Nu Nu looked from one to the other. Two children with sober faces who already knew much too much about life. Did they have any idea what they were saying? What challenges awaited them? Until now they had barely been able to manage sharing a meal. What business did they have in a neglected field?

THE PARCEL LOOKED worse than Nu Nu had feared. It was overgrown with weeds, a carpet that in sunlight shimmered in myriad shades of green. The intervening rainy seasons had abolished any trace of the irrigation system that Maung Sein had so painstakingly laid out. The sun burned in the sky. The shelter her husband built had collapsed. Nu Nu stood motionless, as if paralyzed, surveying the landscape from atop an embankment. How would she ever be able to make this piece of earth productive again? They had four weeks tops before it would be time to sow. Four weeks. It would take a dozen hands or more even to have a chance. How would she feed her children if they did not manage it? Gathering firewood and selling it? Weaving bamboo baskets? While she was busy wondering if it would be better to turn back and maybe rent the land for a small sum, her sons were setting to work. They knotted their lon-gyis up and started ripping the weeds out of the earth and turning the soil with their bare hands. Within a short time Ko Gyi's fingers were bloody from the unaccustomed work.

That evening a great pile of weeds stood by the side of the road. And yet their work had made little visible impact on the field. To Nu Nu it seemed that they had bailed a bucket of water out of a lake. There was no sense in what they were doing. No sense at all. She had to think of something else.

The next morning Thar Thar shook her shoulder gently. He had already gotten everything ready to go. Packed provisions, brewed tea, fetched water, cleaned the tools, a job they had been too weary to do the previous evening. Nu Nu hesitated. Why prolong their agony? They didn't stand a chance. But for lack of any better idea, she followed her children to the field.

By midday her sons' hands were so swollen that they grimaced at every touch. Still they would not stop. The two of them would pause only when she compelled them to. They returned to their hut with agonizing headaches.

By the third day Nu Nu's arms and legs hurt so badly that she could hardly move. Every muscle in her body ached. Ko Gyi, too, was noticeably slower than he had been at first.

Walking at dawn to their field after a week, they could spy the pile of weeds from a long way off, so much had it grown. Nu Nu gazed across the land, and for the first time she could detect a significant change: one corner of the field gleamed dark black in the rising sun.

After two weeks they made some provisional repairs to the shelter and decided to sleep there for the next few days in order not to lose any time on the long walk back and forth. Nu Nu still doubted whether they would manage it, but her sons' optimism and zeal had left their marks on her. Whenever she watched Ko Gyi and Thar Thar working hand in hand in the field she had the growing feeling that anything was possible. They had only to keep their courage up.

And she discovered tokens whose significance she could not ignore. The thinnest and weakest of their three hens had hatched a chick on the very day they had started to work. It was so small, Nu Nu was certain it would not survive its first day. Yet it grew and throve.

The banana plants had sprouted an exceptional number of shoots for this time of year.

The incident with the snake was especially suggestive. It lay right in their path one morning as they made their way to the field. That was already remarkable for these shy animals. It let Thar Thar approach to within a few yards without taking flight. That was more remarkable still. It raised its head, staring at Nu Nu and her sons, and rather than disappearing into the brush, it turned around and wound its way through the grass as if showing them the way. They followed the animal. Just before they got to the field it turned around again, paused, and then disappeared into the tall grass.

Nor did the omens disappoint. After four weeks there was nothing left of the green carpet. They stood together in the field, arms black to their elbows, longyis stained with grime and sweat. They looked around in silence, as if themselves unable to believe it. The air was redolent of fresh, humid, fertile soil. Nu Nu knelt down and dug into it with both hands. She handed a clod to Thar Thar. He smelled it, smiled, and crumbled it slowly between his fingers. It almost seemed to her that he was caressing the earth.

What had the midwife said that time? A child's soul knows all. Whether it forgives she did not say.

But there was no time to lose. They had borrowed money and bought cauliflower, potato, and soybean seeds that needed to get into the ground as soon as possible. When they returned the next day rats and birds had stolen half the seed. They spent the night at the field again, driving off the vermin, working as long as the sun allowed. Planting seed beside seed, seedling beside seedling. Plowing furrows. To mollify the spirits of the field they built a little altar, where they made daily offerings of a banana and a small mound of tea.

Nature and the spirits smiled upon them. The rains came on schedule that year and in moderate quantities. The other farmers could not remember the last time they had brought in such a rich harvest. Nu Nu even borrowed a water buffalo and cart to bring the vegetables from the field to the village. Ko Gyi sat proudly on the back of the beast, directing it with a switch as if he had been doing so all his life.

When she saw him with all those vegetables Nu Nu recalled the words of her late husband. Time had borne them out. He had told her, and she had not wanted to believe it: We have the power to change ourselves. We are not condemned to remain who we are. No one can help us do this but ourselves.

Fate had asked the three of them a question. The cultivated field and the abundant harvest were their answer.

The copious crops helped them through the dry season. During the hot months, when there was nothing to do in the field, they sat in their yard weaving roofs, walls, baskets, and bags. The money allowed them to restore their own roof and to replace a few rotten beams.

The second year, too, there was no shortage of food. What nature denied them by way of rain they made up for through hard work and skill.

The third year they were confident enough to plant rice, and Nu Nu discovered that Thar Thar had inherited not only his father's powerful build, but also his great uncle's agrarian talents. While the neighbors lamented the poor harvest, their field was more productive than ever.

The thing that did not change was his need for solitude. As before, there were days when he withdrew from them.

He would work alone in another part of the field, speaking not a word, ignoring mother and brother. Or he sat on a bank and played with his slingshot. She had never seen a better aim. He shot mangoes from trees, put pinpoint holes in leaves, drove birds from the field without injuring a single one.

These moods would disappear as quickly as they came, and after a few hours he would be available to them again as if nothing had happened. Nu Nu found it a strange mixture, her son's temperament. He could be taciturn, composed, and caring like Maung Sein or volatile and melancholy, as she herself had once been.

In the fourth year, too, they increased their yield, and Nu Nu began to wonder if she had been mistaken. Maybe we did not come into the world with a limited allotment of luck that would eventually run dry. Perhaps there was some power that could renew our supply at opportune moments.

All the same, not a day passed on which she did not miss her husband, especially at night as she lay awake and the children slept. She would hear his breath, feel it on her skin. She would turn to lay her arm across his chest. The emptiness she felt at these moments made every part of her body ache.

The hole his death had torn in her life had not closed and never would, though it seemed that it might with time become overgrown.

Nu Nu did not wish to be an ingrate. They had been spared from illness in recent years. They were not hungry. On the contrary, they had enough money at the end of every year to make improvements on the house. A new roof. New walls. A concrete latrine in a remote corner of the yard. Next year they were even planning to buy a water buffalo. Or a pig. She was proud of her sons, both of whom were industrious, modest, and obedient.

This is how happiness must look, she thought, when it does not have her husband's mouth. When it does not smell like him. This is how happiness must look when it stands on its own two legs.

Chapter 17

THERE ARE MOMENTS, Nu Nu realized, that a person remembers as long as she lives. They burn themselves into your soul, leaving unseen scars on an unseen skin. So that when you touch them later, your body shudders with a pain that seeps into all of your pores. Even years later. Decades. Everything is present again: the stench of fear. The taste of it. The sound.

The moment Nu Nu heard the engines was such an occasion.

A late afternoon. A light drizzle came drifting across the hills and would soon reach the village. The air was warm and damp. It had rained often over the past few days; the muddy road oozed up between her bare toes with every step. Her feet and knees ached from the long day in the field. She and her sons and a few other women and their children were on their way back to the village.

Like the roar of an approaching predator the engines echoed through the valley where machines were otherwise absent.

The women and children froze, rooted to the spot. As if obeying all at once the same command. They all understood what these noises meant. She saw it in their eyes. She saw it in the contorted faces and the motionless bodies.

She gazed in the direction of the noise. In the distance she could make out two trucks and two Jeeps. Approaching quickly. Much too quickly.

There had been rumors they would come. Old U Thant had warned them repeatedly, though few in the village paid him any mind. He was always proclaiming the end of the world, and there had never been anything in it. Now he would be vindicated. The end of the world was nigh. It came in green uniforms and shiny black boots. It came in trucks big enough to cart off the whole village.

And it was coming right now.

Nu Nu looked around again. It was too late to flee. Where would they run, where would they hide? The next settlement was several miles away, and even there they would not be safe. There was no jungle whose brush could save them. Those caught trying to flee seldom survived their detention. So it was rumored at the markets.

None of the women moved. The smallest of the children sought shelter behind their mothers' legs.

Nu Nu's sons stood looking at her a few yards to the side. Their faces, too, she would remember forever.

They knew what was coming. The soldiers would take them away. Hardly anyone ever returned. Their mother could not protect them.

The end of the world was now less than a hundred yards off and coming closer every moment. On one of the trucks stood soldiers armed with machine guns, their faces expressionless and empty. They were too young to look their victims in the eye. Behind them were several spools of barbed wire.

In the first Jeep sat an officer; she could tell by his uniform. Their eyes met, and Nu Nu understood that he was her chance.

Her only hope.

The little convoy rolled past them and stopped in the square in the middle of the village. The soldiers leapt out of the trucks. Some of them took up positions at the entrances to the square; others ran through the village commanding all residents to gather in front of the trucks as quickly as possible.

Half an hour later everyone was there.

The officer scrambled onto one of the trucks. He was tall and muscular, an ethnic Burmese towering a whole head above the villagers. He took up a megaphone and announced what everyone had already feared: that every unmarried male of the village between the ages of fourteen and twenty-two must be standing in front of his family's home waiting for the soldiers within the hour. That his men would collect them and escort them to an improvised camp at the entrance to the village. After which they would thoroughly search each property. Any remaining young men discovered during this search would be summarily executed. There would be no mercy for anyone attempting to escape. Early tomorrow morning they would depart for a barracks in the state capital. The time had come for these young men to fulfill their obligation to serve the Union of Burma. The country was under constant threat from her enemies, and everyone must be prepared to make sacrifices in her defense.

She knew what he meant. Everyone knew what he meant. The army needed more than soldiers (whom they generally recruited in larger localities with the promise of a wage that would feed multiple families). More than anything they needed porters. Young men to lug the provisions and the heavy equipment, the munitions, the grenade launchers of the regiments over the mountains and through the jungle into the rebel territories. In the marketplace you would hear rumors about how dangerous this work was. Those areas were infested with malaria, and the porters' treatment at the hands of the soldiers was bad. Anyone who got sick or wounded would be abandoned, left for dead. Several porters had reportedly been torn apart by land mines.

Who could say whether these things were true? Few who were taken by the military ever returned. Those who returned said nothing.

The officer lowered the megaphone and surveyed the crowd.

The small people before him were even smaller now.

No one said a word.

Nu Nu took her two boys and went home. Her mind was racing. Was there any chance for them to get away or hide? The latrine? The neighbor's shed? The empty hut at the edge of the village? Ridiculous. The very places they would search first. Maybe the monastery on the fringe of the bamboo grove where four elderly monks lived with a dozen novices. Would the soldiers dare to violate its sanctity? Probably not. But what would the villagers say when they learned that she had spirited Ko Gyi and Thar Thar to safety? Most would hold their tongues, cover for her. She did not doubt it. But one voice of betrayal was all it would take. Should envy, resentment, or sorrow prevail in even a single heart, her children would be lost.

No, the risk was too great. No place was safe. Death would take whomever he wished.

Ko Gyi and Thar Thar followed their mother in silence. At home they stood motionless in the hut, watching her every move.

Nu Nu wondered what to pack for her sons. They had nothing but the rubber sandals on their feet. They each owned a second T-shirt, a spare longyi, a jacket, and a toothbrush.

That was everything.

A good-luck charm? They desperately needed some talisman to protect them. The bit of bark sprang to mind, the one her husband had broken off the pine tree beneath which they had kissed for the first time. He had given it to her and promised it would protect her. It was all that she had to remember him by. She had worn through his clothes long ago; she had never owned a photograph of him. In the weeks and months following his death she had often clung to that bit of bark as she fell asleep each night. She felt that it had protected her heart, which might otherwise have stopped from grief while she slept. Now it lay wrapped in a heavy cloth at the bottom of the chest where she kept her few possessions.

She unwrapped the bit of bark. It was thick and firm as ever, hardly broader than Nu Nu's palm. One piece, two children. Would it lose its protective power if once divided?

For just a moment she thought of giving Thar Thar some other thing, but nothing occurred to her. She broke it in two pieces, one small and one large.

With a rusty nail she gouged a hole in each bit. Through each hole a length of string and then a knot. Nu Nu closed her eyes and kissed each charm, then hung them around their necks.

The big piece for the big brother.

The little piece for the little brother.

Soon they heard the soldiers' voices. Ko Gyi took the parcel with his belongings and went outside. Even now not a word had passed between them.

Nu Nu watched them go. They left without a backward glance. Her heart was racing. When she could stand it no longer, she started to follow them. A soldier barred her way, pushing her back through the gate onto her own property. She managed one last time to glimpse them through the hedge. The last she saw of her sons was their two green-and-black longyis.

Two grown children marching off to war.

With bits of bark about their necks.

But she did not despair.

She still had one chance.

Chapter 18

THEY MET IN the evening by the well. In a desolate village where mothers and fathers feared for their sons. Where Dread sat in the trees making faces and casting abhorrent shadows.

Where hearts turned to stone.

Nothing moved on road or path. Not a soul dared venture out. Even the livestock had made themselves scarce. The pigs lay silently in their slop. The chickens vanished behind sheds or piles of wood or into thickets. The rats and snakes took refuge in the latrines.

Over everything hung a reeking silence. Even the candles that otherwise illuminated homes and gardens had been extinguished. The moon alone was free of fear. Big and round in a cloudless sky, lighting up the night.

The commandant was waiting beneath a fig tree, smoking a cigarette and observing her. Nu Nu had put up her long black hair and was balancing a water jug on her head. She wore her best longyi and one of the two blouses she owned. Freshly laundered. She would leave nothing to chance. Her body was no longer that of a desirable young woman. Nor was it yet an old woman's.

She would have to make her best effort.

They had arranged the encounter without a word. A few glances as the soldiers were arriving, a few gestures. Each knew what the other wanted.

Nor did they speak now. Nu Nu set down her jug and began with slow movements to scoop water out of the well. The commandant watched her. She felt his eyes on her body. She felt him sizing her up. Her slender neck, her muscular arms. She felt his eyes working their way down, testing the suggestion of her breasts inside her blouse. Her hips. The trim, shapely backside that had always aroused her husband.

She waited. He did not move.

As she was lifting the jug, he stepped over to her.

"Where?" He did not even bother to whisper.

With a nod of her head she indicated the direction. She raised the heavy jug and led the way. They walked past the empty house where only a few hours earlier her sons had waited for her.

The hut stood on the outskirts of the village, the last house before the fields. It had been empty for years. Old Aung had died there, lonesome and alone. His wife and three children had all predeceased him, and his ghost, full of grief, would return to mourn them at each new moon. But tonight was a full moon. And she had no alternative.

She climbed the few steps up onto the veranda. The door was ajar, as she had anticipated. Cold moonlight fell through a hole in the roof. In the middle of the room was a pile of straw.

They were not the first. They would not be the last.

Nu Nu set the jug on the floor. She saw the desire in his expression. The lust in his eyes. That was not going to be the problem.

He set his rifle down, took off his uniform, and left his shiny black boots beside the bed of straw. She examined his athletic body out of the corner of her eye. The army fed its soldiers well. At least its commandants.

She loosened the knot of her longyi and let it slip to the floor. With a deft motion she pulled her blouse over her head.

He could not stand to wait. She made an effort to draw things out. The hotter his passion, the better her chances, she thought.

Worst of all were the pictures in her head when he entered her. She saw her dead husband before her. She saw her sons. She saw her parents. To drive these images from her mind, she fixated on the boots standing next to her. There was neither forgiveness nor love in the world reflected in that shiny black leather. There was only fear and hatred.

There are moments that we simply cannot endure. They transform us into someone else.

She did not want to look, but it was too late.

Even still, Nu Nu was ready to take him again. She would have slept with every one of his superiors and with all his subordinates, too. With every soldier in his company.

Just to save her sons.

They were all she had left in life.

"What do you want from me?" A question. The question every moment of the evening had been leading up to. That first, brief glance. The coy looks that followed. And then the provocative ones.

All without a word. Only gestures whose intent was beyond all doubt. Each motion, each touch, each kiss, each thrust that she had tolerated culminated in this one simple, life-altering question.

"What do you want from me?" Snorted, expelled, not asked. As if he were driving a pesky fly from his upper lip.

She stroked his black hair. Examined the scars on his chest.

She could seduce him again. Perhaps it would leave him more favorably inclined. She kissed a nipple, teasing with her tongue.

"What do you want?"

He was not in the mood. And that was what everything depended on. Ko Gyi and Thar Thar. Their laughter. Their tears. Their deaths. His mood.

"My sons," she whispered. "Nothing more. Just my sons."

My life.

"Impossible."

He crossed his arms behind his head and looked at the ceiling. Soon he would be wandering off in his thoughts. To the next village. The next battle. Or his chances at a transfer out of the damned rebel area to somewhere on the coast. He was already on his way; she was about to lose him. She sensed it.

"I need them."

"So do we."

"Without their help I can't tend my field. Can't bring the vegetables to the market." Just don't mention love. The way a mother feels watching her sons go off to their deaths. Nothing could interest him less. Emphasize the practical value of her sons. This was the language he understood.

No other.

"So what?"

"My husband is dead. I have no one else." She added quickly: "Who can help me." Explain. Don't ask. Whatever you do, don't plead. Save that for later.

She let her hand slip slowly down his chest and stomach, lower and lower. That's where the fate of her sons would be determined. Nowhere else.

His breath quickened.

A swelling member does not lie.

She might still have a chance.

He was her first man since Maung Sein's death.

She made every effort. Her hands and her mouth. Her tongue and her fingertips.

His skin was raw, his thrusts course and arrhythmic, the second time, too.

Her lean body quivered. Not with excitement.

He lay on top of her, arms tensed. Saliva ran out of his mouth, tinted red from the juice of betel nut. Drop by drop he drenched her features with the colors of death. And of life.

When he pulled away from her he was satisfied. She heard it in his quiet breathing. She sensed it in the way his body relaxed.

"Please." Sometimes one word is sufficient. Six letters enough to depict a world.

He lit a cigarette. It glowed brighter with every drag.

Please.

Please.

Please.

"How many sons do you have?"

"Two."

"Healthy?"

"Yes."

"How old?"

"Sixteen and fifteen."

He thought about it. Seconds with life and death in the balance.

"You keep one. We'll take the other."

"Which one?" It slipped out.

"I don't care. You pick."

And so he rent her in two.

On that clear, moonlit night. A small farmer's wife. A big heart with surprisingly little room to spare. But it was the only one she had.

You keep one.

We'll take the other.

Ko Gyi and Thar Thar. Fated to die. Or live.

She had given them life—now she would have to take it from them.

From one of them.

Chapter 19

KHIN KHIN HAD ceased talking a while ago. Now U Ba, too, fell silent. Softly he had spoken, ever softer all the while, until the final sentence was but a whisper, and his voice failed utterly.

I regarded Khin Khin out of the corner of my eye. The wrinkles on her cheeks and brow had deepened; her dark eyes had narrowed to small buttons. I noticed unusually thick veins in her neck through which her blood pulsed vigorously.

My brother crouched beside me, slumped over, head down. He glanced my way, tears in his eyes. I felt as if I might burst. A pressure had been building in me over the past few hours until I could hardly bear it. How long had we been listening? Three hours? Four? It was still light out. Hens cackled in the next yard. Somewhere a dog was barking.

The smell of a spent fire. Khin Khin poured cold tea, rose and fetched a plate of roasted melon seeds, rice cakes, and a packet of crackers. She opened the plastic wrapper and offered me one. In her eyes was such desperation that I could not even manage a "No, thanks."

What had become of Nu Nu? Had she found a way to save both sons? Surely she hadn't . . . ? How had she lived through this nightmare? Although nothing interested me more than the answers to these questions, I did not dare to ask. We sat together in silence. I waited for U Ba or Khin Khin to say something. Minutes passed.

I needed to get outside. The confines of the hut had become unbearable to me. The suffering and sorrow that dwelt therein. The chasms that yawned all around me.

Before me I saw Nu Nu. For the first time I had a picture of her in my mind. Her lanky, quivering body beneath the lieutenant. The red juice of the betel nut on her face. The fear for her sons' lives.

You keep one.

We'll take the other.

I wanted to vomit. I took deep breaths to keep from throwing up. I felt short of breath and had a stabbing pain in my breast.

Eventually I tried to get up and nearly fell on my brother in the process. My legs had gone to sleep and would not support me.

"I need to go into the yard," I whispered.

He coughed and nodded slightly. "Wait for me there."

I crawled on all fours to the porch, stretched, and sat for a few minutes until the tingling in my legs dissipated. I climbed down the steps and squatted on the ground in the shadow of the hut. What had they done to Nu Nu? How had she decided? I felt the tears running down my cheeks.

Above me I heard U Ba and Khin Khin whispering, her story punctuated from time to time by his burning cough. By her tone I could tell that her sorrow had been far from over.

AT SOME POINT my brother, too, climbed down the steps. He kept a firm grip on the railing. I had the impression that his entire body was quivering. With a nod he signaled me to follow him.

We walked in silence along a path so narrow that we had to go single file. In the distance I saw columns of smoke rising into the air. It was late afternoon, and we met many farmers who greeted us amiably on their way home from their fields.

Behind them a boy riding atop a water buffalo smiled at me with white teeth. I nodded to him.

We turned right on the road at the banyan tree, soon after which we were overtaken by a military Jeep. Their brakes squealed as they stopped and then backed up until they were level with us.

I went weak at the knees. What did they want with my brother and me? Had they been following us without our noticing? Had we put ourselves into danger? Would the voice prove right in the end?

They'll come to get you. No one can protect you from them.

In the Jeep sat four soldiers. Curious looks. Red teeth. Green uniforms. Shiny black boots.

She had warned me. *When they come, don't look them in the eye. Don't look them in the boots. They have magical powers. In them is reflected all of the cruelty, all of the evil we are capable of.*

Bloodred saliva dripping onto a face.

The soldiers pointed at me and asked my brother a question. He laughed mechanically. They laughed back. I turned away, unable to bear the sight of them.

The exchange was brief, punctuated by laughter and surprised faces, and then they drove on.

"What did they want?" I asked, breathless, as the Jeep drove out of sight.

"To know who you were and where we were going," he answered in strained tones.

"Why?"

"Just because." U Ba hesitated briefly. "One doesn't often see a Western visitor walking about with a native around here. They were curious."

"What did you tell them?"

"The truth. That you are my sister and that we are on our way back home. They offered to give us a lift. They speculated that you were not accustomed to hiking in a hilly landscape. I respectfully declined."

"That was all?" I wondered.

"Yes," he replied a touch too curtly. Too loudly. It was not his style.

When we got to the teahouse my brother suddenly stopped in his tracks and coughed so violently that it interfered with his breathing.

"We've got to get you to a doctor," I said, horrified.

He raised both hands dismissively without managing to get out a sound.

"U Ba! There must be a doctor here who could take a look at you. You need a lung X-ray."

"There's no one. Besides, it's not so bad, and it will soon pass. Trust me. Or did you think we should go to a military hospital?"

I said nothing.

"Are you hungry?" he asked.

I shook my head. "Not really."

"Do you mind if I stop here for a quick noodle soup?"

"Of course not."

There were only a few guests left at the teahouse. We picked an out-of-the-way table.

The waitress shuffled over to us. U Ba ordered two glasses of Burmese tea and a soup.

I was waiting for him to report on what Khin Khin had told him, but my brother said nothing, and I dared not ask.

The waitress brought the tea and soup. He bent low over his bowl and started to eat in silence.

I stirred my tea.

"U Ba?"

He looked at me.

"What did Nu Nu do?"

He spooned up more soup. "After the lieutenant had gone back to his troops?"

I nodded.

"She wanted to kill herself. But then the military would have taken both her sons. She had the opportunity to save one of their lives. Ought she to have passed it by simply because she lacked the strength or the courage to make a decision?"

He looked at me inquiringly, paused for a moment without expecting an answer, and then continued: "No. That same night she went to the prisoners' camp and got one of her sons out of there."

"Who?"

"Ko Gyi."

I closed my eyes and felt dizzy. I held on to the table with both hands.

"She told herself that even though he was older, he was also smaller and weaker. He would never have stood a chance among the soldiers. They would have found little use in him and quickly sent him to his death. Thar Thar was bigger and stronger. If anyone could survive, it was he. She had *no* choice. She *had* to keep Ko Gyi. So she told her sister. Sometimes three times a day. 'I had *no* choice. I *had* to keep Ko Gyi.'"

"And Thar Thar?" I asked in a whisper.

"The soldiers took him the next morning."

I searched for the words, but there was no language to express how I felt.

I sipped at my tea. U Ba downed his in one vigorous gulp. His hands were shaking.

"No mother can . . . survive that," I managed to say.

"No," he repeated softly, "no mother can survive that."

"Why did she . . . ? I mean, couldn't she . . . ?" I never finished these sentences. How did I know what she could or could not have done. I tried to imagine the scene that night. The two brothers taking leave of each other. How Ko Gyi took his things and left Thar Thar behind. What must he have thought or felt? A child with a piece of bark around his neck. What had become of him?

"Do you think he came out of it alive?"

"His mother spent years afterward consulting with all the astrologers and fortune tellers. One claimed that Thar Thar had gone over to the rebels. Another declared that he was roaming the country as a wandering monk. A third disclosed that the stars had shown him plainly that Thar Thar had fled to Thailand, where he had married into money. All agreed that he would send word soon. At some point, Nu Nu lost hope."

"Perhaps he became a soldier and is still alive?"

"In that case he would certainly have gotten word to his mother or brother, don't you think? It has been nearly twenty years now since they hauled him away, and that was the last she heard of him. Besides, the army has enough soldiers. They prefer to deploy these young men as mine detectors."

"Mine detectors?" I did not understand what my brother meant and looked at him, puzzled.

"Well, we're in the midst of a decades-long civil war. Not everywhere, as you can see, but in several provinces. Ethnic minorities are fighting in the jungle for their independence. Most regions are mountainous. There are no streets, not even paths where the army can drive their trucks and Jeeps. They need men to carry provisions, ammunition, and weapons. Khin Khin hinted at it, but did not tell the whole story. The rebels frequently mine the area. The soldiers then send the porters ahead and follow them at some distance."

"Why don't they just run the detection equipment themselves?"

U Ba shook his head and said, so quietly that I could barely hear: "They don't have any detection equipment."

"How are the porters supposed to find the mines?"

He leaned far over the table to me: "By stepping on them."

It took a few seconds for me to process what he had said.

"You mean the army uses them as . . ." I left the sentence unfinished. "How . . . how do you know that?"

"Now and then someone comes back alive."

I leaned back, eyes scanning the teahouse, as if I might here find some confirmation of the atrocities I was hearing about. At the far end three men were deep in a lively conversation. From time to time one of them spat red betel nut juice into the grass. I shuddered every time. Beside them sat a young couple, whispering, shy, in love. The waitress, deep in thought, swept the floor between the empty tables. Below the altar with the gilded Buddha and the flowers, the cook sat sleeping with her head on the table. Did they know what I knew? Probably.

Perhaps they even had a brother, a brother-in-law, a nephew, an uncle who had been forced to look for mines in the jungle. And found one.

Or did their brothers, brothers-in-law, nephews, or uncles wear shiny black boots?

I suddenly realized how little I knew about my father's native country. How strange it was to me. How little I could read in the laughing faces of its people.

"What are you thinking?" U Ba wanted to know.

"How little I understand about this country."

"You are mistaken," he contradicted. "You know everything anyone needs to know."

"What do you mean?" I replied in surprise.

"Later."

He made a curious noise with his lips, like blowing a drawn-out kiss. The waitress immediately looked our way. My brother tucked a worn thousand-kyat note under one of the tea glasses and stood up.

Darkness had fallen. We walked down the street in silence. In front of one teahouse stood a large television. Two dozen young men sat in front of it cheering along to a soccer game. I couldn't help but think of Nu Nu and her sons.

"U Ba?" I thought I might tell by the tone of his voice whether or not he was ready to tell me more.

"What would you like to know?"

"How did Nu Nu and Ko Gyi get along without Thar Thar?"

"They tried to survive together. They did not succeed."

"Is Ko Gyi dead, too?"

"No, but the two of them, inseparable for fifteen years, began suddenly to quarrel. Odd, isn't it? The dutiful Ko Gyi neglected his obligations. He refused to go with his mother to the field. He preferred instead to go to pagoda festivals in other villages, from which he always came home drunk.

"Khin Khin believes that he never got over the shock of learning what his mother was capable of. She seemed to him now strange and sinister. In his inebriation he often claimed that Thar Thar was stalking him. Said he was sitting by the fire with them. Going with them to the market, watching them cook and eat. He spoke less and less, and in the end he wished that she had held on to his brother instead of him. After three years most of the field was overgrown. The hut deteriorated, and Ko Gyi decided to move to the nearest city to look for work."

We had arrived at U Ba's house. He fetched water from the yard, lit candles, and asked if I would like another tea.

I thanked him but declined and lowered myself onto the sofa beneath the kitschy oil painting of the Tower of London. He sank into the armchair and continued the story.

"Ko Gyi soon relocated to the capital and found employment as a sailor on a freighter. He made good money and sent some of it to his mother at irregular intervals. Not much, but enough to survive. Nu Nu eventually moved in with her younger sister who had no children and whose husband had died young. They came to Kalaw together a few years ago because no one knew them here and because the place held no memories for them. She was a broken woman.

"On the day Nu Nu died, she and Khin Khin were on their way to the market. They ran across a young man whom Nu Nu took for Thar Thar. The shock was so great that her heart ceased to beat. I think I mentioned that incident in my letter."

I nodded.

"Khin Khin reported that Nu Nu's health had been failing for years. She had begun to imagine things, her memory failed her, she would go for a stroll and lose her way back to the hut. The moment she spotted soldiers or even just a military Jeep, she would be frozen with terror. She could not bear the sight of black boots. She frequently woke in the night screaming loudly, disconsolate. Her body was completely covered with red splotches. She ate very little, as if trying to starve herself to death. Her heart was weak. A troubled spirit. Her death was no surprise. Only the circumstances were out of the ordinary."

"And Ko Gyi? Why didn't he return to look after her?"

"The last they heard from him was five years ago, when he contacted them from Australia and sent them some money. Apparently he has settled there. No word since then. Though it's possible that his letters have gotten lost or been opened."

My brother's eyes drooped shut, and I, too, felt over-whelmed by a profound weariness.

"Would you like to listen to some music before going to bed?"

"I'd rather not."

For a while we said nothing. For the first time I found the silence between us pleasant.

"Do you think that the voice inside me has been silenced?"

"I don't know."

"Of course not. But what do you think?"

"We shall see," he replied evasively. "Did she have any-thing to add during Khin Khin's story?"

"No."

"That's a good sign, don't you think?"

I shrugged, clueless. "I guess so."

With effort he stifled a yawn. "Forgive me. I'm dread-fully tired. The day has taken a toll on me."

"On me, too."

"Do you need anything else for the night?"

"No."

He rose and approached me, took my head gently in his hands and kissed me on the forehead. "Sleep well."

"You, too."

"Wake me if you have any bad dreams."

Chapter 20

I WAS AWAKENED in the night by a loud whimpering. Was that my brother crying? I got up and felt around for the flashlight next to the sofa. In its dim light I tiptoed to his room, where I could hear behind the curtain the peaceful, even breathing of his sleep. Had I imagined it? Or had the voice returned? Had she woken me? I listened intently. Insects. A dog barking in the distance. Another barking in reply. Silence.

I lay back on the couch, listened for another minute, and then fell back asleep.

When I woke for the second time that night, it was the voice that roused me.

Where's Thar Thar?

I sat bolt upright and stared into the shadows. It sounded as if someone were speaking to me out of the darkness.

What's happened to my son? What have they done with him?

A chill ran down my spine, and I groped for the flashlight but could not find it.

Why didn't you listen to me? Why didn't you go back to New York? This is not going to end well.

Suddenly the light came on, and there was U Ba standing in front of me.

"What happened?" he asked in a worried tone.

I was too surprised to answer.

"You cried out in your sleep."

"The voice." I peered around the room. "I heard the voice."

He sat down beside me. "Are you certain?"

"Yes. No. I don't know. It sounded like her."

"What did she say?"

I was too wound up; I couldn't concentrate.

"Did she want to know where Thar Thar is?" my brother asked.

"Yes."

"What else?"

"She said I had better go back to New York. That our search would end badly."

U Ba nodded. "How did she sound?"

I tried to recall the tone of her voice, but began to doubt myself.

"I'm not sure anymore. Maybe," I hesitated a moment, "maybe it was just a dream."

"I don't think so."

It was cold. I pulled the covers up to my chin and slid deeper and deeper into the cushions, lowering myself gently to the side until I lay with my head on his knees. I was simultaneously wide-awake and dead tired. Had everything been for naught? Had the monk been mistaken, or had I been too gullible ("two souls in one breast") in following a silly superstition?

"The monk said that the voice would stop when I found out who it belonged to and why she died," I said. "We've done that. Do you think he was wrong? Or that we got the wrong person?"

"Neither nor." My brother was silent for a long time, then continued: "But I think that she will not go away until we know the whole truth. How else can this restless soul find peace?"

"The whole truth? Did Khin Khin lie to us?"

"No. But we have to find out what happened to Thar Thar. A mother wants to know how her child died. She wants to know where he is buried. She won't let go of it until then."

U Ba brushed my hair out of my face and looked at me pensively.

"Is there some clue you haven't told me about yet?" I asked cautiously.

"Not a clue. More of a rumor. Khin Khin alluded to something that I did not pay much attention to yesterday."

"What was that?"

"It is said that one of the boys later escaped. Such attempts seldom succeed. No one in the village, she said, would ever discuss the details or let on that they knew anything. Death awaits all deserters, their families, and anyone who assists them. But still the rumor persists."

My brother was suddenly agitated. He stroked my head a couple of times more, but his thoughts were elsewhere. I heard his breath quickening, his stomach growling. Suddenly he stood up and disappeared into his room without a word, only to return moments later fully dressed.

"The sun is about to rise. I need to talk to Khin Khin again. I did not inquire about it yesterday. Perhaps she knows the fate of this boy."

I did not wish to be alone. "Can I come along?"

U Ba shook his head. "I think I had better go alone this time. I won't be long. Wait here for me. Should anyone come and ask for me, no matter who it is, tell them you don't know where I am or when I'll be back."

I nodded uneasily.

He scurried down the steps and across the yard.

Through the open windows the first light of day was spilling into the house. Roosters were crowing, and the pigs below the house were awake now. I wanted to get up, light a fire, boil water, and make a little breakfast, but I felt too exhausted. Instead I just crawled deeper under the covers. I couldn't get Thar Thar out of my head. He must have been an extraordinary individual. About my age. I wished I could have met him.

I was reminded suddenly of my brother and my mother. We had spent a lot of time together just the three of us, because my father frequently traveled or worked late. I remembered the events of a particular summer's day. My mother, my brother, and I were at the beach on Long Island.

I must have been six or seven years old. I saw them before me sitting on their towels and applying sunscreen on each other. Backs. Arms. Legs. Faces. Then they stood up and ran to the water, forgetting all about me. I ran after them and floundered in the waves, and while they swam farther out, I dug holes in the sand. That evening my thighs, arms, and nose were so red that my father took me to the doctor.

First- and second-degree burns.

More than skin-deep.

We weren't close. Never had been. My brother and I, definitely not. But not my mother and I, either. Why, I never knew. I suspect that she didn't, either. Maybe I, like Thar Thar, had crashed a party for two. I wondered whether they had planned to have me or whether I had been an "accident." I didn't know. It was not something anyone in the family ever talked about.

A full-grown New Yorker? With a small heart? Without much room to spare? But it was the only one she had.

I still lay wrapped up on the sofa when I heard U Ba coming back. He was out of breath and more excited than I had ever seen him. I detected a shadow of disappointment in his eyes when he saw that I was still in bed.

"She thinks the rumor is true." He took a deep breath.

"One of the boys managed to get away?"

"Yes."

His eyes turned to my big backpack.

"Can you pack just a few things for a short trip in your small bag?"

"Sure. Why?"

"We need to be on our way."

"On our way? When?"

"Now. At once."

"For how long?"

"A couple of days."

"Where to?"

He considered it for a moment. "To the island."

"Which island?"

"*Thay hsone thu mya, a hti kyan thu mya a thet shin nay thu mya san sar yar kywn go thwa mai,*" he said in Burmese.

"I don't understand a word of it."

Chapter 21

WE DIDN'T HAVE much to go on. The man we were looking for had apparently lived for years in Thazi, a city on the rail line between Rangoon and Mandalay, five hours by bus from Kalaw. He was married, had two or three kids. His father-in-law owned a garage on the main drag, where he supposedly worked as a mechanic. He was one of the young men hauled off by the military that morning in the village. After a few years he had managed to escape. Would he be able to tell us anything about Thar Thar?

We hitched a ride in the next pickup truck to Thazi. U Ba clambered onto the roof, where half a dozen young men were crammed among shopping bags and sacks. Someone lifted me onto the bed, where there seemed at first to be no space at all. The other passengers pushed closer together; a child sat on his mother's lap, and I squeezed in between them and an old woman on a wooden pallet. We were so cramped that I began to sweat immediately and felt short of breath.

The road wound steeply in tight serpentines into the valley below. My anxiety increased with every turn. I felt sick and was on the verge of throwing up. Out. I had to get out. At the first stop I pushed my way into the open and climbed onto the roof with my brother. We sat in the very front above the driver, clenching the grill that we were sitting on. The vehicle was desperately overloaded. It leaned threateningly on every curve.

The road was full of potholes broadened by the rainy season. The shoulders dropped off precipitously. There were no guardrails or any other kind of safety structures. In the brush below us we could see the occasional wreck. My increasing panic was threatening to overpower me any moment. My brother sensed my fear.

"Look up at the sky. Breathe deeply and think of something else," he said.

I tried it. Looked up, concentrated on my breath, and thought of New York, of Amy, my apartment. It didn't make me any calmer. I thought of the sea. Of a long beach, the monotonous roll of the gentle waves, of U Ba's voice coming to me in an endless stream of talk. I heard the singing of the novices at a monastery in the early morning and gradually felt calmer.

THE FIRST WE saw of Maung Tun were his long, thin legs. He was lying under a van, hammering away at something.

The other mechanics with their longyis tied high and their sweat-soaked T-shirts regarded us with curiosity.

"Hey, Maung Tun," one of them eventually called.

The hammering stopped. An oil-smeared man crawled out from under the vehicle.

He was as tall as I was, and he stared at us in surprise. A haggard man with close-set eyes, bushy brows, a narrow face, strong cheekbones, and a deep scar on his forehead. Lips and teeth stained red from the juice of betel nuts. He was missing two fingers on his left hand.

Maung Tun's eyes flitted back and forth between my brother and me. U Ba asked him something. He nodded, irritated, grabbed a rag, and tried without much success to clean his hands.

U Ba spoke again, and though I did not understand a word, I knew approximately what he was saying. We wanted to invite him to a teahouse or, if he was hungry, to a nearby Chinese restaurant.

Maung Tun nodded and said something to the other men, who returned to work.

"He's not hungry," my brother whispered to me, "but he'll gladly join us at a teahouse."

IT WAS MUCH hotter in Thazi than in Kalaw. The glaring light was blinding. I put on my sunglasses and then took them right off again. It made me uncomfortable being the only one with protection against the sun.

U Ba and Maung Tun walked a couple of yards ahead of me, deep in conversation. We crossed the main street bustling with traffic. Vans, tractors, trucks, and buses rolled past amid oxcarts, a horse-drawn carriage, pedestrians, and bicycles. The surface of the road was dry and sandy. Every passing car kicked up a cloud of dust. In the middle of the street U Ba suddenly stopped, held firmly on to me, and started to cough. Maung Tun gripped him under one arm and led us both safely to the other side.

In the teahouse Maung Tun lit a cigarette, took two deep drags, turned and said something to me.

I looked at my brother for help.

"He would like to know why you are interested in Thar Thar," he translated.

I had been expecting that question, and in order not to make a fool of myself by admitting that I heard voices, I had concocted an elaborate story about distant relatives of Thar Thar who now lived in America and were coincidentally my neighbors and who had asked me to . . . but before I could make any reply U Ba was answering for me.

"What are you telling him?" I interrupted.

"That you hear the voice of his dead mother and that you need to know what happened to Thar Thar if the voice is ever going to leave you in peace."

Maung Tun nodded to me, full of understanding, as if my circumstance was the most natural thing in the world. He paused for a long while before saying a few words and gesturing to my brother that he should translate.

"He says that he does not like to talk about his time as a porter. Not even his wife knows anything about it. But for Nu Nu he will make an exception. She deserves to know what happened to Thar Thar. She deserves to know what a hero her son was."

I thanked him. Also on Nu Nu's behalf.

Maung Tun put out his cigarette, leaned forward, and started to tell.

Chapter 22

THE SOLDIERS HAD rolled out barbed wire in a field just outside the village, and they used that to pen us up. It was a cold night. We sat in a tight circle to keep warm. Thar Thar and Ko Gyi were sitting right next to me. I knew them both well. We were the same age, and we used to play together as kids. Thar Thar took his brother, who was shivering from head to toe, in his arms. The soldiers had forbidden us to speak. No one said a word. I heard nothing but the loud wheezing of fear. Suddenly a soldier shouted into the night that Ko Gyi and Thar Thar should come to the gate. They both stood up, and I recognized their mother waiting for them in the moonlight. They stood whispering not far away. Ko Gyi shook his head again and again. Nu Nu was crying. At some point she took him by the hand and tried to lead him away. He wouldn't go. Then the two brothers stood face-to-face one more time. Ko Gyi put something around Thar Thar's neck. Two soldiers

came and ordered Nu Nu to clear out and drove mother and
son away into the darkness.

Thar Thar watched them go. He stood at the barbed wire,
motionless. For minutes. The guards kept calling out for him
to go back to the others and sit down—immediately!—but
Thar Thar did not react. Only when a soldier shoved the
butt of his rifle with full force into his side did he shudder,
turn around, and come back to us. I was horrified when I saw
his face. His eyes looked bigger, his cheeks were sunken, he
was pale, and now he was the one shivering.

He stood there in the middle of us all and kept looking
toward where his mother and brother had disappeared. The
soldiers were making vile threats and some of us tried to
pull him down by his hands, but he shook us off. Eventually
things quieted down, and I fell asleep. Thar Thar was still
standing there when I woke up at daybreak.

Thar Thar and I huddled side by side in the truck that
brought us to the barracks. He sat slumped on the boards, not
holding on. The truck was jolting severely and his head kept
smacking into the wall until the blood ran into his face. It stank
something awful in the truck because some of us had vomited.
Thar Thar seemed not to care about the blood or the stench.

At the camp an officer divided us into two units. Some
of us went straight onto another army transporter and then
drove on. I wound up with Thar Thar in a smaller group
that stayed at the barracks. I found out only later that that
had saved our lives, at least for a start. The others went

straight to the front, and as far as I know, not one of them got through the next few months alive.

The officer split us again into smaller groups. If you had any experience as a metal worker or a mechanic they would put you in the workshop. Others went to the laundry. They asked Thar Thar if he could cook. When he nodded they shipped him off to the kitchen and me with him.

We spent nearly two years in the barracks. Compared with what followed, that was the good life. They rarely hit us without cause; there was almost always enough to eat; we slept on pallets in one of the barracks. In winter we even got a few blankets that we shared.

Thar Thar quickly earned a measure of respect, because he was an extraordinarily good cook. His specialty was a sweet rice cake. I'm pretty sure his cooking was about the only thing between us and the front; the officers didn't want to miss out on his food.

My survival depended on his. I made every effort to make myself an irreplaceable assistant: cleaned, peeled, and cut vegetables, cooked rice, slaughtered hens when the higher officers had a hankering for meat.

I think that some of them found Thar Thar creepy after a while. He hardly spoke more than a handful of sentences during the whole two years. He did his work in silence, no matter what they assigned him, answering with a nod or a shake of his head, avoiding all conversation. He never laughed at jokes. If they were at his expense he just ignored them. Threats got no reaction at all out of him. A commandant smacked him in the face and threatened to send him to the front the next day because a meal was not ready on time. Thar Thar stared at him in silence until the commandant turned away uneasily.

There were some who took his lack of fear as a sign that he was simpleminded. Others thought he was mute. I knew he was neither, and I was already in awe of his courage even before I had any idea of what was to come. Thar Thar was the bravest person I've ever met.

Even when he got injured he never said a word. One time he tipped over a pot of boiling water. It ran down his legs, but he winced only briefly. He looked at the scalded flesh as if it belonged to someone else.

IN OUR QUARTERS the pallets were packed so close together that you could hear your neighbor's stomach growl. During the first year I heard him crying at night now and again. Sometimes he would reach out for my hand in the dark and squeeze it so tight that it hurt. He always held on for a long while.

Whenever I asked him whether I could do anything for him he would always answer "No, thank you."

Thank you.

I had practically forgotten that those words even existed.

Only sleep would loosen his tongue. In the night he would call out to his mother or father. Or mutter sentences where I could make out only fragments.

I always wanted to ask him what happened that night when his mother came to get Ko Gyi, but I never dared to.

When the military started to prepare for a big offensive against the rebels, Thar Thar and I ended up getting shipped off to the jungle, too.

By that time we'd heard enough stories from the soldiers to know that our chances of coming back alive were next to none. Fear gnawed at me. As our departure approached I was unable to help him in the kitchen because I had diarrhea and vomiting. You wouldn't have known from Thar Thar, though, that anything was different. I started to suspect what turned out in the jungle to be true: it just didn't matter to him. He feared neither death nor dying. By the time I figured out what he was actually afraid of it was too late.

WHEN THE FATEFUL moment arrived, the soldiers crammed us onto two open trucks. We drove the whole day without a break until we reached a base camp late in the evening where a regiment was stationed. From there we would set off in smaller units on days-long—sometimes weeks-long—marches into the jungle.

The atmosphere in the encampment was completely different from the atmosphere in the barracks. The soldiers were nervous and aggressive, kicking and punching us without cause. If we had been beasts of burden they would have treated us better. At night we would wake up to shots fired into the darkness by guards who feared a rebel attack.

We slept on the ground in bamboo huts. There were no toilets for the likes of us. We had to do our business in a corner behind the huts where the shit was piled high. At dusk and dawn the mosquitoes would come after us. Whoever did not yet have malaria would be infected soon.

There wasn't much to eat, almost always rice, some vegetables, and occasionally a bit of dried fish. The thirst was worse than the hunger. They rationed out the drinking water. We got whatever was left. Not much. Medication was only for soldiers. Festering wounds, bouts of malaria, pneumonia, snake bites. Any time one of us was seriously ill they would bring us to a hut at the far end of the camp. Precious few ever came back. We called it the Death House.

The daily routine was monotonous. We did the soldiers' laundry and cooked, worked on the camp fortifications, repaired watchtowers, or deepened ditches. The rest of the time we sat around and waited. Only half the porters would return from any given deployment. At most.

A week after our arrival we got orders for our first mission. With twenty other porters we were to accompany two dozen soldiers who were supposed to be delivering food and ammunition to an outpost two days' march away.

We set out at dawn. I was carrying a fifty-pound bag of rice; Thar Thar had an even heavier crate of hand grenades. He was the biggest and most muscular of us all, towering a couple of inches over even the captain, who was not what you would call short.

After the first couple of hundred yards our road plunged directly into the forest. Despite the early hour it was warm and moist. After a short time shirts and longyis clung drenched with sweat to our bodies. The hungry mosquitoes swarming all around us would not be driven off. We followed a dirt track that led deeper and deeper into the jungle. Maybe two hours had passed when I started to feel that I couldn't go on. My shoulders and legs ached miserably. We walked barefoot, and my feet were bloody because I had stepped on a branch full of thorns. I had no idea at that point just how much I was capable of.

Thar Thar was walking right behind me, and he saw that I was exhausted. He offered encouraging words, told me I would make it, it wouldn't be far now, we'd be taking a break soon. When no one was looking he carried my sack of rice for a while.

The soldiers ordered us to take turns going in front. They would follow the first three or four porters at some distance, machine guns always at the ready. They were at least as scared as we were. If we walked into an ambush their chances of survival here in the jungle were not much greater than our own.

When my turn came my legs were quivering. Every step I took might trigger a mine. I felt paralyzed, incapable of setting one foot in front of the other. A soldier brandished his weapon threateningly, barking at me to pick up the pace. I cast Thar Thar a terrified look. He stepped forward and said that he would take my place in the lead. The soldiers looked at him suspiciously. A nutcase? A trap? An attempt to flee? Who was crazy enough to volunteer? In the end they didn't really care who was risking his life for them, and Thar Thar took the lead. He stepped thoughtfully, but not slowly, his gaze intently scanning the ground and underbrush for anything suspicious. All at once he paused. A few yards in front of him the ground had been disturbed. Had someone buried something, or was it just some animal looking for food? We backed away, a soldier fired a couple of rounds at the spot, nothing happened. Thar Thar went forward and we followed a few yards behind.

EARLY IN THE afternoon we reached the edge of the wood. In front of us were fields where the rice stood knee-high in water. We had to get across. I could see by the soldiers' reactions that they feared this stretch more even than the jungle. The captain shouted some orders. Each of the soldiers took a porter as a shield and walked close behind him. We walked along a causeway and were about halfway across when the shots rang out. At first I didn't know what was happening, then I saw a bunch of the porters fall; the soldiers screamed in confusion, we jumped into the field and sought cover in the rice. I lay flat on the ground and dug my fingers hard into the mud. Thar Thar lay not far off.

On the road above me a porter gasped and groaned. I dug myself still deeper into the muck so that it practically covered me. The shots dropped off, and at some point I heard soldiers' voices commanding us to check on the wounded. I didn't move. They just wanted to see whether the rebels would open fire again. Beside me Thar Thar roused himself and crawled up onto the road. I held my breath, dreading the next shot, but all was quiet.

The soldiers had used us to stop the bullets. Four of us lay wounded on the road. A fifth was dead. Two officers briefly discussed what to do next and then ordered us to leave the wounded behind. They would only slow us down.

The wounded begged us to take them with us. One of them got to his feet to prove that he could walk on his own, that he wouldn't be a burden. He stumbled two steps before collapsing unconscious right in front of me. Blood flowed from a gaping wound in his belly and seeped into the ground. A captain bellowed that we should ignore him and get a move on if we didn't want to come under fire again. Fifty yards on I turned around again and saw two of the wounded trying to follow us on all fours. When they started to cry out, begging us to wait, not to leave them alone, the captain himself opened fire. Four shots later a dreadful silence lay over the paddy.

Now I had to carry a rice sack from one of the dead porters, and it wasn't long before my strength failed. My legs buckled a couple of times, until at some point I just fell down.

I lay on the ground, the sickly sweet taste of blood in my mouth, listening to my heart beating while insects swarmed around my head. It was the end of the road for me.

Get up, get a move on, the soldiers commanded, but I could not. One of them rolled me with his foot onto my back, put the barrel of his rifle in my face, and threatened to pull the trigger. I mumbled something and closed my eyes. Suddenly Thar Thar was whispering in my ear, telling me not to give up now, it wasn't far now, another hour tops, that's what the captain told him, and he, Thar Thar, would carry both of my sacks. He took my hand and lifted me up.

I have no recollection of how I made it to the outpost.

We had thought we would be safe there. What a mistake. Rebels had attacked it twice in recent days. The soldiers were expecting another attack anytime. They weren't much older than we were, but they were more brutal than anyone I had ever met. They beat one of us half to death over a spilled bowl of rice. The next morning they forced another of us to stand in the sun on one leg until he passed out. They were placing bets the whole time on how long he would last.

On the way back we lost a porter to a mine. He was the youngest among us and had only recently relieved Thar Thar at the front of the party. I heard the explosion and thought at first that it had been Thar Thar. The soldiers took cover in the brush. We porters threw ourselves to the ground. When no shots or explosions followed I looked up and saw Thar Thar wriggling over to the wounded boy. He had lost a foot and he died a few minutes later in Thar Thar's arms.

This first mission changed every one of us. Up until that point, I think most of us still harbored hopes of getting out of that hell alive. Now we understood that there was no way out. We were doomed to die. If we weren't torn to pieces by a mine on the next mission, then we'd get struck by a bullet or beaten to death by a soldier. It was a question of weeks, months, maybe a year if the cards fell right. There was no other outcome. The military did not send people home, only to death.

Even Thar Thar seemed to be changed.

I had the feeling that he was only now ready to put fate to the test.

After our return from that first mission they caught one of us with a handful of stolen rice. Since he had stolen the rice from our rations, we were supposed to cane him as punishment. They bound his hands and tore off his shirt. A captain showed us how to do it. He whaled the boy so viciously with a bamboo stalk that he cried out, and his skin tore open in long lines. Then it was our turn. If you didn't thrash hard enough, they warned us, you could share the same punishment side by side with the thief.

The first porter hesitated initially, raised the bamboo reluctantly, and looked to us for help, as if we could tell him what to do. The officer screamed. Two soldiers moved to take the cane away from him, but he shook his head fearfully and struck a mighty blow. The skin burst open in two places and spurting blood ran down the boy's back. He bellowed in pain. After ten strokes his back was just one open wound from his neck to his hips. It was my turn. My hands clenched the stalk. I concentrated, took a big windup, and struck as hard as I could. My victim sobbed loudly. Relieved, I passed the bamboo to Thar Thar. He took the stick and wound up just as big as I had, then let loose a mighty swing. He brought it up short at the last second, looked coldly at the captain, and tapped the boy lightly on the back of his head.

Nobody moved. Not even the soldiers.

The officer drew his pistol, walked up to Thar Thar, and shoved it forcefully in his face, his finger on the trigger. I saw his body shaking with rage and am amazed to this day that he did not fire.

Thar Thar yielded not an inch. The two of them stared at each other, and the captain must have seen something in his eyes that kept him from shooting. Several soldiers ran up, bound Thar Thar, and threw him to the ground. They gave us more bamboo canes and commanded us to beat him. They kept a special eye on me because they knew we were friends. I struck him with all my might.

When we couldn't go on—he had passed out, and the skin on his back was in tatters—the soldiers picked up where we left off. When they were through with him four of us carried him to the Death House.

The next day, though it was forbidden, I slipped in to see him. I was sorry for what I'd done, and I was ashamed, even though I knew that I wouldn't behave differently the next time. I was no hero. Would never be one. I didn't want to die.

Thar Thar lay semiconscious on a straw mat with half a dozen other porters. Some of them had severe malaria.

Others had gunshot wounds, infections, or diarrhea so extreme that it was going to kill them. The place reeked of pus, urine, and shit. The sobbing in the hut was just about unbearable. Thar Thar lay curled up in one corner. Dozens of flies had settled on his open wounds. He recognized me and whispered that he was parched and did I have any water for him. I promised to get some. On the way back to the Death House some soldiers stopped me and demanded to know who the water was for. They drank it in one gulp and threw the cup on the ground at my feet. I picked it up and turned around without a word.

That evening I saw them carrying six dead bodies out of the Death House and burying them in a shallow grave.

After that I gave that part of the camp a wide berth.

Ten days later there was Thar Thar, standing in the doorway to our hut again. Stooped. Haggard like an emaciated ox.

But alive. He had not left the Death House as a corpse.

We took care of him as best we could, sharing our food with him and our water, washing him, driving off the flies and mosquitoes that plagued him. Gradually he showed signs of improvement, and a couple of weeks later he was ready for action again.

But he was not the same Thar Thar. He was aggressive and volatile. He spoke nary a word with us; he had not forgiven us.

On our missions Thar Thar always marched right up front. Voluntarily! No light steps for him. He stamped his feet as if to make sure that any mine he stumbled on would be sure to blow. He sped along with a sack of rice on his shoulders. The soldiers had to order him to slow down because none of us could keep pace with him.

More than anything we feared the paths overgrown with plants, where the underbrush was thick and the ground was covered with leaves. Here, too, though, Thar Thar willingly took the lead. The soldiers gave him a machete and he cleared a path for us. He swung like a madman, hacking anything in his way to bits with the long sharp blade. A cobra reared up in front of him; he slashed its head off. A second one he chopped in half with a single blow.

We were all happy that he relieved us of this deadly work. The soldiers let him get as far ahead as he liked. It had long since gotten to a point where they found him unsettling. Sometimes he got so far ahead that we could barely hear his wheezing and the splintering of the wood. Thar Thar could have made a break for it on these missions, but he was always waiting for us at the destination. We didn't understand why until later.

He lost a finger to a mine, at one point, and a bullet grazed his right arm.

There was a phase where I came increasingly to fear him.

A chill would run down my spine when he looked at me. When the others came back alive from an outing you could see the fear of death in their eyes, their joy and relief, their gratitude when they got an extra ration of rice. His expression was utterly impassive. As if he was untouched by all that happened around him.

He no longer resisted the soldiers' instructions. Yet his obedience was different from ours. It still did not seem that he was afraid of them, rather that he was just waiting for the right moment to defend himself.

Or maybe it wasn't indifference at all. The rest of us porters eventually gave up, waiting spinelessly and apathetically for death while he nursed a contempt that spared nothing and no one, that kept him alive. I had the feeling that there was ultimately not much distance between his contempt and the brutality of the soldiers.

All that changed when Ko Bo Bo showed up in the camp.

He was one in a group of boys that had been hauled straight from their village to the front. He was the youngest and physically the weakest of them all. His delicate wrists and ankles, his big dark-brown, almost black eyes reminded me of my sister. I felt sorry for him. He was a kid. I had seen a few of his kind, with his constitution, come into the camp. Not one of them had lasted more than a couple of weeks.

During the first few days he didn't dare to leave the hut. Huddled in a corner the whole time. Even at night. We set a little bowl of rice for him, but he didn't touch it. Whenever we asked him a question he just lowered his head and held his tongue. A couple of us crouched around him and tried to get him to open up, but he gave no answer. On the third evening Thar Thar took the sleeping lad in his arms and laid him on the mat next to him.

During the night I heard whispering. I recognized Thar Thar's voice, but the other one was strange to me. That morning, for the first time, Ko Bo Bo ate some rice and dried fish.

Two weeks after his arrival he had to go on his first patrol with us. The soldiers wanted to search a village. They suspected the farmers had stashed some weapons for the rebels. The settlement was only a few hours away, and you could get to it easily on broad, beaten tracks that the farmers traveled regularly with their oxcarts, so we didn't have to worry about mines. The trip out was uneventful. Ko Bo Bo was carrying a jug of water. Thar Thar walked beside him with a crate of ammunition on his shoulder. Seeing as how the soldiers had told us to keep our mouths shut, no one said a word for almost three hours.

The first ones to spot us were kids climbing in the trees on the edge of the village. The soldiers dispatched the first farm; six of them searched the house and property. Two other porters and I were made to turn over the soil in a couple of places, but we didn't stumble into anything fishy. Three women with babes in their arms, an old man, and a couple of kids were watching us in silent dread. I saw them holding hands and shivering with fright.

We didn't find anything at the second farm, either. But the tension there was even thicker than at the first place. Two boys, maybe ten or eleven years old, kept running excitedly back and forth, and I imagined that I saw more than fear in the glances of an old woman, but I couldn't have said what it was. One young woman was screaming hysterically. Her mother was able to calm her only with considerable effort.

The third farm stood there as if its occupants had just up and left it. Longyis and shirts were hanging on a line to dry; the smoke of a flickering fire rose out of the hut; cackling hens flitted about. No trace of the farmers. Two soldiers mounted the steps, guns at the ready, looking warily around the house. It was empty. An officer ordered us to dig under the hut, but we didn't find anything there, either. Suddenly a soldier called us to the outhouse. Shining his flashlight into the cesspit, he had seen what he thought was the barrel of a rifle. We were commanded to tear down the straw building, and within a few minutes we had an open view of the pit.

It might have been a stick. Two porters had to climb down. They stood chest deep in the shit, rooting around. A few seconds later they held up a rifle. And another. And another.

That's when the first shots rang out. An officer stumbled headfirst into the excrement. Two soldiers next to him fell stricken. The others returned fire without knowing which direction the shots had come from. I heard loud shouting, rifle rounds; everyone was trying to find some kind of cover. I threw myself on the ground, rolled to the side, and crawled as fast as I could behind a pile of wood under the house. Other porters were already huddled there, including Ko Bo Bo and Thar Thar. A soldier who tried to join us got a bullet in the back. He lay unconscious two yards in front of me. I saw the earth darken beneath him. We heard a dull crash above us, followed by ashes drifting down onto us. A few seconds later blood was dripping through the bamboo floor. Next thing we knew, the hut above us was in flames.

Thar Thar took Ko Bo Bo by the hand and ran for the hedge. I followed them. We tripped over a dead body, stumbled, and kept going on all fours. Thar Thar threw himself with all his weight into the hedge and cleared a way for us into the neighboring farm. There, too, lay bodies, and the hut was ablaze. Gunfire on all sides. The soldiers had lost their minds. On the hunt for rebels, they were going from hut to hut shooting anything that moved. Chickens, cats, dogs, people.

We crept past the burning hut into the first farm, where we hid behind a haystack. The old man lay in front of us, his back full of holes and two dead kids beneath him. One of the young women lay bleeding against a palm tree, mouth and eyes open wide. Her baby floundered in her arms. Without hesitating, Ko Bo Bo left his cover and crawled over to her. Thar Thar tried to stop him, but he was too quick. He took the baby from its dead mother's arms and came back to us.

The baby wailed in a raw voice, but then calmed down and eventually was quiet. From our hiding place we could hear kids calling for their mothers, loud bawling, screams for help, one blast, then several. I wondered if there was a chance to get away, but the settlement was too isolated. The army would find us before we could get anywhere.

At some point, a silence fell over the village that was more terrifying even than the gunfire had been.

The rebels had fled or been killed. We saw soldiers looking for their porters, and we crawled out of our hiding place. Thar Thar tried to take the baby from Ko Bo Bo, but he held on as tightly as if it were his own.

We gathered in a group in front of the first farm, the surviving porters, soldiers, and a few villagers. One of the soldiers spotted the baby and commanded Ko Bo Bo to set it down immediately. He did not react.

The soldier cocked his pistol and screamed that he would shoot it on the spot if he didn't put it down immediately. Ko Bo Bo still did not respond. Not out of disobedience. I could see in his face that he couldn't do otherwise. The soldier raised his weapon and aimed. Thar Thar spoke softly to Ko Bo Bo until he loosened his grip. Then he took the baby from him, walked slowly over to a young woman, and put it into her arms.

AFTER THAT MISSION the two were inseparable. Maybe Thar Thar saw in him a younger brother he needed to look after. Or maybe just someone who needed his protection. I don't know what it was, but the two of them were always together. They washed their laundry together at the river, cooked, cleaned rifles, buried the corpses from the Death House. Somehow they always managed to get assigned to the same group. They slept next to each other, and I often fell asleep to the sound of their whispers. Thar Thar the Taciturn had suddenly started to talk again. His bad moods evaporated, as did his aggression. He had forgiven us porters for what we had done. Between him and Ko Bo Bo something had developed for which there was no room in the world we occupied. I don't know how I should describe it. They conversed with each other long after the rest of us had retreated into silence. They laughed together. During the whole time that I spent in the camp they were the only people I would see smiling occasionally. They helped each other. They watched out for each other in a world where everyone who lived past the first couple of weeks was only looking out for himself. I envied them. There was some secret that bound them and that kept them alive. I'm sorry to say that I never discovered what it was. Thar Thar and I were no longer close enough.

And there was some power that protected them. Six months passed, and Ko Bo Bo was still alive. Most of us figured it was destiny. The stars were smiling on them.

Months passed and turned into a year and then another. We were among only a dozen or so porters to live so long. Maybe it was luck, instinct, or intuition to do the right thing in dangerous situations. Or maybe it was just our karma, though I'd be hard-pressed to say whether it was a good karma or a bad that kept us alive for so long in that hell.

Most of us wondered what we had done in a previous life to deserve such torture. We suspected that we had been soldiers ourselves, and that we had killed people. Or drunkards. Murderers. Animal abusers.

Thar Thar and Ko Bo Bo never indulged in these speculations. I have no idea whether they followed the teaching of the Buddha. I never heard them mention it. I never saw them meditating, and I don't remember ever seeing them leave an offering at our little altar in the hut.

THE DAY OUR luck turned started with an extra ration of rice. That was not a good sign. Any time we got something more to eat it meant that we were slated for a special mission. A colonel came into the hut and picked a dozen porters. Thar Thar and I were the first two. Ko Bo Bo volunteered.

We had to accompany ten soldiers who were chasing down a rumor that the rebels had built a bridge over a nearby river. They had retaken large stretches of our territory in recent months, and they had more than once managed to cut off our supplies for days at a time. The commandant was anticipating a major offensive against our camp. Anxiety was growing among the soldiers, and there were even plans to abandon the camp. We porters were hoping the rumors would prove true. A rebel victory over our camp, should we survive it, was our only chance of ever getting away.

As on many other missions, Thar Thar and Ko Bo Bo willingly took the lead. I was walking maybe ten yards behind them. A good omen, I thought. In this formation we had so far always come back alive. The march through the forest passed peacefully, and when we came out of the trees the river lay right in front of us. It had swollen with the seasonal rains to a mighty current.

And there was a bridge.

The soldiers ordered Ko Bo Bo to investigate whether there were any explosives underneath it or we could get safely across the river. He was our best climber. Gracefully and skillfully he climbed a few yards down the bank, balancing on stones and pieces of wood without holding fast. He had nearly gotten under the bridge when he suddenly straightened up, threw his arms into the air, swayed, lost his balance, and fell.

In the roar of the river I had not heard the gunshot.

He rolled down the steep slope. The other porters and soldiers took cover. I stood there unable to move. Thar Thar let out a cry and sprang down the embankment, tumbled over, slammed into a boulder, righted himself, took flying leaps over tree trunks and stones, fell again, struggled to his feet.

Ko Bo Bo slid toward the river. Curiously there was no second shot, as if both sides were engrossed in the drama that was unfolding before their eyes. Seconds before Thar Thar reached his friend his body slipped into the water and went under at the first eddy. Thar Thar dove headlong after him and likewise disappeared in the surge.

A few yards farther on I saw Ko Bo Bo's head resurface briefly in the white froth, then Thar Thar's. The water flung them into an outcropping of rock, they went under, Thar Thar's arm jutted for one moment above the water and then disappeared again. I felt a dread come over me like none I had known since those first missions. I couldn't take my eyes off the waves and eddies. Fifteen, maybe twenty yards farther downstream the trunk of a fallen tree rose out of the water. It was their only hope. Beyond it the river became a raging sea of white. Seconds passed without any sign of them.

The colonel crawled through the tall grass to me and cast a wary eye down the embankment.

A hand. An arm. I could see them clearly on one of the branches. Thar Thar's head. A second one, both above water. Underwater. Above. Under.

The colonel barked at me to rush to their aid. I finally overcame my paralysis and started to clamber my way down the slope, keeping a sharp eye on Thar Thar the whole time. I saw him making his way toward the bank. Where was Ko Bo Bo? Thar Thar had solid ground beneath his feet by now. He straightened up, and in his arms I saw a limp body emerge out of the waves. He dragged him ashore and collapsed in exhaustion beside him.

The second shot was meant for the colonel. I have only vague memories of what followed. I know that I turned immediately about face. Where Thar Thar and Ko Bo Bo lay there was no protection. I scrambled back up the bank and took cover behind a boulder. I lay there between the fronts. After a grenade exploded near me I passed out.

When I came to again I found two rebels squatting beside me. My ears were still ringing, I had a dreadful headache, and I could hardly understand what they were saying.

They helped me to my feet. I had abrasions on my head and arms, and I was so stunned that I was dizzy. They took me with them, and at the edge of the forest I could see the bodies of porters and soldiers, could not imagine that any of us had survived this battle, and lost consciousness a second time.

I came to in a rebel camp. They treated my wounds, gave me plenty of rice and water, asked me a few questions about our encampment's weaponry, troop strength, and layout, but otherwise left me in peace. After two weeks it was for me to decide whether to fight with them or have them drop me off in the nearest city.

MAUNG TUN LIT a cigarette and looked at me, sizing me up. A waiter set melon seeds and a thermos of fresh Chinese tea on the table.

I waited for my brother to pose the last, most important question, but he said nothing.

I was finding it difficult to think clearly. What I had just heard was too monstrous. At the same time I felt disappointment, fear, that Maung Tun would not be able to tell us who or what killed Thar Thar.

"Can you tell us," I raised my voice, "where and how Thar Thar died?"

U Ba glanced at me, hesitated briefly, then leaned far over the table and translated.

"How Thar Thar died?" asked Maung Tun, as if trying to make sure he had understood correctly.

I nodded.

He shook his head. Said something.

My brother's eyes opened wide. "He's not dead. Thar Thar is alive."

Part Three

Chapter 1

MY BROTHER HAD fallen asleep next to me. His head lay lightly against my neck, his mouth half open, a quiet rattle in his throat with every exhalation. I took a towel and wiped the sweat from my face. I laid my hand carefully on his forehead to feel whether he had a fever. It was very warm. He had had a severe bout of coughing before falling asleep. I was worried. In Thazi, too, he had refused to go with me to a doctor, insisting that his cough was an allergic reaction that would soon pass. It affected him every year at this time, no reason for concern. I didn't believe a word of it.

Now we were sitting on a train to Mandalay. The carriages rocked and rumbled. Reading was out of the question. Through the open windows a gentle draft provided a bit of refreshment, but it was too hot for that to make much difference. It smelled of food, sweat, and a pungent deodorant that a Chinese traveler in the row in front of us applied repeatedly.

U Ba had somehow managed to arrange seats for us in the "upper class." We sat in two wide armchairs with adjustable footrests and seat backs that were nevertheless dreadfully uncomfortable. I could feel every spring, but I knew better than to complain: most of the passengers in the rear cars were sleeping on wooden benches between crates and boxes full of fruit, vegetables, and chickens. Or on the floor. Compared with the pickup truck, this was pure luxury.

Men and women kept passing up and down the aisle with buckets and baskets, hawking their wares. Boiled eggs. Peanuts, rice cakes, bananas, mangoes, betel nuts. Little plastic bags filled with a brown liquid. Hand-rolled cigarillos. Cigarettes. One merchant thrust a bowl under my nose. Deep-fried chicken legs swimming in a greasy sauce and surrounded by dozens of flies. I shook my head in disgust.

Outside, the sun set slowly. The train rolled through a town at walking pace. Two young boys drove a water buffalo along between the rails. Behind them a woman balanced a half dozen clay jugs in a tower on her head. There were fires burning in some of the yards. Naked children splashing in a pool.

I thought of Maung Tun. *He's not dead. Thar Thar is alive.*

It had taken a moment for the meaning of those two sentences to sink in. Neither my brother nor I had considered that possibility for a second. We had assumed we were on the trail of a dead man. Nu Nu had imagined her son was dead. As had Khin Khin and Ko Gyi.

Maung Tun had not learned anything from the rebels about the whereabouts of Thar Thar and Ko Bo Bo. They had left them in peace. The powerful man had eventually stood up, taken the limp body lying next to him in his arms, and headed off downstream.

Years later Maung Tun heard reports from a number of truck drivers of a monk who lived with several children and dozens of chickens in an old monastery in the vicinity of Hsipaw. An utterly extraordinary man who looked after the children. He was missing a finger on his right hand. Under his chin was a birthmark, and on his right upper arm a long scar. The result of a gunshot wound. Apparently he had lived for years as a soldier in the jungle. Supposedly he had been a dauntless warrior.

Two bus drivers later confirmed the tale. Maung Tun was convinced that it must be Thar Thar. U Ba, too. I was skeptical.

Now we were on the way to Mandalay. We planned to sleep there and then continue on to Hsipaw the next morning.

The train stopped with a jolt. My brother woke up. He looked around quickly, licking his dry lips. I gave him my water. He drank in small sips and exchanged a few words with a neighbor across the aisle. "We arrive in Mandalay in two hours," he said, turning to me. "Are you hungry?"

I nodded.

"Me, too. Shall we go for a bite to eat?"

"In the train?"

"There's a dining car."

I looked doubtfully at my armchair's grimy upholstery, the sticky floor. "I'm not sure it's a good idea."

"We'll have just a bit of fried rice and coffee. The water is boiled. Don't worry."

U Ba rose, and I followed him reluctantly.

The train was rocking violently. I staggered along the aisle, bumping my head twice.

There were still two seats free in the dining car. My brother made for them single-mindedly and sat down. I hesitated at the entrance. A group of soldiers were eating their dinner at the next table. I saw their green uniforms. I saw their shiny black boots. Their bloodred teeth.

U Ba indicated with a glance that I should sit down with him. I couldn't decide. My hesitation aroused attention. Curious looks. Abandoned conversations.

It was too late to turn back. I didn't want to leave my brother alone, so I walked over to him.

"They won't bother us," he said quietly. "They can't even understand what we're saying."

The soldiers looked at us with interest. U Ba responded with a smile that they returned. I stared out the window.

When the waiter came U Ba ordered coffee and rice with chicken and vegetables. In the kitchen I could see several men in filthy, sweaty T-shirts working over an open fire spooning something out of a trough.

"May I ask you something?"

"Anything," he replied with a wink.

"Why do people always laugh here, even when they don't really feel like it?"

He tilted his head to one side and looked as if he had long been expecting this question. "Laughter has many meanings here. We laugh when something is unpleasant. When we are afraid. When we are angry."

"Is it a kind of mask?"

"You could call it that. If you look closely you will quickly recognize what lies behind it, what kind of laugh it is."

The waiter brought two glasses of hot water and packets of instant coffee. The rice followed shortly. It looked more appetizing than expected. U Ba dove in hungrily, burned his tongue, and laughed at himself. "How can someone my age still be so greedy?"

The rice was nicely seasoned, dusted with coriander and other herbs. Delicious.

"Do you think we're going to find Thar Thar?" I asked him after burning my own mouth.

He nodded.

"Maybe this monk with the missing finger is someone else."

"Maybe."

"Or Thar Thar has died in the meantime. The story with the truck drivers is already a few years old."

"It's possible."

"You still think we're going to find him?"

He nodded confidently.

"Why?"

"Intuition."

"Intuition can be misleading."

He shook his head. "You should never doubt intuition."

I had to laugh. "Unless you're me. My intuition is not very reliable. It's always letting me down."

"I don't believe it. Intuition is the incorruptible memory of our experiences. We have only to listen closely to what it tells us." With a smile he added: "It does not always speak plainly. Or it tells us things we don't want to hear. That does not make them untrue."

I ate my rice thoughtfully.

U Ba was finished long before me and ordered a second coffee. He looked tired, more haggard than usual. His face seemed to have grown leaner in the past few days.

At first I thought he had choked on the coffee. I stood up and whacked him between the shoulder blades, but he waved me off. Another severe coughing fit. He could hardly breathe, was turning red in the face, gripping the table tightly. Even the soldiers looked at us with concern. I got scared and took his hand, rubbed his back. When it was over, he looked even more exhausted.

"I'm taking you to a hospital as soon as we get to Mandalay," I told him authoritatively.

He tried to calm me. "It's not so bad."

"U Ba, stop it," I answered, annoyed. "The whole time I've been here it just keeps getting worse. That's no allergic reaction."

"It is," he contradicted weakly.

"To what?"

"I don't know."

"You need to be examined."

"And if they find something, what then?"

"Then we'll see that you get treatment."

"They can't treat it. I've already told you. What good is a diagnosis?"

"If they find something they can't treat we'll take the next flight to Bangkok," I declared with certainty. "They've got top-notch hospitals there."

He smiled. "Julia, my dear, I don't even have a passport."

"Then we'll get you one," I said, unimpressed by his objections.

"That's kind of you. We'll have to go to Rangoon for that. Processing an application for a passport can take months here, sometimes years. And I'm not even sure I would get one in the end."

"Months? For a passport? I can't believe it. I'm sure there's some way to expedite it for urgent cases."

"Maybe so. But not for people like me."

"What do you mean, people like you?"

"People without connections to the military."

"We'll find a way. First of all we need to get you examined."

"I don't know . . ."

"U Ba! In Mandalay we're going to step right into a taxi and take you straight to the best hospital. Until then I'm not going to any hotel or boarding any trains for Hsipaw or anywhere else."

"But we have to . . ."

"I'm serious. I'll just stand there in front of the train station."

My decisiveness apparently made an impression on him. He sighed and gazed off into the evening. The streets were getting broader. There were more people on the roads, more houses, more lights. We were approaching Mandalay.

"So why don't you have a passport?" I wanted to know.

"Why would I need a passport?" he challenged.

"To visit me, for instance."

"You are right."

"Will you try to get one when we get back?"

"We'll see."

I was disappointed. "Wouldn't you like to visit me in New York sometime?"

"Of course." After a long pause he added, "But it is a long, arduous journey."

When we got back to our seats, U Ba took another short nap. Looking at him, I was filled with tenderness.

There were few people I felt so close to, so comfortable with. He was so utterly without guile, without ulterior motives. What would I do if it turned out his cough was a symptom of something serious? Fear for his well-being was taking hold of me. The thought of losing him was unbearable to me just now.

Chapter 2

THE MANDALAY GENERAL Hospital was only a few blocks from the main train station. A betel nut monger pointed out the way. I cinched up my backpack and relieved my brother of his bag. To my surprise he made no objection.

The entrance to the hospital was bustling like a market. Several stands offered bananas, pineapples, coconuts, and mangoes. You could get drinks, magazines, and books. Pedestrians stood and read by the light of bare bulbs. Between them rickshaw drivers and taxis waited for customers. A young man approached me, hands loaded with freshly woven wreaths of jasmine blossoms. He handed me one, and its intense fragrance immediately filled my nostrils.

"You like the scent of jasmine?" asked my brother.

"I love it," I answered, looking for some money, but the young man just smiled and disappeared into the throng.

On the street in front of two fully equipped food stands a dozen folding tables and plastic chairs had been arranged.

Curries simmered over blazing fires; skewers of meat, mushrooms, and peppers roasted on a grill.

U Ba stopped abruptly to look at a group of men playing a kind of checkers with bottle caps on a homemade board. One of them had tattoos over his legs, arms, hands, even his neck.

"What's that about?" I whispered.

"The tattoos protect him from evil spirits," U Ba answered.

I pulled him along. We crossed the hospital forecourt and entered a biggish hall, a kind of emergency room, and for a first long moment I doubted whether it had been a good idea to bring my brother to a hospital.

It was hot and humid, and it stank. Two sluggish fans turned on the ceiling. Lurid neon lighting illuminated the crowded space. People huddled on chairs, sometimes two to a seat. Others leaned against the wall, sat on the tiled floor, or lay on blankets they had spread out. Mothers clutched infants in their arms. One child cried softly. Some of them gave us a once-over; most were too exhausted or sick to pay us any mind.

I could see that my brother felt ill. He dropped back, leaning against a column by the entrance, not even pretending to have some other purpose. I set about finding a doctor, stepping right over patients, treading unintentionally on a leg. Someone groaned; I apologized immediately and profusely, went on, spoke to a nurse who listened attentively, smiled, nodded, and then disappeared again without

a word. I had no confidence that she had understood a word
I had said.

A few minutes later a young doctor came and waved to
me to come into a side room. U Ba followed us reluctantly.
He sat down on a stool right next to the door. As if he had
nothing to do with the whole affair.

"How can I help you?" the doctor asked in surprisingly
good English.

"My brother has had a severe cough for some time now,
and it gets worse day by day. When he's coughing he can
hardly breathe."

The doctor regarded U Ba skeptically. "Is your brother
Burmese or foreign?"

"Burmese," I replied, annoyed. "Why?"

"Our hospital is quite full. You have seen so." He
paused briefly as if weighing his words carefully. "In an
emergency I could offer a foreigner preferential treatment.
Not so a Burmese. Would you be able to come back in a
few days?"

"A few days?" I wasn't sure I had understood correctly.

"Yes. This evening, tomorrow, or the day after would be
very difficult. I'm sorry," he said, smiling. Even I could tell
what kind of smile it was.

"Let's go, Julia," I heard U Ba say behind me.

"No," I declared authoritatively, "we cannot come back
in a few days. My brother is sick. He needs help."

The young doctor was still smiling, but I was no longer
sure what lay behind it.

"There are many patients right outside the door who need our help." He paused briefly again. "I am truly sorry."

"Julia, please."

I pulled two hundred-dollar bills out of my bag and laid them on the table.

The doctor looked for a long time at the money, then looked back and forth between my brother and me. A sad smile lined his face. Behind me I heard U Ba sigh deeply.

The doctor hesitated, eventually stood up, pocketed the cash, and went to the door. "Follow me, please."

We walked down a corridor that was likewise lined with patients. U Ba slunk, head bowed, behind us, not returning my look. The doctor led us into a room where four other patients were already being examined. He asked my brother to sit and to bare his upper body, to inhale and exhale deeply while he listened. He prodded his head, neck, shoulders, and chest, looked down his throat and in his ears, and then wrinkled his brow. U Ba let it all happen without glancing up.

"Do you have pain in your chest when you inhale deeply?" he asked in English.

"No," replied my brother softly.

"In your armpits, maybe?"

"No."

"Do you cough up mucus when you have an attack?"

"Sometimes."

"A lot?"

"Sometimes more, sometimes less."

"Is there blood in the mucus?"

U Ba shook his head mutely.

"Are you certain?" asked the doctor, looking to me.

I shrugged my shoulders.

"I suspect your brother has severe bronchitis. I'd like to get an X-ray of his lungs."

The X-ray machine looked like a holdover from British colonial times.

A good hour later, during which time U Ba and I sat beside each other in silence, the doctor reappeared holding a couple of papers in one hand. He sat down next to me.

"Your brother does indeed have severe bronchitis. The X-ray also revealed a nodule in one lung. That could be the cause of the infection."

"A nodule?" I asked, alarmed.

"A kind of circular shadow on the lung."

"What does it mean?"

"It can mean many things," he answered evasively.

"Such as?"

"It could indicate acute tuberculosis, which for various other reasons I think unlikely. A healed tuberculosis is also a possibility. Or the shadow could be a remnant from an old, healed infection. In that case it would be completely harmless. Or . . ." He pursed his lips and faltered.

"Or?"

"Or it is a symptom of some more serious disease."

"What kind of more serious disease?"

"There are a handful."

"Which ones?" I was impatient to know.

"In the worst case, lung cancer."

I felt a pang in my stomach. Shortness of breath.

"There are tests one can perform to determine whether it is malignant," he added quickly. "But we can't do them here, not for all the money in the world."

I caught the drift. "Where, then?"

"In your country."

"Not even in Rangoon?"

"No. Maybe in one of the military hospitals, I can't say for certain. But your brother would have no access. Or do you have a Burmese army general in your family?"

I shook my head and didn't know what to say. My brother was sitting a short distance away. I was sure he could understand what the doctor was saying. I tried to exchange a glance with him, but he fixed his gaze on the floor.

"So what do we do now?" I asked, flummoxed.

"Wait."

"For what?"

Clearly he was disconcerted by my questions. He avoided making eye contact. His legs were perpetually bouncing, and he was rubbing his left hand with his right thumb so that it was clicking.

"For the next symptoms."

"And what might those be?" I asked tentatively.

"I'll give you some antibiotics. If it's just bronchitis, he'll feel better in a few days."

"And otherwise?"

"Otherwise he'll eventually have blood in his mucus. Probably sooner rather than later. Pain in his chest, pain in his armpits."

"And then?"

The doctor lifted his head. Our eyes met. There was not the least trace of a smile on his face.

"And then?" I repeated softly.

He didn't answer.

WE GOT A taxi in front of the hospital. U Ba asked the driver to take us to the nearest hotel. It was still quite hot. The car had air-conditioning, but it didn't work. Some of the potholes jolted us to the bone; the driver smiled at us in the rearview mirror. The streets were full of people strolling around or crouching in sidewalk restaurants.

"I'm sorry," I said. "I didn't mean to . . . I just wanted to know . . ."

My brother gazed out the window, deep in thought. He took my hand and stroked it.

"It was the first time I ever bribed anyone," he said suddenly, as if to himself.

"You didn't bribe anyone," I contradicted.

"Of course I did. The doctor."

"Why you? *I* am the one who gave him the money."

"That's irrelevant."

"How is that irrelevant?"

"Because you did it on my behalf. I profited from it."

"But it was my money and my idea. You couldn't do anything about it. I never even asked you."

"I ought to have stood up and left."

"But U Ba!" I didn't know what to say.

"No, no. I let it happen and am therefore complicit," he said, reflecting. "We are responsible not only for what we do, but also for what we fail to do."

"I . . . I'm sorry. I didn't want to make trouble for you. I only wanted to help."

"I know." He pressed my hand again.

I took the pills out of my pocket. "You need to take one of these every morning and evening."

He looked at the bottle, shook his head, and gave them back to me.

"They're antibiotics. If it's bronchitis, they'll help you."

"I don't take pills."

"Why not?" He was being stubborn like a child.

"Because most of our medicines are counterfeits from China. What's inside the bottle has nothing to do with what's on the label. They do more harm than good."

I looked incredulously at the packaging with its Chinese and Burmese script. "But we got these from a doctor. I can't imagine, I mean, he wouldn't . . ."

"What else could he give us? That's all he's got. In the hospital in Kalaw patients die from pills like these."

The taxi stopped in front of a rundown building with a flashing red neon sign over the entrance. Above it plants were growing out of the facade. The windows in the lower stories were dark and barred. There was a pile of trash in front of the door.

I looked doubtfully at my brother. "Maybe there's some other hotel in the vicinity?"

He regarded the entrance with skepticism equal to my own. He exchanged a few words with the driver. He nodded quickly, and we were on our way again.

A few minutes later we turned into the driveway of a modern six-story hotel. A footman hurried solicitously to the car and opened the door. A second footman relieved me of my handbag and backpack. Still two more bid us welcome in chorus and held open the heavy glass doors. The spacious lobby was cold and empty. In the middle of it stood a Christmas tree whose artificial candles and red balls were reflected in the glossy, polished floor. Several hotel staff bowed. The concierge greeted us yet again and escorted me past a lush flower arrangement to the reception desk. A young woman offered me a moist cloth and a reddish-yellowish cocktail. I requested two quiet, adjacent single rooms, non-smoking, as far from the elevator as possible, ordered a wake-up call for six the next morning, and laid my credit card on the counter.

Only then did I notice that U Ba had not followed me. He stood as if lost at the Christmas tree, fingering the knot of his longyi, looking at the door as if he were already on his way out. I waved him over to me, but he didn't move.

I recovered my baggage from the befuddled bellhop and walked over to U Ba.

"What's wrong?"

"I could sleep elsewhere, there's another . . ."

"Out of the question," I interrupted him at once. "We have two single rooms. They'll wake us at six tomorrow morning, we'll have breakfast and then catch the next train to Hsipaw."

He nodded and followed me to the elevator that one of the staff had already summoned for us. We rode in silence to the sixth floor, walked down a long corridor, and parted ways outside our rooms.

"Do you need anything?"

He shook his head wearily.

"Is there anything else I can do for you?"

"No, thank you."

"Then sleep well."

"You, too."

MY ROOM WAS much too cold. Chilled, I turned off the air conditioner and had a look around. A big bed with fresh sheets. Minibar. A desk, writing paper, two telephones, wi-fi, color television, bouquet of flowers. A bowl with fresh fruit. It all felt dreadfully familiar. How often had I stayed in similar rooms on business trips? Dallas. Miami. Chicago. Houston. San Diego. The hotel rooms, offices, and conference rooms I worked in looked the same wherever I went. It was an anonymous, interchangeable world. Even-tempered, sterile, odorless, non-sensual. A world in which I could find my way without difficulty. In which I had until now felt neither good nor bad. In which I felt, to be honest, nothing at all. In which I functioned. Conducted negotiations. Accomplished tasks. This room was a reminder of it, and in a disconcerting way I suddenly found myself feeling out of place in it. Alienated. As if, after a long absence, I were visiting dear friends only to find that we no longer had anything in common.

I fell enervated into an armchair, put my feet up, and waited. For what, I didn't know. I had actually been looking forward to a hot shower and a soft bed. Now I was too exhausted to get undressed. I don't know how long I sat there. At some point I heard U Ba coughing. As the attack went on and on I decided I had better check in on him. His door was ajar. In the corridor stood his shabby flip-flops. He had taken the blanket off the bed, folded it in half, and laid it on the floor. The bag with his two shirts and longyi served as his pillow. There he was, sleeping on his side, his knees pulled up almost to his chest. The coughing had not woken him, or else he had fallen right back to sleep. I closed the door softly, sat on the bed, and gazed at my brother. His thin legs, his callused feet. His rib cage rising and falling in the even rhythm of a sleeper. Lying on the floor, resting, he looked still older and more haggard. Needy. Vulnerable.

I thought of the ten years that separated my two journeys and during which we had not seen each other. How could I have failed to notice how much I missed him? Suddenly I understood why he had never visited me in New

York. I could not picture him there with his longyi and sandals any more than I could imagine him walking the streets of Manhattan in jeans and shoes.

Why had I brought him to a hospital against his will? Why had I bribed the doctor without consulting him? I wanted to help. I was afraid for him. How could I imagine that I knew better than he did what was good for him?

I was reminded of something our father used to say, something I never understood when I was little: "In the hell of the well-intentioned." That was how he referred to the charity balls my mother helped organize. "Hell" and "well-intentioned" were for me incompatible concepts. They stood in irresolvable contradiction to each other. Only much later did I understand how apt his description was. How difficult it was to resist the well-intentioned. It was impossible to make a clean getaway. The shadow of the guilty conscience was too long.

My father's jibe might just as easily have come from Amy. I wondered how she was getting along. Since my departure ten days earlier we had had no contact at all. It had been years since we had gone so long without speaking. What would she say if she could see me sitting on this bed? If she could hear the tales we had heard?

I wonder whether this voice might also have some purpose?

Yes, Amy, it might. It does. And an important one at that.

I missed her I-wonder's.

I wonder whether it makes sense to drag your brother to a hospital that can't do anything for him?

I wonder what you were thinking, subjecting an honest doctor to such temptation?

I wonder whether "well-intentioned" is ever a cover for something else?

Why didn't I just call her? It had to be early afternoon in New York. Her voice, a few words with her to help me manage my fear for my brother, that's all I wanted. I walked to the desk, picked up the receiver. One of the few numbers I knew by heart: 001-555-254-1973. I paused, hesitating. The thought that I could dial a few numbers and be connected to Rivington Street in Manhattan was absurd. As if my world were separated from this one by no more than the push of a couple of buttons.

If only it were that simple.

U Ba wheezed and coughed a bit. I crouched beside him and put my hand on his arm. Eventually I rose, fetched my blanket from my own room, and lay down on his bed. I'm not sure which was stronger: my unwillingness to leave him alone when he was so sick, or my desire to be close to him.

Chapter 3

THE BREAKFAST BUFFET was opulent. We were the only guests in the dining room at this early hour, and more than a dozen waiters and cooks hung on our every move. U Ba closely examined the various kinds of cheese and sausage, bent low over the diverse rolls and jams, wanted to know what croissants, muesli, and cornflakes tasted like, and in the end ordered a Burmese noodle soup.

My cheese omelet didn't taste like anything. Probably because I had no appetite. I felt queasy. I had an uncomfortable pressure in my stomach. I had slept badly, and my shoulders were tense. I couldn't get the images from the hospital out of my mind. The doctor's face as I laid the two hundred dollars on the table.

"Is it true that you have never bribed anyone?" I wanted to know.

He sipped his tea and nodded.

"I thought the authorities here were so corrupt."

"That they are. But I had no children for whom I had to purchase better exam scores. I own no shop for which I need permits. I have never been seriously ill. In my whole life I have never yet had dealings with the police. I require nothing from the authorities for which I would have to pay."

"Except a passport," I said.

"Except a passport," my brother confirmed with an expression that I could not interpret.

The waiter brought a steaming noodle soup. My brother slurped at it, savoring it. I had the impression he was doing somewhat better.

"Is it good?"

He nodded. "Yours isn't?"

"I'm not hungry."

"Why not?"

I shrugged.

"You're worrying too much."

"What would I be worrying about?" I countered, forcing a smile.

"I am not deathly ill. Trust me."

"How can you be so sure?"

"I sense it."

"Intuition?"

"Intuition!"

He saw me laughing. "What a beautiful woman you are."

"Oh, U Ba, stop," I replied wearily. "You're not taking me seriously. I'm worried about you."

"Why?"

I wasn't sure whether he meant it seriously, or whether his innocence was feigned. "Because it might be that you are very ill."

My brother finished off his soup before answering. "It's true. That is a possibility. For you, too."

"I don't have a nodule on my lung."

"You woke up this morning with a headache. It might be a tumor in your head that you are as yet unaware of."

"It's a tension headache. I know what they feel like."

"Or it might be . . ."

"I could get hit by a car on our way to the train station," I interrupted him. "That's not what it's about."

"What then?"

"It's about the fact that you have severe symptoms. That you might . . . that we have to do something . . ."

"We are waiting. The doctor explained it to you. There's nothing else we can do at the moment."

"I don't believe it. I can't imagine it."

"If there were something we could do, would it frighten you less?"

"I don't know. At least I wouldn't feel so helpless. Waiting to see what happens: I can't bear it. There's always something that can be done."

"Who am I to contradict you?" he answered with an impish grin. His ironic undertone was suffused with tenderness.

The worlds we came from were too different for us to reach agreement on this point.

"Have you heard anything from the voice?" he asked.

I shook my head. "No. She's had nothing to say, not even about Maung Tun's story."

"Curious. I would have thought she would have spoken up by the time we learned that her son was still alive, if not before then. Perhaps it is enough for her to know that he survived it."

"Either that or she's just as anxious as you and me to see whether we'll find him."

IN HSIPAW WE sat down in a teahouse near the train station. My brother ordered Burmese tea and struck up a conversation with the waiter. Patrons at nearby tables quickly joined in, and a few minutes later he turned back to me, very pleased.

"They all know him. He lives with a dozen children and youths in an old monastery that had long stood empty. It's just a few kilometers from here in the direction of Namshaw. We have to follow the main road and turn right at a white pagoda. The waiter will take us there on his moped."

Half an hour later the three of us were squeezing ourselves onto a Honda Dream II. I sat at the back with the luggage wedged between me and U Ba. The waiter opened the throttle. The first few yards were a wild zigzag all over the street until he finally got control of the moped. By the white pagoda just outside the town we turned onto a dirt road. In my excitement I was shifting so restlessly back and forth on the seat that the driver had difficulty keeping the moped on the track. Were we about to meet Thar Thar? What might he look like? Would he be willing at all to talk with us? Had he really survived that hell in the jungle? What marks had that time left on him? Nu Nu's decision? His father's early death? What kind of person would we find? What had become of Ko Bo Bo?

We climbed a hill and saw the monastery in the distance, a large, dark wooden structure, standing on pillars, with a tin roof and several turrets on whose gables bells and flags were hung. It was situated among trees and protected, it seemed, by a large bamboo grove that towered several yards above the turrets.

The young waiter stopped and pointed to it, as if it were our last chance to turn back. U Ba coughed briefly, gestured to him, and we rolled down the hill.

A few minutes later we pulled into the sandy courtyard to be greeted by two barking dogs and dozens of hens cackling vociferously and running about excitedly. We dismounted. The driver turned around, and we thanked him, but my brother nipped in the bud my attempt to pay him for his trouble.

"He is happy that he could do us a favor."

We looked around full of curiosity. The courtyard was teeming with flowerbeds and hedges blooming in stunningly beautiful colors. I saw rosebushes, yellow and red hibiscus, oleander, violet bougainvillea, gladiolus, and amaryllis.

The monastery itself was not in very good condition. Many of the pilings looked rotted, there were boards missing from the walls in several places, brown rust was eating through the corrugated tin roof, and one wing of the building was partially collapsed. A broad staircase with crooked railings led up to the entrance. At the back of the courtyard reddish brown monks' robes hung to dry on a bamboo framework. U Ba called out, but there was no answer. The chickens and dogs had settled down. We heard nothing but the gentle tinkling of the bells on the roofs.

A boy and a girl appeared at the top of the stairs. They wore the red robes of novices and looked at us inquiringly. A moment later a monk appeared behind them. He put his hands on their shoulders, whispering something to them. They laughed. He descended the staircase slowly and approached us with deliberate steps that had, at the same time, a gentle spring in them. I felt my heart pounding. Could that be Thar Thar? Of whom I knew so much, and then again almost nothing? He was even taller and more muscular than I had imagined. His hair was closely cropped, his teeth as white as the jasmine blossoms of the day before, a shapely head, full lips, powerful arms reaching out of his monk's robe. I immediately recognized the birthmark under the chin. The scar on the upper arm. The missing finger on the right hand. He welcomed U Ba with a friendly "*Nay kaung gya tha lah*," then turned to me. He offered me his hand and looked me straight in the eye, speaking English with an accent similar to that of an Italian friend of mine: "Welcome to my monastery, Signora. How are you?"

Chapter 4

THAR THAR LAUGHED. Apparently I was not the first visitor to be caught off guard by his greeting. He had a wonderful laugh. A laugh he had no right to, given his past.

The next thing I noticed was his eyes. I had never met anyone with eyes like that. Unusually large, dark brown, focused on me in a calm way, a way that I found pleasant. More than pleasant. In them dwelt such power and intensity that I got goose bumps. He was someone in whose company I would feel at ease without being able to explain why.

My brother would have called it intuition.

Our hands touched. For one moment we stood silent, face-to-face. I had no idea what to say.

"Do you not speak English?" he asked, perplexed.

"No, I do . . . of course."

"What brings you to us?" Thar Thar looked first at U Ba, then at me.

My brother looked at me with a question in his eyes. I hesitated.

"We have come . . ." U Ba began.

"Out of curiosity," I interrupted.

Astonishment in my brother's eyes.

I did not want to tell Thar Thar the truth. Not yet. Maybe because I feared it would mean the end of our journey. Or because I didn't know how he would react. Would he think we were crazy? See me as some kind of medium through which he could quarrel with his mother? Turn away from us, send us packing so that he would not have to be reminded of his past? I really didn't know what was holding me back.

"Did you hear about us in the city?" asked Thar Thar, apparently oblivious to the confusion between my brother and myself.

"Yes, exactly," I quickly confirmed. "That's why we're here."

"Just as I thought. We have . . ."

He was interrupted by my brother's coughing fit. U Ba turned away. Thar Thar regarded him with concern and waited until he had recovered, then carried on: "We have curious tourists visiting us from time to time. They hear of us in Hsipaw. But you are Italian, aren't you?"

I shook my head, surprised. "No, I'm American."

"*Che peccato.*"

I was stumped. "I'm sorry . . ."

"How unfortunate."

For a moment I doubted it was Thar Thar standing there before us. Why should he, who as far as I knew had never gone to school, why should he know two foreign languages? "Do you speak Italian?"

"*Un poco.* A little."

"Where . . . where did you pick that up?"

He was tickled by my growing confusion.

"From an Italian priest. He taught me English, a bit of Italian, and much, much more."

"Where? Here in Burma?"

"Yes. But that is a very long and regrettably also rather uninteresting story that I would not wish to bore you with. I'm sure that you did not come here to hear my life story. I imagine you'll want to see the monastery and meet a few of the children, no?"

U Ba nodded, embarrassed.

"Follow me, then."

Thar Thar led the way and we followed. My brother seemed to be just as irritated as I was.

I kept expecting to hear from the voice. Here we were, face-to-face with her son. Why silence now? Shame? A guilty conscience? What does a mother say to the unloved child she sent to his death, but who beat the odds and survived? Maybe it was enough for her just to see him alive. To see that he was doing well. Would she find her rest here? Without another word? Without asking for forgiveness?

~~~~~

THE GROUNDS WERE more expansive than they initially appeared to be. Behind the monastery was a well with a walled creek, a shed with a stack of chopped wood in front of it, and a soccer field with two cockeyed homemade goals. Beside the field was the bamboo grove. In the distance I could see a couple of people working in a field. A gentle wind brushed the bamboo stalks against one another. Their creaking groans mingled with the bright tinkling of the bells into a singular song.

In the other corner of the monastery stood a grayish-white stupa with a gilded steeple. Large chunks of plaster had broken off. Two novices sat in front of it among dried leaves and branches, weaving baskets. Thar Thar called to them. They put down their work, rose with difficulty, and came over to us. One of them walked with slow, tentative steps, head bowed, as if looking for something. The other walked bent beside him, a large hump in his back. Both were barefoot, their feet and legs riddled with scars and scratches. When they stood before us, they put their hands together and bowed politely. On top of his other difficulties, the younger one had a severe cleft lip, and when the older one lifted his head a shiver ran down my spine. His eyes were milky white. He was blind.

U Ba took my hand.

"This is Ko Aung and Ko Lwin," said Thar Thar. "No one can weave baskets like they can. I used to have clever hands of my own, but I was a klutz by comparison."

They whispered something in chorus that sounded remotely like "How are you?"

"I instruct them in school subjects every other day," Thar Thar explained with a hint of pride in his voice. "Including a bit of English."

I answered that I was doing well and that I was happy to be here. Inscrutable smiles crossed their faces; they bowed and went back to their work.

Thar Thar explained that the other novices were in the field and invited us to join him for a cup of tea in the monastery.

We climbed a rickety staircase and entered the main building. I stood frozen in amazement. It was a spacious hall. Across from the entrance a dozen diverse Buddhas stood on a podium. Some of them glinted golden in the light of the electric bulbs; others were made of a dark, almost black stone, and still others of a light-colored stone. There was a reclining Buddha, head propped up on one arm, an erect and also a sitting Buddha, one hand raised in admonition. Another statue had him plump and clownish, like a sumo wrestler laughing himself silly. In vases were red gladioli, jasmine, hibiscus boughs; rose blossoms floated in a bowl. Above the altar hung paper lanterns and a yellow valance with colorful stones stitched onto it. Offerings lay on plates—rice, tiny plastic packets, candies, batteries, pastries. Smoke from incense drifted across it all, mingling its perfume with the fragrance of the fresh flowers. On the wall behind it, two crucifixes caught my attention. On one column there was a gilded poster of the Virgin Mary, and on another column a similar poster of the Magi. I wanted to ask my brother about it, but he was crouched on the wooden floor, coughing and spent.

"I believe your companion is exhausted. I'll make us some fresh tea," said Thar Thar, disappearing into a room at the end of the hall.

I sat down beside U Ba.

"I'm sorry. I need a little rest," he said.

"Did you see the Christian crucifixes?" I whispered.

He nodded. "Surely presents from the Italian priest."

"But why would they be hanging in a Buddhist monastery?"

U Ba shrugged his shoulders and smiled wearily.

Thar Thar returned with a tray, a thermos, and three small cups. He fetched a flat table and a pillow for me.

The tea was hot and bitter.

"I would be grateful for an opportunity to rest, if it's not an imposition," U Ba said softly.

Thar Thar rose immediately, fetched a mat, and draped a blanket over my brother.

"Do you have a hotel in Hsipaw?"

"No," I said.

"You are welcome to stay with us."

Skeptical, I looked around for beds or anything that resembled a place to sleep. "Do you have room for us?"

He laughed again. "Ample. We roll out mats in the evening. If you want your privacy, I can set up a sleeping area in the corner for you. There's a curtain. Sometimes tourists stay overnight. That's where they sleep. We even have two sleeping bags that someone left here for us. I think it would do your companion good."

"He is my brother."

He faltered briefly. "I don't see any resemblance."

"My half brother. I live in New York and am visiting him here."

Thar Thar nodded, accepting my explanation without further questions.

Dusk was falling outside. I heard voices under the building. Rustling. Rattling. Cheerful, rollicking laughter, as only children can produce, I thought.

Soon afterward they came up the stairs. Ko Aung and Ko Lwin I knew already. They were followed by two young men, both hobbling. A girl with a staff that served as a crutch. She was missing a leg. A girl with only one hand. Another girl accompanied by a boy, neither of whom bore any physical injury that I could discern at first glance. All of them greeted me earnestly but warmly and disappeared into the kitchen. Soon enough I could hear the crackle of a roaring fire, the clatter of crockery.

"How many are you altogether?" I asked.

"Thirteen."

"And you are the abbot of the monastery?"

"No. Strictly speaking we are not a Buddhist monastery."

"What then?"

He pondered. "A family. We live together. My twelve children and I. All of them have, how should I say it . . . all of them are different from other children. Ko Aung is blind, Ko Maung deaf. Ko Lwin has a cleft lip and a hunchback. Ko Htoo limps, Soe Soe lost a foot. Moe Moe is missing an arm, Toe Toe has seizures, Ei Ei a rigid leg. Whatever the difficulty, their families could no longer care for them, and the other monasteries in the vicinity would not accept them."

"Why not?" I wondered.

"Many Buddhist monasteries are loath to take in novices with disabilities. The monks believe they have bad karma. Only physically and spiritually unblemished individuals can become monks. That is why these children have come to me."

"And what do you do with them?"

He refilled my tea and regarded me, puzzled. My question seemed not to make sense to him. "What families do: caring for one another, no? I instruct them as well as I can. We grow vegetables, weave baskets, roofs, and walls that we sell. We pray and meditate together. We cook and eat together. Don't you have a family?"

I swallowed and gestured to the sleeping U Ba. "Of course I do. My brother."

"And in America?"

"No one I live with."

"No husband?"

"No."

"No children?"

I took a deep breath.

"None."

"You live utterly alone?"

Not since I was a little girl had anyone looked on me with such pity.

I cleared my throat. "Yes, and I like it that way."

He tilted his head to one side and rocked his upper body slightly without making any reply.

A girl's voice called us to the table.

We sat around the fire on three wooden beams, twelve children, Thar Thar, and I. Each of us got a bowl of rice with some vegetable curry and a fried egg on top. Some of them stole furtive glances at me over the tops of their bowls; others were too hungry to give much thought to me. The curry tasted somewhat bitter, but good. The rice had not been cleaned thoroughly. Now and then I felt a bit of sand or a small stone between my teeth.

A satisfied silence spread throughout the room. The crackle of the fire, the rustling of the bamboo outside.

Only now did I notice that one of the girls trembled as if she had Parkinson's. She raised the spoon to her lips, but before it got halfway there it was empty. She tried again, and again some of her food fell off. She held her hand, but that failed, too, which only aggravated the trembling.

Beside her sat the one-armed Moe Moe. She was clenching

her bowl between her knees. She put it aside, took a spoon, and started to feed her neighbor, who at once felt calmer. Moe Moe and I exchanged looks. She was the only one who did not avert her eyes. With a gesture I indicated that I would help her. She shook her head almost imperceptibly. A smile flashed across her face, and she thanked me with her eyes. Hers was the most beautiful, the saddest smile I have ever seen.

I brought my brother a bowl of rice, but he had no appetite and wanted to go on resting.

We decided to spend the night.

Thar Thar arranged our sleeping area. He swept the floor, dug several mats out of a chest along with several blankets and the two sleeping bags. He spread them out in the corner behind the curtain. He made my bed doubly thick because I, he suspected, was not accustomed to sleeping on a hard floor. He took the bowl with the rose blossoms from the altar and placed it between our mats. They would drive off bad dreams and ensure a sound sleep, he claimed.

The thoughtfulness of this gesture touched me.

I went to my brother and sat down beside him. He smiled, exhausted, took my hand, and fell asleep within minutes.

I went outside and sat on the steps. Darkness had fallen over the yard. Above me stars were twinkling. So many that it took my breath away. From inside I could hear U Ba coughing in his sleep.

After a short while Thar Thar joined me on the steps. I was struck by his broad, powerful feet, which did not seem to match his long, slender fingers. He had brought a candle, tea, and two cups.

"Care for some tea?"

"I'd love some."

"Your brother has a terrible cold," he remarked while pouring for us.

"I hope that's all it is."

"What else would it be?"

I told him about a doctor with sad eyes. About a dark spot on a lung. About medicines that do not heal.

"Are you blaming yourself?"

"Mostly I'm just worried."

"I understand, but it is not necessary. Your brother is not dying yet."

"That's what he says, too. What makes you so sure?" I countered uncertainly. "Are you soothsayers? Astrologers?"

"No. But I recognize his cough. It sounds familiar. Many people here cough that way when the cold weather sets in. And in his eyes, in his face, there is no sign of death."

"You believe you can recognize impending death in a person's eyes?"

"Yes," he said calmly.

"How?" I asked skeptically.

Thar Thar thought about it for a long time, all the while stroking his shaven head slowly with both hands, as if petting himself. "It depends. In some eyes you see the fear of death. A last flicker, very desperate and alone. Life has already drained partially out of others. In them you catch a glimpse of the emptiness to follow. In your brother's eyes is nothing to indicate the approach of death."

"The doctor was not so sure."

"Doctors don't look into your eyes."

I didn't want to talk any more about it, so I asked him again about the Italian priest.

"That really is a long story," he replied.

"No matter. I have time."

"Then you're the first Westerner I've met who does," he laughed.

"Do you know many?"

"What does 'many' mean? We get visitors from time to time. Father Angelo also frequently played host to tourists. They were always in a hurry. Even on holiday."

"Not me," I claimed.

He looked at me, sizing me up. "How long are you staying?"

"We'll see. We have no plans."

"No plans? Things are getting more and more unusual," he said, grimacing. "A few days?"

"Why not?"

"But whoever lives with us has also to pitch in with the daily work."

"Which means . . . ?"

"Cooking. Cleaning. Laundry. Gathering eggs. Feeding chickens."

"Of course. If you tell me how you found your way to the priest."

"Why are you so interested?"

I thought briefly of telling him the truth now. But I was afraid that if I told him now we wouldn't talk about anything else, and I definitely wanted to learn what happened since the time he had walked downstream along the riverbank with Ko Bo Bo in his arms.

Thar Thar was a riddle to me. He was in no way the man I expected to find, even if I would not have been able to say what kind of picture of him I had formed based on the tales of Khin Khin and Maung Tun. I had imagined an embittered soul. A troubled spirit. Raging. Haggard. Suspicious. A sullen man, perhaps deeply depressed, who hated the world.

"It must be an unusual story. I'm curious about it." That was not a lie.

He accepted that answer, refilled our teacups, and sat quietly.

In the silence a rooster crowed. Another answered.

I watched him out of the corner of my eye in the flickering candlelight. He radiated a profound, soothing calm. His features were relaxed. He sat bolt upright, as if meditating.

"I was," he began after a long pause, "how should I say it, I was in distress. I had lost my family and I was searching."

"For what?"

He grinned. "See how little patience you have?"

I had to laugh at myself and nodded as a sign that I had understood.

"In a teahouse," Thar Thar continued, "I heard of Father Angelo and learned that he helped people like me.

He had lived here for a long time. He had come as a missionary back when it was still officially called Burma and the English were in charge. During colonial times many clergymen came from America, England, Spain, and Italy in order to convert us. Some of them spent the rest of their lives here. Father Angelo was one of those. He took me in without my having to plead with him. I kept house for him, cleaned, went to market, cooked, did laundry. In return he gave me a place to stay, and he instructed me. He taught me reading and writing and a bit of arithmetic. Mathematics was not his strong suit. He preferred to teach me English, and sometimes a bit of Italian, too. He was the first person ever to put a proper book in my hands. I learned from him what power words possess. He had a small library in his house. I had a lot of time, and I devoured just about every book I could get my hands on. I know who Robinson Crusoe is."

He savored the astonishment in my face.

"Moby Dick. Oliver Twist. Even Cain and Abel. The good Father and I studied the Old and New Testaments together. I assisted him at burials, baptisms, and weddings. We celebrated Christmas together, and Easter. He held services in an old church, and there was a small but growing Christian congregation in the town. In eight years I never missed a single sermon of his."

"As I see, though, he was never able to convert you."

"What do you mean?"

"The monastery. The Buddhas, your robe . . ."

"Those are superficial. Don't let them fool you. The children who come to me grow up in Buddhist families. They feel safer when the Buddha has an eye on them. You are right, but then not really. Father Angelo did manage to convert me. But not to Christianity."

"Why not?"

"Because I am not a sinner." He smiled at these words.

"What did he convert you to, then?"

Thar Thar hesitated. "That's another story."

"I have time . . ."

He shook his head. "It's not a subject for this evening. I'm not sure I could tell it at all. It's not a story I have ever put into words."

He gave me a look I could not interpret. Was it full of tenderness, or was that just my imagination?

"Why did you leave Father Angelo?"

"He was old and fell ill. I took care of him for almost a year after he had a stroke. One day after his ninetieth birthday his heart ceased to beat. I was sitting on his bed. He took my hand and laid it on his chest. I could feel it beating slower and slower. Eventually it just stopped."

We looked in silence into the dwindling darkness that was gradually surrendering the grounds and the trees and the bushes: above the bamboo the moon was rising and casting its wan light.

I was reminded of the village where Dread sat in the trees making faces and casting abhorrent shadows.

Where hearts turned to stone.

Of a hut with a hole in the roof.

Of shiny black leather boots.

Of a powerful body and a frail body that shivered. Not with arousal.

Of spittle running drop by drop out of a mouth with bloodred teeth.

Of seconds that pass with life and death in the balance.

You keep one.

We'll take the other.

He sat there next to me, beaming at me. How could eyes that had gazed so deeply into the heart of evil, that had seen so many people die, that had seen a man they so loved fall from the top of a tree, how could such eyes shine like that?

What was their secret?

I felt truly as if I had landed on an island. It was not the Isle of the Dead. Nor the Isle of the Lonely.

It was a different island.

An island no one had ever told me about.

Chapter 5

MORNING CAME EARLY. I heard the novices whispering. Laughter at the crack of dawn. Rolling up their mats. Thar Thar's voice, singing. He was leading them in a mantra. The tiny bells on the gables tinkling in a gentle breeze. Hens clucking. The babbling of a brook I had failed to notice the day before.

I stretched. The invigorating sensation of a well-rested body.

My brother was still asleep. He lay on his back, lips parted slightly, cheeks sunken. His nose looking thinner and sharper than usual. A hint of a pause in the rhythm of his breath. I sat up terrified, listening. His wheezing put me at ease.

Don't let U Ba die.

Please, no.

Please, please, no.

I caught myself doing something I had not done since I was a child: I was seeking the aid of a higher power. Back then I would sometimes lie awake in bed asking "Dear God" for help. When my best friend, Ruth, moved to Washington. When my guinea pig lay dying. When my mother holed herself up in her darkened room for nearly a week.

Who should I turn to now? Fate? The stars? The local spirit known as Nats? The Buddha?

My prayer was not directed at anyone in particular. Let anyone answer it who had the power to help me!

After one fervent recitation I listened to the sounds of the morning. Heard the rattling in the kitchen, subdued voices, a crackling fire. After some time I heard the others descending the steps on their way to the fields.

I crawled out of my sleeping bag. It was colder than I had anticipated.

Two girls had stayed behind in the monastery. They lay on their mats covered with old blankets in the middle of the great hall. They looked miserable. One of them was the one-armed Moe Moe. Thar Thar squatted beside her.

"What's wrong with them?" I asked. "They were healthy only yesterday."

"They are feverish with colds," he said.

"Do you have any medicines?" I thought I knew the answer.

He shook his head.

"None at all?"

"Sometimes tourists leave fever and headache pills. But the children cannot tolerate them. They get stomachaches from them. If there's no improvement, we'll fetch a medicine man from Hsipaw. He has herbs and salves that generally help. At least they do no harm, unlike the Chinese pills."

"I could put cold compresses on their calves."

"What does that do?"

"It lowers a fever."

He brought me a bowl of water and a couple of cloths. I dipped them in the water and wrung them out, pulled back the covers and gasped. The girl next to Moe Moe—I think it was Ei Ei—had a rigid leg. It peeked out from under the covers, scrawny and hard as a stick, without muscles, without contours. Would it ease a fever to wrap a crippled leg? Was there any point to cooling only one of them? The two girls raised their heads and gazed at me skeptically. I sensed that the situation was as awkward for them as it was for me.

They shuddered briefly as I lay the cold cloths on their calves, pulled them snug, and wrapped them in towels. When was the last time I had made cold compresses for anyone? Probably Amy, when she had a bad cold a few years back.

I pulled the covers back over the two girls. They shivered a bit. Moe Moe rewarded me with a feverish smile.

THAR THAR WAS waiting for me in the kitchen. He was kneeling in front of the oven, fanning the flames. In one corner stood several bowls, pots, and baskets with potatoes, tomatoes, cauliflower, carrots, and ginger. Beside them hung strands of garlic and dried chili peppers. On a wooden beam were arrayed a handful of cans and bottles containing brown and black liquids.

Breakfast was the same as dinner the evening before but with two eggs on the rice, sunny side up, and strong black tea that left a fuzzy feeling on the roof of one's mouth.

"I keep the cooking mild for the children. Would you care for something spicier?"

"I would."

He picked up a plastic jar of ground chili pepper and sprinkled a teaspoon of it over my curry.

It was a pleasant spiciness that spread immediately throughout my mouth. After the second spoonful my lips were burning, but not so that it hurt.

In the meantime Thar Thar peeled ginger and cut it into thin slices.

When I finished eating he said, "Your choice: sweeping, cooking, or washing?"

"Cooking."

"Good. We can do that together. First we have to gather eggs." He gave me a basket, and we went into the courtyard. The chickens made straight for him and ran clucking about his feet as if they had been waiting for him.

"How many chickens do you have?"

"I don't know. More and more all the time. I've stopped counting."

"Do they have names?" I inquired without thinking.

He turned sharply on his heel. "Who names chickens?"

"Kids," I replied hastily and with embarrassment.

Thar Thar smiled. "Some of them have names, others don't. There are too many of them."

He gave a short whistle, and out of the bushes strolled a dark-brown, slightly ruffled hen. "This is Koko. It all started with her."

He bent down, and the bird hopped onto his outstretched arm. She sat there like a parrot, tipping her head to one side and staring at me the whole time.

I took a step back.

"Don't worry, she doesn't bite," said Thar Thar, putting her back down. "She's very trusting. That's unusual for a chicken."

We collected two dozen eggs from depressions in the ground, piles of leaves, nests of brushwood—Thar Thar knew all of their hiding places.

In the kitchen he gave me a cutting board and a sharp knife, then produced a basket full of tomatoes for me to quarter.

He himself was peeling a mountain of potatoes. His measured movements radiated an almost meditative serenity.

"You know how I live, but I know nothing at all about you," he said suddenly without looking up from his potatoes.

"What would you like to know?" I asked, surprised by the degree to which his interest delighted me.

"Whatever you want to tell me."

"Ask me a question; I'll answer it."

"I can't."

"Why not?"

"It would be very impolite. I can't simply ask questions of a stranger."

"But it would be easier for me," I countered. "If I ask you to do it, it's not impolite." I cast him a sidelong glance. Amy would have called it flirting, I suppose.

Thar Thar answered with a playful laugh. "Okay." He lowered his hands, put the knife down, and thought for a while. Then he said: "What is important to you?"

I nearly cut myself. That was not the kind of question I had been anticipating. I was expecting the usual routine about my career. Where I live, family, age, income. Instead: What was important to me? I thought about how I might answer. My work? Of course. My friendship with Amy? U Ba, of course! My mother? My brother? Both in their own way. Is that what he wanted to know?

Thar Thar sensed that he had embarrassed me. "Forgive me," he said. "You see. I have no practice asking questions. That was a stupid question."

"No, no, not at all," I protested. "It's just not so easy to answer."

"Oh," he said, surprised. "It was the simplest one I could think of."

"It's a rather personal question."

"And one should not ask that kind?"

His guileless candor reminded me of my brother. Both of them were free of malice. How was that possible after all he had been through?

"No, it's all right, but perhaps not so quickly . . ."

"I see. Later?"

"Later!"

"For now, then, I would just like to know"—he was thinking hard about it—"how many rooms your house has."

I wanted to hug him.

"Two. I live in New York City, in Manhattan, to be precise." I looked at him inquiringly.

"I know where Manhattan is," he said. "I read it in a book."

"My apartment is on the thirty-fifth floor," I continued. "It has two rooms, a bath, and an open kitchen where I also eat."

"Like here," he remarked.

I tried to read in Thar Thar's face whether or not he was serious about the comparison. He was looking me straight in the eye, and I was caught off guard by the intensity as our eyes met.

A subtle twitch of his lips suggested that he was probably joking.

"Like here," I confirmed. "Just like here."

He smiled. "I knew it. And what kind of work do you do?"

"I am a lawyer at a high-end firm."

"A lawyer? Really? They don't have a very good reputation here in this country," said Thar Thar.

"Not in ours, either," I said. The allusion went over his head.

"Who do you defend? Robbers? Thieves?"

"No, I don't do criminal defense. I'm a corporate lawyer specializing in intellectual property. Patents. Product piracy. Copyright infringements. That kind of thing. Do you know what I mean?" I wanted confirmation.

He shook his head.

"Product piracy," I said again, enunciating slowly and carefully, hoping that a mere repetition would suffice. I did so want him to understand what I did.

More head shaking. An apologetic expression because he couldn't follow me and was disappointing me.

"How can I explain it? Product piracy is when, for example, you're producing a very expensive handbag, and . . ."

"How expensive?"

"Let's say a thousand dollars . . ."

"There are handbags that cost a thousand dollars?"

"Sure, or much more, even, but that's not the point," I said somewhat impatiently. "It's just an example. So you're making these handbags, and someone comes along and just copies them and sells them for a tenth of the price."

"But that would be good."

"No!"

"Why not?"

"It's totally unacceptable. It's robbery."

"I see. So they are stealing the handbags and reselling them?"

"No!" I said. "Just the idea. They are stealing *intellectual* property. Which is just as bad. Companies have to protect themselves against it. That's what they need lawyers for. In

China, for instance, there's loads of illegal copying. They even knock off entire shops . . ." I faltered. His furrowed brow betrayed his utter lack of comprehension.

"It would be as if someone took . . ." I was looking for a practical example, a counterpart from his own world. I gazed around the kitchen to see if I could find something suitable. My eye wandered from the open fire to the sooty kettle to Thar Thar's threadbare robe. The longer I thought about it, the more ridiculous I found myself. "Forget it," I said in the end. "It's not so important."

"Of course it is," Thar Thar contradicted me. "Tell me more. If the pirates are important to you, then they are important. It's that simple."

"I don't really care that much about them," I replied, almost crossly.

"You cared about them a minute ago."

"I thought I cared about them a minute ago."

He rocked his upper body back and forth in silence, his left hand stroking his right hand all the while.

What was important to me?

A simple question, Thar Thar was right. Very broad, but I should not have found it difficult to answer. In New York I could have answered it without a moment's hesitation. Why was it stumping me now?

Something had happened to me without my noticing. Is it true that we can count the moments in which something really happens in our lives? Do we notice it right away, or only in hindsight?

One of my brother's coughing spells interrupted my thoughts. I rose and hastened to his side.

He stirred from his sleep and gazed at me bleary-eyed, still somewhat groggy. As if he was not quite sure where he was.

I knelt beside him and stroked his hand. I was comforted by its warmth. "Did you sleep well?"

"Not too badly," he answered softly.

"Are you hungry?"

"No, only thirsty."

Thar Thar brought a cup of tea and a wooden bowl containing the dregs of a glistening ointment that smelled strongly of eucalyptus. "I found a bit of salve from our medicine man. You should rub it into his chest and back. It will help him."

U Ba straightened up and slurped at the hot tea.

I hesitated a brief moment.

"Shall I do it?" asked Thar Thar.

"No, thank you," I replied, surprised that he had immediately sensed my uncertainty.

Thar Thar removed himself discretely. I crouched behind U Ba, pushed his shirt up, dipped two fingers in the ointment, and spread it with circular motions between his shoulders. His skin was warm and soft, much softer than I had expected. Almost like a child's. His back was speckled with tiny liver spots, the kind I remembered my father having. The kind I found on myself in the mirror.

When I was done, he lay back down and I applied the salve to his chest. He closed his eyes and breathed peacefully. I could feel his heart beating beneath my hand. Slowly and evenly.

The fragility of bliss.

I wondered what my father would have likened the sound to. Drops from a leaky faucet? The ticking of a wall clock? Strings plucked on a violin?

"Are you sure you don't want anything to eat?"

I fetched water from the kitchen, but by the time I returned my brother had fallen asleep again.

THAR THAR HAD peeled all the potatoes and put the rice on when he turned to help me with the tomatoes. I had never seen anyone cut vegetables so deftly.

"Tell me about your brother and yourself," he asked. "Why does he live here and you in New York?"

"It's a long and complicated story."

"You have said that you're in no hurry."

"We have the same father. He's from Kalaw. When he was a young man, before U Ba was even born, a rich relative brought him to Rangoon. Later that same relative sent him to college in the United States. That's where he met my mother. They married, and he became a successful lawyer."

"Is he still alive?"

"No. He returned to Kalaw decades later and died there."

"He wanted to see his son again?"

"No. He did not even know he existed."

"Are you certain?"

"Quite," I said. "How could he have known about his son? My brother lived with his mother, and they had no contact."

"Is she still alive?"

"No. They died together one day after my father's return. They hadn't seen each other for fifty years."

"How beautiful!"

"What's beautiful about it?"

"The fact that they got to see each other again. The fact that they did not die alone. Is it for her sake that he returned to Kalaw?"

"I think so. She was deathly ill. He must have sensed it."

We said nothing for a while.

I felt a gnawing jealousy rising in me. Not of Mi Mi, but of the love between her and my father.

Jealousy and loneliness.

Would anyone ever love me that way?

Would I be able to stand it?

Would I recognize it when I encountered it?

U Ba had once told me that "we acknowledge as love primarily those things that correspond to our own image thereof. We wish to be loved as we ourselves would love. Any other way makes us uncomfortable."

Was he right? And if so, what did it mean? What manner of love would I recognize? What way did I love? Was it possible that even at thirty-eight I was still unable to answer that question?

Thar Thar must have felt my growing sorrow. He reached out and stroked my cheek tenderly. I took hold of his hand and held it tightly for a moment, letting my head rest in it for a few precious seconds.

Without any preamble I said: "My father could hear heartbeats."

I knew he would believe every word I said.

I told him of a small boy whose father died young, whose mother left him, and who toughed it out for seven days and nights sitting on a tree stump, eating nothing and drinking nothing so that he would not miss his mother's return.

A boy who nearly died, because hope alone cannot keep someone alive indefinitely.

I told of a young woman who learned that we do not see with our eyes, that we do not travel with our feet.

I told of butterflies identifiable by the beat of their wings.

Of a love that brings sight to the blind.

A love stronger than fear.

A love that causes us to flourish, and that knows no bounds.

He followed my tale intently. When it was over he gazed at me for a while, then asked: "Can you also hear heartbeats?"

I shook my head.

"Are you sure?"

"Completely."

He pondered. "Your brother?"

"No."

"Too bad." Thar Thar looked at me, deep in thought. "I once knew someone who could tune a heart."

"Tune a heart?" I asked, wondering if I had understood him correctly.

"Yes, like an instrument. If a heart was out of tune, he would retune it."

"Any heart?"

"Not just any heart."

"How can a heart be out of tune?"

Thar Thar cocked his head to the side and smirked. "The daughter of a heart listener really ought to know that."

Was he making fun of me?

"Alas, there are many ways. Have you never heard of irregular heartbeats, rapid heartbeats, premature heartbeats? If life has made you mean, or if disappointments have made you as bitter as a slice of tamarind, your heart beats too deeply. If you are afraid, it starts to flutter like a young bird. If you are sad, it beats so slowly that a person might expect it to stop completely any minute. If your spirit is overwhelmed by confusion, it beats most irregularly. Is it different in America?"

"No. But when we have arrhythmia we go to a cardiologist."

"That's a different matter. They are mechanics of the heart. They have nothing to do with tuning a heart."

"Who does, then?"

Thar Thar cleared his throat, stuck the knife into the cutting board, and fell silent. A shadow swept across his face.

"How does one tune a heart?" I asked quietly.

He did not answer.

"Does it require a special gift?"

He looked past me. His lower lip began to quiver.

Where was his wonderful laugh? The one he had no right to, given the life he had led.

"What does it take to be a heart tuner? Who can do it? A magician? An astrologer?"

He shook his head. Without a word.

He rose, turned, and went into the hall. Shortly thereafter I heard him conversing with the chickens in the farmyard.

What was all the fuss about heart tuning? Who was the heart tuner he had known? Ko Bo Bo? Father Angelo? Why did his face darken at the memory of him?

I cut up the rest of the tomatoes, then sliced dozens of carrots and waited for his return. In vain.

When I was finished, I noticed him through the kitchen window sitting in front of the shed chopping kindling.

THAR THAR DID not return until he came back with the others later that afternoon. He asked me, as if nothing had happened, whether I would be willing to teach the children a few sentences of English. I would surely be more capable than he, and having a real American for a teacher would be an extra incentive for them, he suggested.

Before long the twelve of them were sitting in three rows of four on the floorboards in the middle of the hall. I folded my cushion in two in order to sit up higher and perched my-self in front of them. Thar Thar stood beside me and said a few words to them in Burmese. His pupils nodded, a ner-vous smile flitting across many a face, then he sat down in the last row. A dozen pairs of eyes gazed at me expectantly.

I said nothing.

What moments earlier had seemed so simple, chatting a bit with them in my native language and teaching them a few useful phrases, seemed suddenly to be an impossi-bility. An arrogance. An excessive burden. English lessons without pencil and paper. Without a blackboard. Without books. Without a lesson plan. The curiosity in their faces. What did they expect from me? What could I give them?

They waited patiently.

The silence was troubling to me, but not to them.

I looked from one to the other. Moe Moe, who despite her fever was sitting in the first row. Beside her Ei Ei, her stiff leg stretched out toward me. The deaf Ko Maung focused on my lips as if all the secrets of the world rested on them. Behind him Ko Lwin, sitting up straight in spite of his hunched back, the quivering Toe Toe nuzzled up right next to him.

At that moment it dawned on me why I felt so nervous; it was their eyes. They had seen more than mine. They had endured miseries that I knew only from hearsay. If at all. Their souls were wiser than mine. They were not expecting anything from me. I had no need to prove myself. To ac-complish anything. Whatever I might give them would be enough. They were grateful for the time I was devoting to them, whether it be minutes, hours, or days. They radiated humility and dignity, a modesty that took my breath away.

I swallowed. Cleared my throat. Wrung my hands so that it hurt. Looked down at the floor.

"How are you?" I said softly.

Silence.

"How are you?" I repeated.

"How are you?" came the echo. In unison.

Whispered.

Shouted.

Murmured.

Mumbled.

I had never heard such an array of variations on that sentence. Each voice put a different face on it. The sincerity with which they pronounced it. The meaning with which they imbued it. Out of their mouths, in this half-collapsing monastery, it lost its how-are-you-I'm-just-fine-how-about-yourself ring.

"How are you?" I said, emphasizing each word carefully.

"How are you?" they repeated. Enthusiastically, loudly, clearly.

I smiled, relieved. They smiled back.

"My name is Julia. What is your name?" I asked, looking at Moe Moe. I saw the gears turning in her feverish head. Searching her memory to see whether the question rang a bell. Carefully considering the possible meanings of each word, weighing them against one another, making decisions. Gathering courage. She moved her lips with the same deliberation as hands caressing a newborn.

"My name is Moe Moe," she sang.

"Very good!" I cried.

The pride in her eyes.

"What is your name?" My eyes turned to Ko Lwin.

His gears were turning, too. He bit his lower lip, furrowed his brow. His thoughts were running in circles. My words were opaque to him.

"My name is Julia. What is your name?" I said again, only deepening the mystery for him.

He took his time, and I was in no hurry. The others waited patiently.

"I am very fine," he said so quietly and imperfectly that I could barely understand him.

Moe Moe turned around and whispered something to him. A flicker in his eyes. The courage for a second attempt.

"My . . . name . . . is . . . Ko . . . Lwin?" he ventured cautiously, as if his life depended on it.

I nodded. "Good. Very, very good!"

The delight they all took in his accomplishment.

I asked them their names. How they were doing. Where they were from.

Thar Thar smiled at me from the back row.

Whether I liked it or not, that smile made my heart pound. Harder than I had felt it pound for a very long time.

AS I LAY in bed I thought about Amy. Heart tuning. She would like that. She would probably dedicate a whole series of paintings to it. *Heart Tuning I. Heart Tuning II.* Or *The Art of Tuning Hearts. The Heart Tuner. A Heart Out of Tune.* I imagined red canvasses. With circles. Black notes in the middle. Or a white paper with a red circle, lines above it suggesting a tuning fork.

Or was I wrong? Amy always said there were themes one could neither paint nor put into words. Themes so vast that only composers could even approach them. If at all. All other artists must practice humility before them.

With these thoughts in mind I drifted off to sleep.

In the night I awoke to the sound of dull blows. As if someone were pounding posts into the ground with a sledgehammer. They made their way to me from a considerable distance, had their own particular rhythm, sounding sometimes lighter, sometimes darker. I listened briefly but was too tired to pay them much heed, and after a few minutes I fell back asleep.

Chapter 6

THE NEXT DAY Thar Thar asked me to help them in the field. It was time to harvest the ginger, carrots, and potatoes. The more hands the better.

We marched off together bright and early in the morning, right after breakfast, laden with baskets, trowels, rakes, cultivators. The sun was still hidden behind the mountains. It was chilly. A thin layer of frost covered the grasses and leaves. The air was clear and fresh, the sky deep blue and cloudless. A cuckoo called.

"You should make a wish," said Thar Thar, who was walking behind me.

"Why so?"

"It's a custom of ours. If you hear the first call of the cuckoo in the morning, then you can make one wish."

"Will it come true?"

"Only if you run into two potatoes that have grown together during the harvest."

"You believe in these signs?" I asked, surprised.

"Doesn't everyone? In their own way?"

THE FIELDS BEYOND the bamboo grove extended farther than I had suspected. Some of them had been freshly turned over; in others various vegetables were growing. The potato stems had already partly withered. Moe Moe, who was feeling better, showed me how to harvest.

"You see?" she said, grasping a cluster of leaves with her one arm, then pulling it out, stalks and all. Potatoes hung from the bottoms of the stalks. She knelt on the ground.

"You see?" She blinked at me proudly and started to dig in the earth for more tubers.

It must have rained heavily a few days earlier. The ground was still soft and wet. With both hands I rooted in the furrows. Moe Moe took the potatoes and set them in a basket.

Together we had quickly found more than two dozen. We scooted along, pulling the next plants out. I dug and she gathered. After a couple of yards we were a well-oiled machine.

She looked at my dark black hands and arms, muddy to the elbows. "How are you?" she asked.

"I am fine, just fine," I answered.

"You are fine?" asked Moe Moe, and I could see how difficult she was finding it to keep a straight face.

"Yes, I am fine," I said. I couldn't help laughing. Moe Moe joined in, and we laughed until we cried.

The sun rose above the peaks, and soon it was warm. Sweat ran down the back of my neck. I was the only one without any kind of hat. When Moe Moe saw how profusely I was sweating she took her straw hat and set it on my head. I wanted to give it back to her. Her eyes implored me not even to try.

My brother would have said that she was grateful to be able to do me a favor.

The pleasure of giving.

When our basket was full, I was ready to haul it back to the monastery. It was so heavy that I couldn't carry it more than a few yards on my own.

"Heavy," I said, setting it down with a snort.

"Heavy," Moe Moe repeated, paying careful attention to each sound. "Very heavy?" Her inquiring face.

"Very heavy!" I confirmed.

"Need help?"

"Yes, I do need help."

Her eyes beamed. I realized that every word was not just a new vocabulary item for her; it was a gift, precious and unique. Something to be tended and preserved. That's why we would so often see her repeating words. Something that helped her to open a new door or window, to unlock a strange world for her, to communicate with me.

We each took hold of a handle and lugged the basket together through the bamboo grove.

That afternoon, during the English lesson, every bone in my body was aching from the unaccustomed work. It was a good feeling to have my body announcing itself to me in such a pleasant way.

By evening I was so tired that my eyes were falling shut already at dinner.

So passed the time. In the morning we worked in the field. In the late morning Thar Thar and I would return with one of the girls to the monastery. We spent nearly every minute there together. He helped me when I tended to my brother; we cooked and did the laundry together. When, as if by chance, we happened to touch, in the kitchen or at the well, it meant more to me than I cared to admit. I saw in his eyes that he felt the same way.

In the afternoon we taught our lessons, which now primarily consisted of my English instruction. I looked forward to it all day long, especially Moe Moe, whose contagious thirst for knowledge was gradually affecting everyone. Thar Thar always sat in the back row. His presence uplifted me.

We both tried to stay close, but still we could not find a quiet moment for conversations such as we had enjoyed during the first two days. Sometimes I even had the feeling that he was avoiding them. When I would sit on the steps after dinner, he would join me, but always with Moe Moe or Ei Ei or both in tow. Although I would have preferred to be alone with him, I was not disappointed. When the time came, I would have another chance to spend time with him. I had no doubt.

I felt better in the monastery than I had for a long time, in spite of the physical strain, in spite of having a wooden crate for a toilet, in spite of the absence of a shower. I slept well. Had neither backaches nor headaches. At times I was filled with a lightness that I had not felt in years. Amy would probably have described me as "deeply relaxed."

Moe Moe brought hot tea and a fresh hibiscus blossom to my bedstead every morning. Later she would tuck the blossom into my hair. Once I carelessly mentioned to Thar Thar that in New York I preferred coffee to tea. The next morning she appeared with hot water and a packet of instant coffee that, as I later learned, she had fetched from Hsipaw especially for me. Her breathless "You are very welcome" and the attendant smile, the loveliest, the saddest I had ever seen, accompanied me throughout the day.

U Ba, too, was slowly recovering. I was applying ointment twice a day, checking the mucus from his cough mornings and evenings without finding even a trace of blood. He experienced pain neither in his chest nor under his arms.

Thar Thar claimed that the coughing was not only less frequent, but now had a different quality, and that it was a good sign. I could not hear any difference.

Those first few days my brother had done little but sleep. Now he was recovering his strength, getting out of bed, and making an effort to help us. We fed the chickens together, gathered eggs, swept the house, cleaned and chopped vegetables. Only when doing laundry did he tire quickly.

I wanted to show him the fields from which I was always returning with overflowing baskets and muddy hands. We walked through the bamboo grove. He was still shuffling a bit. He would take my arm, and I would hold him fast.

We came to the end of the grove, before us a hilly landscape and the cultivated fields.

"How long have we actually been here?" he asked suddenly.

"No idea. A week? Ten days?" Normally I had a keen sense of time.

U Ba rested his head on my shoulder for a moment.

"It's beautiful here," he said.

"Very," I agreed.

"Who would ever want to leave?"

I wasn't sure what he was getting at, and I didn't react.

"How much longer are you thinking of staying?" my brother wanted to know, gazing at the field.

I had been dreading that question. I had been avoiding it for days because I didn't have an answer to it.

"I don't know. What do you think?"

U Ba looked askance at me. "It's up to you."

"Why?"

"I have no office to return to. No one is waiting for me. As far as I'm concerned we could stay another week. Or two. Or three . . ."

"How long we stay," I said quietly, "depends on what we are looking for here."

He nodded.

Another question I had no answer to. The voice had withdrawn, just as the old monk in New York had foretold. I did not expect to hear anything more from her now that we had found Thar Thar. So what was keeping me here? I didn't want to think about it. I wanted to harvest potatoes and ginger with Moe Moe, wash vegetables, teach English.

I wanted to learn from Thar Thar the secret of the heart tuner.

"Don't you want to return to America at some point?"

"Of course," I answered. "But there's no hurry."

I had arranged with Mulligan for an unlimited unpaid leave. Two or three weeks one way or the other did not matter. My visa was good for four weeks, but I had read online and in several travel guides that overstaying one's visa would not cause difficulties at departure time, aside from a modest fine at the airport.

Who or what was waiting for me?

Amy. Anyone else?

"What is your intuition telling you?" my brother asked.

I gave his arm a little squeeze. "No idea. I've told you that mine doesn't always work so well." After a brief pause I bounced the question back to him: "And yours?"

"That we will leave soon," he said gravely.

"Why?"

"Because I fear that we will otherwise bring unrest to this place."

"What do you mean by that?" I asked, astonished. "What kind of unrest?"

"I find it difficult to put into words. That's how it is with intuition."

"You're being evasive."

"Perhaps."

"What kind of unrest?" I insisted. "I have the feeling that everyone is happy to have us here. But maybe I'm missing something. Am I misreading their cues? Is their laughter when they see me not an expression of happiness, but of uncertainty? Discomfort? Are they afraid of me?" I made no effort to disguise my disappointment.

"No, no. You haven't misunderstood anything. It's only . . ." He paused, started again, sighed deeply. "I mean . . . that is to say . . . we're not going to move into the monastery, are we?"

"No, of course not."

"And our departure will only become more difficult the longer we stay."

"You think it will make me too sad . . ."

"Not only you," he interrupted me.

IN THE MIDDLE of the night I was woken by a steady, rhythmic scratching or brushing. As if someone was sweeping the courtyard in the dark. I listened intently. My brother's breath. Nearby sleepers. The sound receded slowly, gradually trailing off until it ceased. A short while later I heard again the dull, forceful blows of the previous nights, accompanied by groans of strain and the splitting of wood.

My watch showed 3:32. I rose and crept into the hall. Thar Thar's sleeping mat was empty.

Outside, the moon bathed everything in a cold white light. The bamboo cast a dancing shadow on the clean-swept

courtyard. Thar Thar stood in front of the shed, swing-
ing an ax, lighting with brutal force into the end of a log.
The blade drove itself into the wood. He spread his legs,
heaved it high above his shoulders, struggled with it above
his head, and then let the ax and the log speed down onto
a second, larger log, so that the smaller log burst into two
pieces under its own weight.

I pulled a jacket around me and went outside.

It was a curious sight: a monk, barefoot, chopping wood
in a reddish-brown robe that he had tied above his knees.
Thar Thar was so engrossed in his work that he didn't notice me approaching. To the left and right of him were big
piles of freshly chopped logs.

"What are you doing?"

"I'm chopping wood," he answered without turning.

"I can see that. Do you know how late it is?"

"No. Does that matter?"

"Why don't you do it by day?"

The ax fell with such force into the next log that the
ground vibrated beneath me.

I was startled by the expression on Thar Thar's face.
Sweat drenched his brow, running down his cheeks and
neck. His lovely eyes were small and narrow, his full lips
pressed thin. He was out of breath. In the pale light of the
moon he looked older. Wearier than by day. Lonelier.

"I had a bad dream. It happens sometimes. Chopping
wood helps."

"Helps against what?"

"Against bad dreams. Evil spirits. Memories," he said, wheezing.

"What kind of memories?"

Thar Thar paused, ax over his head, and looked at me for the first time.

"You wouldn't want to know."

"And what if I did?"

He hesitated, turned away, and chopped again with full force.

"And what if I did?" I repeated. Loudly and provocatively.

He ignored me.

Crash. Splinters flew through the air. Part of a log landed right at my feet. I took one step toward Thar Thar. And then another. If the wood were to split again as it just had, it would injure me. This might be the moment, I thought. Perhaps this moonlit night was the right moment to tell him what I knew. What the true purpose of my journey was.

I thought about Nu Nu.

About fists pounding a belly.

About offerings for an infant death.

I saw the blade sail through the air and pictured it falling on a chicken held in the hands of a child.

Thar Thar struck the ax lightly into the stump and turned to me.

"What do you want?" he asked, out of breath.

"To talk to you."

"About what?"

"Bad dreams. Memories."

"Why?"

"Because I have to tell you something."

He wiped the sweat from his face, leaned with both hands on the haft of his ax, and looked at me in silence. With eyes on which the past had left its mark.

"I'm not a run-of-the-mill tourist."

"I know."

"How?" I asked, surprised. Had U Ba told him something after all?

"Intuition."

"Do you also know why I have come?"

"No. And I'm not at all sure that I want to know."

"Why not?"

"It's been years since I've had nightmares like the ones I've had these past few nights."

"And you think it has to do with me?"

"Yes."

"What makes you think that?"

"Because something emanates from you that makes me uneasy."

"It might not be me that's making you uneasy," I said.

"Then who?"

And so I began my story.

Of a voice that would give no rest. And of a young woman who suddenly and unexpectedly stood up. Because something inside her was talking back.

Of a mother whose heart was not big enough. But it was the only one she had.

Of an old woman who could not keep a grim tale to herself.

You keep one.

We'll take the other.

When I was done I collapsed exhausted onto a tree stump. My whole body was shaking.

An eerie stillness surrounded us. The wind had died down. Even the insects had broken off their chorus. I heard Thar Thar's heavy breathing.

"Do you think I'm crazy now?" I asked warily.

Thar Thar sat down on a stump across from me. Our knees were touching. He shook his head.

I could see tears running down his cheeks, and I took his hands. They were ice cold. I rose and put my arms around him. Pressed his head to my belly. He burrowed into my arms, into my jacket. Into me. His faint sobbing.

Should I not have told him everything?

I pictured Nu Nu, Maung Sein, Ko Gyi, and Thar Thar and thought that some families just have no luck. Or very little. And how long the shadow of misfortune can be. Families in which everyone gives as much love as they can, but still it isn't enough. Where everyone shares as much as they are able, but still hearts go hungry. No one to blame. No malicious intentions. Where injuries occur that cannot be healed within a single lifetime.

The place where it all begins. Love. Longing for love. Fear of love.

The place we can never be rid of. Where hearts are too big or too little. Too greedy or too satisfied.

Where we are defenseless and vulnerable like nowhere else.

Because love knows no justice. Not even a mother's love. Or a father's.

I pictured a straw hut to myself and a building on Sixty-fourth Street on Manhattan's Upper East Side, and I felt grief seize and shake me as if it were a hunting dog and I the long-sought quarry.

I tried with all my might to suppress my tears. I did not want to cry, but my own grief grew with every second I fought the tears.

I don't know how long we sat there. Gradually Thar Thar's breathing settled. I kissed him on the head. He looked up at me. With eyes on which the past had left its mark, but where again a spark shone. In spite of it all. I took his face in my hands and kissed him on the brow.

Once. Twice.

I caressed him. His mouth, his lips. I kissed his cheeks and nose, as if I could drive away my own sorrows with these kisses.

"Is my mother talking to you now?" he whispered.

"No."

"Is she telling you to kiss me?"

"No. No. No."

Sometimes we bond in joy. We become one in our happiness: for a few precious seconds we become one, because one person alone simply cannot bear the intensity of the moment.

And other times we bond in grief. We become one in our pain: for a few precious seconds we become one, because one person alone simply cannot bear the intensity of the moment.

THAR THAR AND I had holed up in the shed. I lay in his arms. An unfamiliar, but not unpleasant scent filled my nostrils. My body was still quivering. His, too.

Two hearts beating fiercely, unable to settle.

I felt hot in spite of the cool night air. He tenderly pushed my sweaty hair out of my face.

A soft smile.

"When did you last hear the voice?" he asked quietly.

"In Kalaw," I answered, pondering. "What would you do if she were to pipe up now? Would you want to talk to her?"

Thar Thar took a long while to answer.

"No," he said at last. "No, I wouldn't."

"Not now?"

"Not at all."

"You have no questions for your mother?" I wondered.

"Not anymore."

"After all that has happened?"

"No."

"Why not?"

"That time is past."

"Do you hate your mother?"

"No."

I thought about his answer and kissed the tip of his nose. "Would you at least want to know why she . . . ?"

"Not anymore," he interrupted me. "If you had asked me in the camp that would have been a different story."

He propped himself up on one elbow. "I was consumed by hatred back then. I was so angry, so bitter, that if you could have licked my heart, you would have poisoned yourself. We were all prisoners in the camp. Even the soldiers and officers. All of us. Except one."

Thar Thar eyed me keenly as if to see whether I could follow him.

"Except one?"

"We were prisoners of our hatred," he continued without addressing my question. "Prisoners of our desperation. Our embitterment. Our sorrow.

"We would have remained prisoners even if they had set us free. Anyone who has been in a camp carries that camp around inside himself for the rest of his life. Anyone who has been the victim of violence carries that violence inside himself. Anyone who has been betrayed carries that betrayal inside himself. How often I quarreled with my mother! Cursed her. Asked her why she kept Ko Gyi and not me. What I had done to her to deserve her coldness already as a child. I wanted answers to questions that have no answer. I would march through the jungle, hoping finally to tread on a mine. To be torn into a thousand pieces. I had no desire to spend the rest of my life in the dungeon of my rage and embitterment. It is a cold, dark, and dreadfully lonely place. Death was the only way out. At least that was what I thought until someone showed me the light.

"In a dream I would often see my brother and mother standing before me. So close that I could feel their breath on my skin. Suddenly they turn and leave. Hand in hand. Without a word. I try to run after them but cannot move. I want to cry out to them to wait for me, but cannot make a sound. They walk along a road, getting smaller and smaller. I want so desperately to follow them, but I am crippled. I think I'm about to die. It's terrible. Then a soldier steps up to me and strikes me in the face with the butt of his rifle. That always woke me up. All of my thoughts and feelings revolved inexorably around the same questions: What had I done to deserve this misery? Why was I cast aside?"

He lay back, arms folded behind his head, staring at the ceiling of the shed. I watched him for a while, traced his lips gently with my fingers.

"And that faded away with time?" I asked in a low voice.

"No, not with time."

"How, then?"

Thar Thar said nothing.

"Today you are no longer a prisoner?" I insisted.

"No. Do I seem like one?"

"Not in the least. How did you free yourself?"

"I resolved to love."

"Is that something you can just up and decide?" I asked skeptically.

"Not just like that."

"Is it up to you at all?"

"No, apparently not," he replied thoughtfully, turning to me. His eyes gleamed as they had those first few days. I wrapped one leg around his hips and pressed him closer to me. "You are right. Let's just say that Love came to me. One day she was standing at the door asking to come in. She had traveled a long way, and I did not refuse her. I felt certain she would not make the effort a second time."

"What does love have to do with your imprisonment?"

"To forgive, one must love and be loved. Only those who forgive can be free. Whoever forgives is a prisoner no more."

Chapter 7

HE HAD TOUCHED me. Where I was most sensitive. He had penetrated into me. Not only physically. Some part of him would remain in me.

The next morning I found a cup of lukewarm tea beside my bed. Beside it a large bouquet of red hibiscus awaited me, and a wreath of jasmine exuding its wonderful fragrance. My brother's sleeping bag was empty. I had overslept.

In the hall, too, the mats had been cleared. Everyone but Thar Thar and U Ba was already working in the field. The two of them sat at the top of the staircase in front of the house, drinking tea. My heart pounded at the sight.

Thar Thar rose the moment he saw me. He greeted me with a shy, bashful look. For a moment we stood there mute, embarrassed like two teenagers.

"Thank you for the flowers," I whispered. "It's very sweet of you."

Him beaming. How I envied him those eyes.

"Good morning, Julia," said my brother. "Did you have a good night?"

I searched his expression for any trace of a double entendre. But it seemed that he was utterly incapable of anything like that.

"Lovely," I answered, smiling furtively at Thar Thar. "Very, very lovely."

Thar Thar could hardly stand still for embarrassment. "Why didn't Moe Moe wake me?"

"We had the feeling that you needed the sleep," said U Ba.

"I'll get you a cup and something to eat," said Thar Thar, hurrying into the house.

With a wave of his hand U Ba invited me to sit down beside him. He was watching me almost as intently as on that day in the teahouse in Kalaw where we first set eyes on each other.

"Is something wrong?" I asked hesitantly.

"You look"—he tilted his head to one side, apparently searching for the right words—"somehow different this morning."

"In what way?"

"Enchanting. Enchanted. More beautiful than usual!"

"Ah, my sweet brother," I sighed, and put a hand on his knee. I longed to embrace him for joy. "I feel just great. It's beautiful here."

Thar Thar returned with a bowl of rice, vegetables, and two eggs. I was so excited that I could hardly eat. We sat in silence on the steps. Chickens cackled in the courtyard. A dog dozed in the shadow of the staircase. It was warm, and it smelled like fresh flowers.

Thar Thar fidgeted with his fingers and breathed unevenly. He wanted to tell me something, but didn't quite dare. At some point U Ba rose and went into the house.

I shot Thar Thar a tender look. "What should we do now? Sweep? Cook? Laundry?"

"Would you care to accompany me on a short hike? We would be back in time for the afternoon English lesson."

"I'd love to. Where are we going?"

"I want to show you something."

WE WALKED ALONG a path that led past brown, newly harvested rice fields, banana plants, palm trees, and bamboo stands. We crossed a narrow valley, balanced our way across a stream, and marched up a wooded hillside. Above us the arch of a deep-blue cloudless sky. We communicated with our eyes and spoke little. Between us was a silence that felt more comfortable with every step.

I wandered in thought back to the night before. I was not sure what to make of what had happened, only that it bore no resemblance to an ephemeral New York affair. Something about this night was different, and I was beginning to sense what it was. He had opened a door in me. He had taken me by the hand and shown me the hiding places of joy. He had relieved me of the fear of my own desire.

I felt an intimacy with him that needed no words. A familiarity that I could not explain. He was a soul mate like no man before him had been.

I felt the desire to take his hand, to stop right where we were, to touch him, to kiss him, but I didn't dare.

Just before the crest of the hill we came to a stupa that had caught my eye even from a distance. The trees had been cleared from a small area around it so that it commanded a broad view of the valley below. There were several little temples and altars on which lay offerings of rice, flowers, and fruits. Devotees had placed dozens of Buddha figures in the recesses of the masonry.

The top of the pagoda was gilded. A few tiny bells tinkled in the wind. The side facing the valley was painted white, but the backside was bare stonework split by a large crack. Out of the crevices grasses and various plants had sprouted. In places they had overgrown the stone, and the rear part leaned so drastically that it ought to have fallen in years ago.

Looking at it from the side, it appeared that the laws of gravity had ceased to operate in this place.

"It looks like it could collapse any minute now," I remarked, regarding it skeptically.

"It does make that impression," replied Thar Thar. "Legend has it that this stupa was destroyed by earthquakes many times over the centuries, and that it was always rebuilt. Some decades ago a new quake left it in the damaged condition you now observe. Since then people have believed it would fall in, but apparently there is some force fending off collapse. That's what all the altars are about. People come here and leave an offering in the hope that this power, this spirit, will also protect them."

He pulled a thermos out of a bag and poured hot water into the cap, dug out a packet of instant coffee and a packet of crackers. He took out one of the crackers and set it in front of an altar. Then he pressed his palms together in front of his chest, closed his eyes, and bowed.

"What did you pray for?" I asked.

"I didn't pray for anything. We merely had a brief conversation."

"Who?"

"The spirit of the stupa and I."

"What about?"

"About the fragility of joy. How it is impossible to preserve it. And crackers. He loves crackers."

"Where did you get those?"

"I was in Hsipaw earlier this morning," he said in a way that suggested it had not been pleasant for him.

We sat down in the shadow of the stupa. It was quiet. A gentle rustling of leaves was the only sound. "Tell me about yourself," he asked.

"Again? About my important battle against patent infringement?" Thar Thar ignored my self-mockery. Smiling, he said, "Whatever is important to you . . ."

I reflected and took a sip of coffee. Looked down into the valley and at some point started my tale: of a young woman who set out on a quest.

Who thought she might be going crazy. Even though madness did not run in her family. Not that kind.

Who had forgotten how fragile love was. How precious. How much light it needs. How much trust. How dark it got when Deceit spread her wings.

Who had forgotten what love thrives on. How much attention it requires.

Who had in recent days rediscovered these things, and who was very grateful for that.

Thar Thar listened attentively. At times I wished he would embrace me or at least touch my hand, but he did not move.

When I was done, I looked at him. Uncertain and with a galloping heart.

I stood up and faced him, took his head in my hands. "Thar Thar." His expression set my whole body aquiver. "I . . ."

He put a finger to my lips, stood up, and kissed me like I had never been kissed before. Why did I have to be thirty-eight before being able to lose myself in a kiss that way?

"Tell me about the heart tuner you knew."

"That was long ago," he answered, hesitating and sitting back down. "Why do you ask?"

"Because I want to know more about you."

"More still? You know so much. More than I do."

"But I don't know the most important thing: What is your secret?" I crouched down beside him.

"What makes you think I have a secret?"

"Why are you not a troubled spirit?"

"I used to be. Most of my life."

"I know, and now you are one no more. Why not? Who taught you to forgive? Father Angelo?"

He shook his head without a word.

"Ko Bo Bo?" I asked.

His eyes fell. The ghost of a nod.

Had he and Ko Bo Bo been lovers? They had shared some kind of secret, according to Maung Tun. I was too surprised to pursue it. And not only about that plot twist: I felt Jealousy swelling up inside me, quickly casting her deep black shadow.

"What exactly did Maung Tun tell you about him?" Thar Thar wanted suddenly to know.

"Not much. That he was the youngest of the porters. Small and wispy, but very brave." As casually as possible I added: "That you two had been good friends."

Thar Thar swallowed several times. "That's all?"

"Pretty much."

"Did he not speculate about the two of us?"

"Well, he said that you really liked each other," I replied evasively.

"That's all?"

"That's all."

Thar Thar nodded as if he had not expected anything else. "Ko Bo Bo had a secret."

I bit my tongue and waited for him to go on.

"I was by chance in the yard when the truck brought him in. We had just hastily buried three corpses from the

Death House and were on the way back to our huts. Most of the new porters already stood nervously in a circle around the vehicle. Ko Bo Bo had curled up in the farthest corner of the payload and did not want to get out. Only when the soldiers kicked at him did he get up and slowly climb out of the truck, a bundle with his things in his hands. I saw at a glance that he was different from the others. The way he moved. The way he looked at the soldiers. In his expression was the same dreadful fear we all shared, but there was also something else. I took it for pride, or a gratuitous defiance, and it was a long time before I learned what it really was.

"He spent the first few days huddled in the darkest corner of our hut, refusing to eat, or even to say a word. Again and again one of us would sit down with him and try to talk to him, but he kept his mouth shut. I was afraid he was trying to starve himself, and one evening, when he was already asleep, I carried him over to sleep beside me. He was so light. At some point he suddenly clasped my hand and refused to let go. He was awake and wanted to know how long I thought it would take a person to die. A second? An hour? A day? A lifetime? I didn't understand his question, and we fell into a long conversation. I liked his voice, especially when he whispered. It sounded so soft and melodic, almost as if he were singing.

"Ko Bo Bo was not as rough as the rest of us, and we quickly struck up a friendship. At first I felt an obligation to protect him, small and wispy as he was. But our first mission together was so grim, and he was so brave. He saved the life of an infant. Did Maung Tun tell you about that?"

"Yes."

"It was clear to me then that he did not need me to watch over him. At least no more or less than anyone else. We could all have used someone to protect us. From the soldiers. From the rebels. From ourselves. But that's something different; that's not what I mean. Ko Bo Bo could take care of himself. And others.

"I had never in my life known such a kindred spirit. I have since then had a long time to ponder why that was so. I felt good whenever he was nearby. A curious thing to say when you consider our circumstances, but there it was. He brought me peace without need for many words. He gave me joy without cause. Unfounded joy is the most beautiful and most difficult. He gave me the courage to live. His presence, one glance, one smile sufficed, and I knew that I was not alone. It was that simple, that complicated. Does that make sense?"

"Yes," I answered again, although I wasn't really sure it did. I didn't want to interrupt him with a question.

"That was the greatest gift of all. Not to be alone in a place where everyone was thinking only of personal survival. Where they would have beaten you to death if they thought it would buy them one more day. Loneliness is the most severe punishment. We are not built to handle it. I've seen many porters and several soldiers die. Those who had strength to say anything before they died invariably called out for other people. Not for their enemies, but for people who loved them. For their mothers. Their fathers. Their wives. Their children. No one wants to be lonely.

"But Ko Bo Bo had taught me something else. Something more important still."

Thar Thar faltered. I looked at him expectantly.

"What it means to love."

"Were you . . . ?" I didn't dare to finish the sentence.

"That, too." He paused, took a deep breath. "But that's not what I mean. Ko Bo Bo loved someone else besides. His brother. Her brother."

I didn't know what he was talking about.

"Was his brother in the camp, too?"

"Her brother."

"Why *her* brother? Thar Thar, I can't understand a word of it. Help me."

"There was no Ko Bo Bo. That was an invention. Ko Bo Bo's name was Maw Maw, and he was a girl. A young woman."

A catch in my breath. "How . . . how do you know . . . I mean . . ." It took a while before I could form a complete sentence. What was a woman doing in the camp? How had she gotten there? Why had Maung Tun said nothing about it?

Thar Thar said nothing. He fixated on the stupa, tears running down his cheeks, but his face was unmoved.

"I had long suspected he was hiding something from me," he whispered without looking at me. "One day we were washing clothes at the river together. He slipped and fell into the water. Ko Bo Bo was not a strong swimmer. I jumped in after him and pulled him out. For a few seconds we stood there face to face, soaking wet, without a word. His shirt, his longyi, were clinging to his body, her body . . . She might as well have stood there naked . . ."

We sat next to each other, not saying anything while I tried to put my thoughts in order. Thar Thar's eyes were still on the crumbling masonry before us.

"I didn't realize that the military exploited young women as porters, too."

"They don't."

"So how did Ko Bo Bo . . . ?" I asked softly.

"Maw Maw."

". . . Maw Maw end up at the camp?"

"She disguised herself as a boy."

I reached for his hand. "Who would have made her do that?"

"No one."

"She volunteered?"

"Yes."

The more I learned, the less sense it made. What possible reason could a person have to volunteer to go to that hell? Why had she been willing to pay so high a price? For what?

"Thar Thar?"

Still he was not looking at me.

"Why did she do that?"

He ignored my question.

"Why did she disguise herself as a boy?" I asked again.

Thar Thar lifted his head and looked me right in the eye: "Because she loved. And because she understood what that means."

"Who did she love so much? Who did she do it for?"

"For her brother."

"Her brother?" I echoed incredulously. How could a young woman make such a sacrifice for her brother, of all people?

"She had a twin brother. He was ten minutes younger than his big sister. The two of them were apparently inseparable. Right from birth. Their mother told them that as infants they would wail the moment the other one wasn't there, and they wouldn't stop until they lay side by side again. If one of them came down with a fever, it wasn't long before the other one was sick, too. They got their first teeth on the same day. Their second teeth, too. Maw Maw was the first to walk. Her brother took his first steps holding her hand, until they both fell. As children they would never let the other one out of their sight. Sometimes it seemed to their parents as if one soul had been divided into two bodies. They lived in their own world, where they were sufficient unto themselves. When hurt, they did not look to their mother or father for comfort, but to each other. No one in the village had seen anything like it. Everyone called them little barnacles because of the way they clung to each other.

"When the soldiers came, going from house to house and taking all the young men, Maw Maw's parents and brother were working in a field a good distance away. They wouldn't be back before dark. Maw Maw heard the soldiers' voices from afar, and she felt sick with horror. Like everyone else, she knew what would happen, that none of those who were taken would come back alive. She told me she thought her heart had stopped beating out of fear for her brother. Seeing his things hanging on the wall gave her the idea. Maw Maw quickly put them on and pretended to be him. From that moment on, she said, she was very calm. None of the soldiers noticed anything. She went to death for him. Can you fathom it?"

"No." It slipped out quietly. Had I ever loved anyone so dearly that I would have let myself be tortured for him? That I would have sacrificed myself for him?

"I couldn't understand it, either. Not at first. But what did I know about love? Nothing, Julia, nothing at all.

"Maw Maw taught me that a person is capable of anything. Not only of any wickedness. Every sacrifice she made was a small triumph over evil, if you understand what I mean. For me it was as precious as a cup of water to a person dying of thirst. Did Maung Tun tell you what things were like in the camp?"

"Yes."

"It was dreadful. Several of us went mad with fear. Some porters pulled their own hair out, wept incessantly, or banged their heads against the beams until the soldiers came and shot them. A mercy killing they called it. As if we were rabid dogs. Did he tell you that, too?"

"No."

"Maw Maw reminded us with every kick, every blow that she withstood without caving in that there was a power the soldiers could not vanquish.

"When she went hungry because again they had given us no rice, she did it for her brother. When they tortured us and Maw Maw had to stand on one leg in the sun until she fell over, she suffered for his sake. And for ours."

He was quiet for a moment. "She was the bravest person I have ever met. Her sacrifices gave me the courage to live. And through them she brought my heart into tune, a little more day by day, without my realizing it. At some point all of my bitterness had dissipated. My rage and resentment, my anger and my hatred just dried up. Like a brook with no more spring to feed it."

Slowly he turned to me and gently pulled me closer to him. Little beads of sweat dotted his brow and shaven head. I noticed only now that he was shivering, and I put my arms around him. We sat long in silence, side by side, holding each other tightly, as if seeking shelter.

The sun was already low in the sky when he stood up, brushed the hair out of my face, and started to kiss me. On my forehead, my eyes, my lips. He picked me up, I wrapped my legs around his hips, and he carried me behind the stupa.

AND ONCE AGAIN I felt him intensely like no man before him.

Heard his rhythmic breathing. Lost myself in his unfamiliar, exhilarating scent.

Amid flowers and fruits who told their stories silently.

Behind a pagoda that refused to give in to the laws of gravity.

Amid temples and altars inhabited by hope.

As if there was something that could shield us and our happiness. Be it spirits. Or stars.

Chapter 8

THE NEXT MORNING Moe Moe woke me again. For one brief, wonderful moment I imagined I was still lying in Thar Thar's arms. His warm hand on my belly.

Moe Moe knelt down beside me, and I saw right away that something had happened. Hers was not the smile of a cheerful person. She set the tea on the floor and cast her eyes down the moment they met mine. On top of the cup was a note that had been folded many times.

"For you," she said, handing it to me.

"A letter? For me? Are you sure?"

Neither my smile nor my English got any reaction. She merely nodded, rose again, and made her way quickly out. Why the hurry? Had she noticed that Thar Thar and I had slipped out again in the night? What happiness I had found in the shed?

With pounding heart I unfolded the paper. Inside I found a scattering of dried jasmine blossoms.

Dearest Julia,

Never before have I written lines as difficult as these. Never before have I held the pen in quivering hand. Never have words occasioned such pain as the ones I must now set to paper.

Foreboding stole over me of what might follow.

By your watch I can see that it is just after three-thirty. Everyone is asleep, even your brother is snoring gently and evenly without coughing!

My heart, by contrast, beats too strenuously. My whole body is quivering. Sleep is utterly out of the question.

So I have sat down beside you and lit a candle. You are lying next to me, and I can hardly take my eyes off you. I can still feel you on me. Your hands, your lips. Whatever have you done to me? What is this place you have carried me off to? A world that I would never have expected to find within myself. Where I would gladly have lingered forever, even though I suspect that it can never last for more than a few precious seconds. I had not known that I had this power in me. I had not known there was a place where fear has no more power.

Where we are so free.

How incredibly beautiful you are! Your brother is right when he says that. Nor does sleep diminish your

grace in any way. You cannot imagine how much restraint
I must exercise not to lie down with you again right now.
Not to feel again your breath upon my skin. Not to kiss
you. Not to caress you.

It causes me physical pain to sit beside you without
touching you, so great is my desire. My craving to return
with you to that place. Right now. Yet were I to continue
giving in to it, I would soon be unable to leave your side.
For that reason I have decided to depart.

By the time you hold this letter in your hands I will
already be on the road. The sun will not have risen yet
when I set off.

Please forgive me.

These past weeks have brought great joy into my life.
A joy that means more to me than I can put into words.
I had never imagined I would encounter anything like it
again. And I am all the more grateful for knowing how
fragile it is. A fleeting visitor in our hearts. No steadfast
friend. No one we can count on. No joy. Anywhere.

I must leave because I fear that my heart would fall
further and further out of step if we were to spend more
time together.

Because I don't know who would tune it again when
you return to your world.

Were I a different person, I might be able to bear such
a tumult, but I have lived for too long with my heart out
of tune. I have no wish to do so again. I could not bear it
even for one more day.

Not one.

A person, once abandoned, bears that loss forever.

A person never loved bears an unquenchable longing for love.

And a person who has been loved and lost that love bears not only that love, but also the fear of losing it again.

I carry a bit of all of those inside myself.

Together they are a like a poison slowly working their way through my body. Penetrating to the remotest corners of my soul. Seizing control of all my senses. Not killing, but paralyzing.

Not killing, but making me distrustful.

Fostering jealousy. Resentment.

How much loss can one person bear?

How much pain?

How much loneliness?

You did not come alone. You brought your brother with you, and a young boy. You tried to hide him, but I recognized him right away.

A boy who would never have existed, had his mother had her way.

A child's soul knows everything.

Lonelier than anyone should ever be. On his hands the blood of chickens that were so much more than chickens. Years would pass before he could look at them again without revulsion. His own hands!

A child's soul forgets nothing.

But it grows, and it learns. It learns to mistrust. It learns to hate. It learns to defend itself. Or to love and to forgive. You had a young boy with you whom I never expected to encounter again.

When you leave he will stay with me, and I will look after him. I will console him when he is sad. I will protect him when he is fearful. I will be there for him when he is lonely.

You have told me that my father dreamt of a life without attachment. He did not succeed. Nor will I. In that sense, I am a failed Buddhist. So be it.

You have shown me that some part of my soul lives still in captivity and will always do so.

Perhaps this is the moment when I must admit to myself that I am not as free as I thought.

Forgive me that error. Forgive me for this letter, if my behavior causes you pain. Nothing could be further from my intention than to hurt you. Yet I must leave. I see no other way out.

I thank you for everything.

Take good care of yourself.

Thar Thar

The letter caught me completely off guard. I scanned it a second time, bit my lip, and turned away. What a coward! was the first thought that shot through my head. What a miserable coward! How could he leave me sitting here with these lines? Not even give me a chance to respond? Not even to ask once how I was feeling? Whether there might not be some other solution than simply to cut out? I was too hurt to formulate a clear thought. What did he mean by the captivity in which he still lived? What was penning him in? His love for Ko Bo Bo? Why had he not told me about that at once? Was he just trying to get me in the sack?

Forgive me that error. Forgive me for this letter, if my behavior causes you pain. What else did he expect? To amuse me? I could have screamed with rage. Where was he? Did Moe Moe know where he was hiding? Would she reveal it to me? Was there any chance of finding him a second time? Did I even want that?

My brother was awake now and sitting up. He drank a sip of water and looked at me over the rim of the cup.

I felt myself starting to cry.

"Did you know what he was planning to do?" I asked, and was startled by my own brusque tone.

"Who?"

"Thar Thar, of course. Who else?" I barked at him.

U Ba shook his head slowly, keeping an eye on me the whole time.

"Did you suspect it? Be honest."

"No. He told me nothing. What's wrong with him?"

I shrugged helplessly and thrust the letter at him.

He read it carefully, shaking his head slightly now and then as if he could not believe what he was reading. When he was done he folded the letter and gave it back to me.

"We're leaving," I announced abruptly.

"When?"

"Today. Now."

"Wouldn't you like to . . ."

"No. You said yourself that the longer we stay, the harder it will be to leave."

He nodded.

"So we're going to leave as quickly as possible."

I stood up, pulled on my jeans and jacket, and hastily stuffed my few things into my backpack. Thar Thar's letter could not have been more clear: He did not wish to see me again. He couldn't stand to be near me. He would return to the monastery only after we had left it. The sooner we left, the better. I quickly folded blankets, rolled up the mats and sleeping bags. When my brother tried to help, I waved him off.

Moe Moe sat in the kitchen, poking at the embers of the fire with a stick. She looked up, frightened, when I entered. "You? Go?"

"Yes, we leave."

"Leave?" she repeated.

"Go. Yes, we go!" I replied sternly.

Her eyes. They locked onto me and expressed such sorrow that I felt embarrassed.

"I am very sorry," I explained more calmly now. "I . . . we . . ." How could I explain to her in a language she barely understood something that I myself could hardly put into words?

"I *must* go!" I said, enunciated each word carefully. "Understand?"

A ghost of a nod. "Why?"

My brother joined us, and I asked him to tell her that my holiday was coming to an end, that I had to go back to work, that I had really enjoyed my visit, that I would miss her tea in the mornings, and that I would be sure to come again. While U Ba spoke to her, her eyes flitted from one of us to the other. Suddenly she interrupted him with a question. He answered something. She repeated, insistently, what she had said.

"Moe Moe would like to know when you will return," he said, turning to me.

"When?" I laughed uncomfortably. "Oh . . . soon. Very soon."

U Ba translated, and I could see in her eyes that that answer was not good enough for her.

"Stay," she said suddenly in a grave voice. It sounded almost like a decree. Where had she learned that word? Not from me.

"That's impossible. I'd love to and all . . . but work . . . the office . . . is waiting . . ." I never finished the sentence. It left too bad a taste to sell her a line like that.

We stood for a long time silently next to each other.

She whispered something, and U Ba hesitated a moment before translating it.

"She asks whether you would like to leave any message for Thar Thar."

Our eyes met, and I sensed that she knew much more than I had suspected.

I swallowed. Hesitated. "No."

"No?" The incredulity in her voice. "No?" she repeated slowly, and in a tone that made me realize that it had not been the whole truth. She had understood more than I had.

"No," I repeated in a thin voice.

"Yes," whispered Moe Moe back. "Please."

I lowered my eyes. "That I am thinking of him. That I will miss him."

U Ba translated. Her smile.

I shouldered my pack, and Moe Moe followed us to the door. We bade farewell with our eyes, and climbed down the steps. In the courtyard the chickens were running around more excitedly than usual. I turned around. She stood on the top step waving. I waved back, went along, turned around again. She was still waving. And she was still waving as we turned onto the road and I lost sight of her behind the bushes.

Chapter 9

THERE ARE MEMORIES we cannot escape. We take them with us wherever we go, however far, like it or not. They pursue us or accompany us in good times and in bad. We smell their scents. We hear their sounds. We delight in them or dread them. By day and by night.

My memories of the monastery were so intense, filled me with such longing, that I could hardly bear it. I missed Moe Moe's smile in the morning. Her bottomless joy. The pride in Ko Lwin's eyes every time a new English word unveiled itself to him. The patience with which they took it in turns to feed the quivering Toe Toe.

Nor could I put Maw Maw out of my mind. The thought of her brought tears to my eyes. My initial jealousy had given way to gratitude. And admiration. She had saved not only her brother, but also Thar Thar. If not for her he would sooner or later have fulfilled his death wish. He would have stumbled onto a mine. Or have gotten himself shot by the rebels. Or a soldier.

Maw Maw had soothed his troubled spirit, made of him a loving and lovable soul. Maung Tun's account replayed itself in my mind. I pictured Thar Thar being washed down the raging river, Maw Maw's lifeless body in his arms. Had she drowned, or had she succumbed to the gunshot wound, died in his arms? Where might she be buried? I wondered what kind of person she must have been. Where had she drawn her courage, her strength? By the end of Thar Thar's tale I had come to understand how her example, her love, had given him the capacity to tune his heart.

And still there were so many questions. I had not dared to ask Thar Thar a single one.

In my thoughts I was ever with him. I could not comprehend what had passed between us. He had touched me like no man before him. We had spent ten days together, ten days and two nights, half nights. What happened to me during those hours was utterly out of proportion to the short time we had spent together.

Not since my childhood had I experienced the separation from another person so physically. I had no appetite, hardly ate, slept fitfully, and woke up with pain in my back. I had shortness of breath, suffered from a vague pressure in my chest. Sat for hours exhausted in U Ba's armchair while he restored books. Again and again I turned to Thar Thar's letter.

Never before have I written lines as difficult as these . . . Never have words occasioned such pain as the ones I must now set to paper.

My outrage, my disappointment had lessened with each reading. At a few days' distance I could better appreciate why he had departed so suddenly.

I had not known there was a place where fear has no more power. Where we are so free.

Nor had I, I wanted always to interject at that point. Nor had I.

I had dismissed the idea of writing back to him, only to take it up again and then dismiss it afresh. What would I have written? That I was sick with longing? That I would relocate to Hsipaw?

It was touching the way my brother looked after me. He was convinced I was lovesick. According to him I had succumbed to a virus that we all carry, though my own case was especially severe. A virus for which there was no medical treatment. Body and soul would heal themselves. Or not, as the case may be.

A diversion might alleviate the symptoms, but only for a limited time. To that end we hiked to some of the neighboring mountain villages; made an excursion to Inle Lake, where we visited floating gardens and markets and a monastery where we marveled at jumping cats; sat often in our teahouse. Not that it helped me feel better or turned my mind to other thoughts. Try as we might, the memory of the monastery would not leave me.

One afternoon U Ba took me on a long walk. We walked straight across Kalaw and up onto a hill. The road was spottily paved and turned quickly to sand and then to an uneven path. I thought I recognized it. Amid bushes and dried grasses I found the first graves. Gray concrete slabs in the dust, without ornament or inscription, overgrown with brush. There were no fresh flowers, not a single well-tended site.

Here on a windless day the bodies of Mi Mi and Tin Win had been cremated. Two columns of smoke, so my brother told me, had risen straight into the sky, where suddenly they had moved together, blending into one.

Not all truths are explicable. Not all explicable things are true.

I wondered why he had brought me back to this cemetery. "What are you trying to say?" I asked. It sounded more hostile than I had meant it.

"I'm not trying to say anything," he retorted. "I'm only bringing you back to the place where our father . . ." He stopped short and started again. "I merely thought that you might like to come here again, that it might"—he searched for the right word—"help."

I nodded. "Forgive me, U Ba. It's just that I'm so on edge . . . I don't know myself what's wrong with me . . ."

He sat on the ground, took my hand, and drew me down. We sat a long time in silence. My eyes wandered aimlessly through the hilly landscape with its rice fields, forests, bamboo groves, and white pagodas.

"Tell me what to do."

"Who am I to advise you?"

"You're my brother. Besides, I'm asking you."

He gazed at me intently. Something was weighing on his heart. His expression gave him away, the way he pulled his shoulders up and lowered his head. "Perhaps," he began and lingered on the word, "the time has come to return."

"Return to where?" I asked, astonished.

"To your world."

"Isn't this my world?" I made no attempt to hide my irritation. The distance implicit in his wording had offended me.

"Of course," he admitted.

"Are you trying to get rid of me?" I asked half in jest.

U Ba sighed deeply. "Julia, as far as I'm concerned you can stay forever. Only I fear that you will not find what you are looking for."

"What am I looking for?"

"Clarity."

"About what?"

"About yourself."

"And you think I'll find it in New York?"

"I don't know. But sooner there than here, perhaps."

"What makes you think so?"

"Sometimes we must search afar to find what's close at hand."

I was not sure what he meant.

"Sometimes we have to try one thing in order to discover that we want something else."

"And then it's too late . . ."

"Sometimes . . ."

I took a deep breath, in and out, then sank back until I was stretched out next to him.

"What would the Buddha say?"

U Ba laughed. "That a person's truth is in her soul. That is where you will find the answer."

"And if I don't?"

"Then you have not looked thoroughly enough."

I stared at the sky and observed the scattered clouds. Perhaps they, with their flowing forms, would give me a sign, but I saw nothing beyond the misshapen white figures that occasionally blocked my sun.

"Do you think Thar Thar is right that 'a person, once abandoned, bears that loss forever'? And that 'a person never loved bears an unquenchable longing for love'?"

"Yes."

"But then we're all prisoners, aren't we?"

U Ba thought long before answering. "Not so. Whatever we carry within us, each person is responsible for himself, for his deeds, and for his fate. There is no captivity from which we cannot release ourselves."

"I disagree," I contradicted him. "Some shadows are just too long."

"To step out of?"

"Yes."

He shook his head. "We need not always agree," he replied, smiling and lying down beside me.

The question Nu Nu posed to her husband came to mind: Do you think that a person can shed? Can we strip away a part of ourselves once something else has grown in to replace it? Or, I could hear her asking, are we stuck with who we are?

What happens if we try to strip away the old when there is nothing to replace it?

I thought about Amy. It would do me so much good to be able to discuss it all with her. We would sit together on her sofa, drinking wine, eating cheese, analyzing every detail of the situation, carefully weighing all the pros and cons and discussing their every nuance until late into the night. Was it really plausible for me to stay longer in Burma? What would I do here? Set up shop as a lawyer in Rangoon? Open a teahouse in Kalaw? Live in a monastery in Hsipaw? What were the benefits, what the costs? She would give me no peace with her questions, and I imagine that I would quickly discover in talking to her what an absurd idea it was. And yet I was finding it equally difficult to imagine going back to America and back to my office as if nothing had happened.

I had already made that mistake.

I did some math: my share of the proceeds on the sale of my parents' house, if used sparingly, could last for many years—in Burma probably for the rest of my life. What else could I do in New York? Were there any alternatives to the life I was leading? It was a question that I had never before taken seriously.

I turned to my brother. He was breathing quietly, eyes

closed. I had come here to solve the riddle of a voice inside myself, a voice that was silent now. In its place I heard another, very familiar voice. It was my own voice, constantly whispering contradictory advice.

Pack your things!

Stay!

Trust your intuition.

What business do you have here?

What business do you have in New York?

It's not going to work out.

Don't be afraid.

Listen to me!

No, don't listen to her. Listen to me!

My thoughts ran in circles; I felt paralyzed. Maybe U Ba was right. Maybe I had to try one thing to discover that I really wanted something else.

And hope that it wasn't too late.

Chapter 10

MY BROTHER INSISTED on coming with me to the airport. A friend of his managed to get a car and take us to Heho.

U Ba held my hand the entire time. We didn't say much. A look now and then was enough. How I would miss this amiable silence in New York. This wordless understanding.

Suddenly we were forced to stop. An army truck turned, blocking the narrow road. On the truck bed sat young, armed soldiers staring at us fiercely out of empty faces. Two shiny black boots approached our car. I could see in the rearview mirror how U Ba's friend's eyes opened wider and wider. I did not know that one could smell fear. It stank. It exuded the repulsive stench of fresh vomit. Even my brother was shifting somewhat uncomfortably in his seat.

His friend slowly rolled down the window. Red-stained teeth approached us through the window, curious eyes leering at us.

I thought of Ko Bo Bo. Of Maw Maw. And the longer I thought of her, the calmer I became. There is a force that resists black boots. That is not afraid of red teeth. There is a power stronger than fear. That opposes evil. I was convinced that Thar Thar was right: there was a bit of it in all of us.

The officer and the driver exchanged a few words, laughing a laugh I could not read. Then the street was clear again. The soldier waved us on.

We drove over the top of a hill, and suddenly there was the airport spread out in front of us. My heart was so heavy that I squeezed my brother's hand tightly.

I didn't want this.

The car turned onto a long boulevard—lined with oaks, pines, eucalyptus, and acacias—at whose end the terminal and little tower stood. We drove along slowly. Every fiber of my being was bridling. I felt sick, and I felt myself shivering on this warm day as if it were bitter cold.

We parked in a dusty lot. A tour bus was there ahead of us with a handful of tourists climbing out. None of us said a word.

U Ba got out first, fetched my backpack out of the car, and carried it across the street to an iron-barred gate, where a police officer brought him to a halt with stern words. I stood by passively, as if I had nothing to do with it.

"I can go no farther," said my brother.

"Why not?"

His look made clear that it was a stupid question.

We stood there facing each other. I didn't know what to say. He took both my hands and looked long into my eyes.

"See you soon," he said.

"See you soon," I answered. "Thank you so much for . . ."

He put a finger to his lips and I fell silent. He kissed his finger, then put it to my lips, where it rested for one fleeting moment. Then he turned on his heel and left.

Wait. Don't go. Stay with me, I wanted to call out after him. I felt as abandoned as the little Julia at the window.

I took my backpack and looked around one last time. My brother stood alone on the sandy plaza holding the knot of his longyi in one hand and waving with the other.

His smile. Would I ever see him again? Would I keep my promise to return soon this time around?

I walked slowly up the ramp and entered the building hesitantly.

I didn't want this.

The customs clearance was a small room with three counters that looked as if a carpenter had just now slapped them together as a stopgap measure. They weighed my baggage on an old rusty scale. They filled out my boarding card by hand.

The security officer waved me through a metal detector whose shrill peeping was of no more interest to anyone than my half-full water bottle.

RESTLESSLY I PACED around the sparsely furnished waiting area, unable to sit even for a moment.

The plane was already waiting on the tarmac. A few minutes later our flight was called. My heart was pounding.

I didn't want this.

No departure had ever been so difficult. There was at this moment nothing drawing me back to New York. Not the comfort of my apartment, nor a hot shower in the morning, nor a heated floor in the bathroom. Not even the prospect of talking it all over with Amy. There was nothing to analyze, nothing to assess. The pros-and-cons game no longer held any interest for me. Each word would have been one too many. I had only to decide. U Ba was right: the truth was within me. How free was I? How long were the shadows? What was holding me captive?

I TURNED AROUND and looked for my brother. Behind a fence stood a handful of curious onlookers, a few children playing among them. No sign of U Ba.

There was a baggage truck parked beside the plane, loaded with bags, backpacks, and suitcases. Two airline employees were loading them piece by piece into the front of the aircraft. I spotted my backpack at the very bottom.

I didn't want this.

I stood frozen on the tarmac. A flight attendant called to me. With heavy steps, I was the last passenger to climb the short foldout stairway. She met me with a smile.

I didn't want this.

She asked me for my boarding card. I looked at her without a word. She repeated her request.

"I'm staying here," I said.

Her smile was unaltered. As if I had said nothing.

"I'm not getting on the plane. I'm staying here," I reiterated.

Her eyes betrayed her uncertainty.

I smiled back, turned around, and slowly descended the steps, weak at the knees. I went to the baggage truck and pointed to my backpack. One of the baggage loaders looked first at me, then at the flight attendant, confused. She shouted something to him. He pulled out my luggage and handed it to me.

I walked back to the terminal, perfectly calm.

In front of the building a taxi waited in the shadow of an acacia. Beside it the car we had come in. U Ba was leaning on the trunk, waiting. In his hand was a wreath of fresh jasmine. He didn't move when he saw me. Only his quiet smile betrayed his joy.

I had no plan. But a dream.

Acknowledgments

From the author

My thanks to all the friends in Burma who have accompanied me on my travels over the past twenty years, patiently explaining their wonderful country and taking pains to answer all my questions. They have also been extremely helpful with the sometimes difficult research for this book.

Dr. Werner Havers, Dr. Christian Jährig, and Dr. Joachim Sendker assisted me greatly with the medical research.

Thanks to my sister, Dorothea, and to my mother for teaching me so much about big hearts.

I am particularly indebted, as always, to my wife, Anna. This book would not have been possible without her critical advice, her patience, her unflagging encouragement, and her love.

From the translator

My thanks to Krishna Winston, who first connected me with Jan-Philipp, and also to Sarah, Patrick, and Geneva for all their support, encouragement, and confidence.

JAN-PHILIPP SENDKER, born in Hamburg in 1960, was the American correspondent for *Stern* from 1990 to 1995, and its Asian correspondent from 1995 to 1999. In 2000 he published *Cracks in the Wall*, a nonfiction book about China. *The Art of Hearing Heartbeats*, his first novel, is an international best-seller. He lives in Berlin with his family.

KEVIN WILIARTY has a BA in German from Harvard and a PhD from the University of California, Berkeley. A native of the United States, he has also lived in Germany and Japan. He is currently an academic technologist at Smith College in Northampton, Massachusetts. He lives in Connecticut with his wife and two children.